E.R. PUNSHON
THE DUSKY HOUR

Ernest Robertson Punshon was born in London in 1872.

At the age of fourteen he started life in an office. His employers soon informed him that he would never make a really satisfactory clerk, and he, agreeing, spent the next few years wandering about Canada and the United States, endeavouring without great success to earn a living in any occupation that offered. Returning home by way of working a passage on a cattle boat, he began to write. He contributed to many magazines and periodicals, wrote plays, and published nearly fifty novels, among which his detective stories proved the most popular and enduring.

He died in 1956.

Also by E.R. Punshon

Information Received
Death Among The Sunbathers
Crossword Mystery
Mystery Villa
Death of A Beauty Queen
Death Comes to Cambers
The Bath Mysteries
Mystery of Mr. Jessop
Dictator's Way

E.R. PUNSHON

THE DUSKY HOUR

With an introduction
by Curtis Evans

DEAN STREET PRESS

Published by Dean Street Press 2015

First published in 1937 by Victor Gollancz

Cover by DSP

ISBN 978 1 911095 39 2

www.deanstreetpress.co.uk

INTRODUCTION

"It was dusk, the dusky hour that lingers in the English countryside before the closing in of night...."

"Murder was certainly a dreadful thing, but also, in a way, impersonal. It was like a war in Spain, a famine in China, a revolution in Mexico or Brazil, tragic, deplorable, but also comfortably remote....[Now] Mr. Moffatt was beginning to feel vaguely uncomfortable. Murder seemed somehow to be creeping near--too near. No longer was it merely a paragraph in the paper, something fresh to chat about, an occasion for a comfortable shiver over a comfortable glass of wine."

E. R. Punshon's suspenseful and engrossing ninth Bobby Owen detective novel, *The Dusky Hour*, was not well-received by the Bible of stout detective fiction orthodoxy, originally published over forty years ago but still turned to today for instruction by traditionalist mystery fans: Jacques Barzun and Wendell Hertig Taylor's *A Catalogue of Crime*. In its general dismissal of *The Dusky Hour*, Barzun and Taylor's *Catalogue* even condemns the "adolescent name" of Punshon's series sleuth, Detective-Sergeant Bobby Owen. Evidently in the opinion of the august co-authors of the *Catalogue*, a mystery writer's investigator was not allowed something so vulgar as a diminutive cognomen, even one that, in the case of Punshon's Bobby Owen, calls to mind actual British slang for a cop. Yet despite this later carping from the *Catalogue*, during his lifetime Punshon was a great favorite of two Golden Age stalwarts of Great Britain's Detection Club, the renowned Dorothy L. Sayers and Sayers' esteemed successor as *Sunday Times* crime fiction reviewer, Milward Kennedy. (Punshon became a member of the Detection Club in 1933, three years after the formation of the prestigious social organization, of which Sayers and Kennedy were, along with other notable mystery writers like Agatha Christie, Anthony Berkeley and Freeman Will Crofts, co-founders.) Sayers's rave review of Punshon's debut Bobby Owen mystery, *Information Received* (1933), gave a great lift-off to the Bobby Owen series (see my introduction to that novel), while Kennedy declared explicitly of *The Dusky Hour*, "I do not think that Mr. Punshon, another front-rank man, has ever done better work than this."

Why the divergence between these two pairs of generally discerning critics, Barzun and Taylor, Sayers and Kennedy? Surely it arose from their differing aesthetic views. Looking back at the Golden Age of detective fiction from the vantage point of the 1970s, the pining traditionalists Barzun and Taylor no doubt would have preferred from *The Dusky Hour* a more strictly functional narrative, along the lines of, say, a mystery by Christie or Crofts. *The Dusky Hour*, on the other hand, is a fairly long book for its period, and Punshon's narrative style is expansive, his sentences sometimes structurally rambunctious. In the midst of the 1930s, however, both Sayers and Kennedy had enthusiastically embraced the ascending movement within the mystery genre to merge the puzzle-oriented detective story with the mainstream, literary novel, making it more emotionally compelling and psychologically credible; and they deemed Punshon an important player in this bold artistic advance, an author to be celebrated, not castigated, for his narrative flourishes.

To be sure, Milward Kennedy commended the plot of *The Dusky Hour*, which concerns the discovery of a dead body in a car dumped into a Berkshire chalk pit (in a case of life imitating art, the novel preceded by nine years England's notorious real-life chalk pit murder, committed in the neighboring county of Surrey by the infamous Thomas Ley) and the net of suspicion that tightens around the inhabitants of three nearby country houses, including Sevens, the hideous "sham and inappropriate" Victorian Gothic residence of the local squire, Mr. Moffatt, and his young adult children, Ena and Noll. Also implicated in the affair are some Americans with agendas and denizens of the Cut and Come Again, a dubious arty West End nightclub, introduced by Punshon in his immediately preceding detective novel, *Mystery of Mr. Jessop* (1937). In my own view, the mystery plot of *The Dusky Hour*, which culminates in a final chapter with sixteen pages of elucidation, is of a complexity that ought to please the most exacting of puzzle fans. Whenever I read the novel, I invariably find myself admiring how Bobby, already at the beginning of the story called to the scene by the county constabulary because they believe an emissary from Scotland

Yard may be able to identify the murdered man, fits all the author's intricately cut puzzle pieces together. Yet Milward Kennedy also praised--again most astutely, I believe--the "sharply and economically" drawn characters in *The Dusky Hour*, as well as the novel's writing, pronouncing it "irreproachable in style" and "spiced by the author's wide reading and acute observation."

There indeed are nicely individuated characters and pleasingly unorthodox authorial asides that enhance this fine crime tale. For example, Punshon on several occasions wryly mocks the High Tory, agrarian conservatism of Mr. Moffatt, as in the following passage, which makes mention of a prominent, real-life English newspaper with a left-leaning, working-class readership: "Mr. Moffatt nodded. He knew Norris well enough, the constable stationed at the village, a civil, intelligent fellow, though less active against poaching than one could have wished, and reported, though one hoped untruly, to have been seen reading the *Daily Herald*--a bad sign." Yet again, a Punshon mystery confounds long-prevalent conventional wisdom that the Golden Age English detective novel invariably expressed instinctive longing for the more securely fixed social structures of the Victorian and Edwardian eras.

Through the perspective of the liberal-minded Bobby Owen, the author also indicates doubts about the efficacy of both capital punishment and harsh police interrogation ("It was [Bobby's] experience that one thing told willingly was worth half a dozen resulting from what are called 'third degree' methods"); and he recognizes that English police actually do need to concern themselves, as a matter of law, with obtaining search warrants before conducting a search--surely something that would have come as news to the police characters of Freeman Wills Crofts, whose implacable popular series crime buster, Inspector Joseph French, armed with his startling array of razor blades, bent wires and skeleton keys, routinely flouts English law on this subject with cheerful abandon. In *The Dusky Hour* I for my part was positively thrilled when a character--a chauffeur no less--evicts the police from his abode after they admit to him that they have no warrant to search it.

On this matter I say three cheers for the people! And three cheers as well for Mr. Punshon and his Detective-Sergeant Bobby Owen--a likable, young British cop who once again cleverly cracks a most complex case, adolescent name or not.

Curtis Evans

CHAPTER I

SHARE-PUSHER?

THE LITTLE MAN with the round red smiling face, the soft alluring voice, the ingenuous eyes, sipped with keen appreciation his glass of port, vintage, Dow, 1904; a sound drink.

"Yes," he was saying meditatively, "I sold him those Woolworth shares for £20. He wasn't keen; thought they were speculative; talked about preferring something sounder. But he took them all right. Now he's drawing £20,000 a year from them. Not so bad, eh?" The speaker paused and gave a faint chuckle. "I won't deny," he said, "that if I had had the least idea how that deal was going to turn out, I mightn't have broken my first rule, even though it's to that I owe what success in business has come my way."

"What rule is that?" asked his host, Mr. Moffatt, a big, heavy-looking man with a general air of liking to do himself well and at the same time of trying to keep himself in condition by plenty of open-air exercise.

The other sipped his port again. His name was Pegley—Edward George Pegley, generally known as "Peg" or "Ted," for he was a genial soul and hated all formality. He spoke with a faint American accent. Born in a London suburb, he had spent a good many years in Denver, Colorado.

"My first rule," he explained seriously, "and I've never broken it yet, is that if I know a good thing, I offer it to my clients first. My first duty, I consider, is their interest. In that respect I rank myself with a lawyer, a doctor. The client comes first. Professional duty. Only if my clients pass it do I consider it for myself. Even then——" He shrugged his shoulders. "Lack of capital, and then again—not my business. I'm not an investor. I'm an adviser of investors. If my clients got the idea that I was nosing round for good things for myself, my standing would be gone." He paused, grinned, winked. "But I own up," he said, "if I had dreamed that that £20—good thing though I knew it to be—was going to turn into a steady £20,000 a year, I should have advised it all the same, but when my client turned it down at first, perhaps I shouldn't have gone on pressing it quite so strongly. All the same, I do feel a bit pleased I can say my rule stands unbroken. I don't, for instance, own a single share in Cats Cigarettes, though I've advised three or four clients to make investments in Cats that bring them in at least a hundred per cent—more, when they bought early. I remember one man—a bank manager—was so impressed by what I told him that he went home, mortgaged his house, furniture, insurance policy—raised fifteen hundred, I think it was—sank the whole lot in Cats Ordinary. I was a bit taken aback myself; more than I had bargained for. His wife was furious; thought he was mad; wept, hysterics, threatened to leave him, sent me a letter from her lawyer threatening I don't quite know what. Then he died. Wife thought she was ruined. Talked about learning typing and shorthand.

Now she draws a steady £3,000 a year from that investment, lives in a swell West End flat, learns contract bridge instead of shorthand and typing. I must say she sends me a case of whisky every Christmas and that's more than some clients do, no matter how much they've profited. Of course, I've had my fee, so that's all right."

"It sounds like a fairy-tale," said Mr. Moffatt, listening greedily, his eyes alight, his port forgotten—unprecedentedly.

There was a third man present, sitting opposite Mr. Pegley. He was tall, thin, active-looking, with a small head on broad shoulders and a large imposing Roman nose above the tiny moustache and the small pointed imperial that in these days of shaven chins helped to give him his distinctive and even distinguished appearance. His long, loose limbs ended in enormous hands and feet, and on one hand shone a valuable-looking diamond ring, a solitary stone set in platinum. He seemed between forty and fifty years of age, and at the back of his head was beginning to show a bald patch that he admitted smilingly worried him a little, so that, in an endeavour to cure it, he had taken to going about without a hat. He had a habit of silence that added weight to his words when he spoke; grey, keen eyes; an aloof, imperturbable, slightly disdainful manner; and, when he chose to produce it, a most charming, winning smile that seemed to show a store of geniality and friendliness behind his somewhat formal air. His name was Larson—Leopold Leonard Larson. He was in business in the City, and, though he had listened to Mr. Pegley's monologue in his habitual silence, he had stirred once or twice uneasily in his chair. He was spending the week-end at Sevens, Mr. Moffatt's place near the Berkshire boundary, and Mr. Pegley had not seemed best pleased to find him there when he himself arrived from London to dine and talk business. He was watching Mr. Larson now with eyes that had grown alert and wary as he went on chatting.

" More than I can understand," he said, " especially after living so long in the States, the way people on this side leave their money as good as dead. An American would think himself crazy if he kept half his capital on deposit account or tied up in the good old two and a half consols that may have been all right in our fathers' time, when land was land and brought in a decent return, and all a country gentleman needed was a trifle of ready cash coming in twice a year to meet any delay in the payment of the rents, or any extra estate expense—a new row of cottages, a new wing to the house, or what not. But to keep good money tied up like that to-day—why, it's like a farmer keeping his seed corn in the barn instead of sowing it in the field. Safe in the barn, no doubt, but where's next year's harvest ? "

" Ah," breathed Mr. Moffatt, and he pushed his glass of wine away—a thing that he had never done in all his life before—and he forgot to pass the decanter to Mr. Larson, ruefully aware his own glass was empty, and had been for some time. " Ah," said Mr. Moffatt again.

" I don't know why they do it," Mr. Pegley protested earnestly. " I don't know even how they meet their liabilities in these days, with all the taxes they clap on land. Why, to-day, the five thousand acres in a ring fence our fathers used to dream of—more a liability than an asset."

" Pretty heavy liability, too," declared Mr. Moffatt, still neglectful of that excellent and sound port of the 1904 vintage, still forgetful of Larson's empty glass, " and you've got to pay taxes on that liability, too—talk about four and six in the pound! Jolly lucky if you get off with double that."

"I know, I know," said Mr. Pegley, with a world of sympathy in his soft, caressing tones.

"I admit," said Mr. Larson, but a little as if he deeply regretted having to agree with anything Mr. Pegley said, "I admit the landed classes are at present most unfairly taxed. The trouble is, Moffatt," he told their host, with one of his rare and charming smiles, "you country gentlemen don't command votes enough. I was dining"—he paused, checked himself on the edge of what would evidently have been a breach of confidence—"I have personal knowledge," he went on, "that the Chancellor has been told so himself in the plainest language. He admitted it; all he said was, he could do nothing. As the—the person I am speaking of said afterwards, 'Politicians never can do anything.'"

Mr. Moffatt expressed a brief but lurid hope anent the future of all politicians.

Mr. Larson, twiddling his empty glass, for his host was still far too absorbed to remember the port, relapsed into his accustomed silence. Mr. Pegley went on talking. Mr. Moffatt continued to listen, to listen as uncertain heirs listen to the reading of a rich man's will.

"I mustn't give names," said Mr. Pegley smilingly, "but I can assure you for one list of investments my clients show me that I can O.K., take my fee for examining, and never worry about again, I get half a dozen that are simply deplorable in their neglect of opportunity, and at least one or two where a very slight readjustment can treble the return. Even in a really good list there is often opportunity for a change that may mean a few hundreds extra with equal security—not to be sneezed at these days. I remember after the war—I had just come out of hospital and was trying to pick up the threads again—I was shown a list; £50,000 capital. A lump in the two and a half's—good enough if two and a half suits you and you can meet your social position on it. Another lump in the five per cent war loan—good enough then, but, as I told my client, liable to a cut as soon as the Government was ready."

"Ah," said Mr. Moffatt again, thinking ruefully of his comfortable little £100 a year from war loan abruptly and bewilderingly turned into £70.

"The rest," Mr. Pegley went on, "the weirdest stuff you ever saw. I remember one item. Three thousand in a dead alive old family business that just about kept itself going but had a valuable freehold that made the capital safe. Well, I drew up a scheme for that man. No. Thanked me, but wouldn't change a thing. His look-out. I got my fee. Whether he acted on my advice or not was his affair. I met him a few months back. He was getting twelve hundred a year from his consols. His thousand from war loan had been cut to £700. The rest of his capital brought him about £500. His estate in the Cotswolds put him in wrong a tidy sum every year."

Mr. Moffatt groaned sympathetically. His own land did not "put him in wrong" by any means, but when he looked at his yearly outlay he often believed it did.

"Meant he had under a thou. to keep up his position on—couldn't be done, of course. Well, believe me or not," said Mr. Pegley, using a favourite expression of his, "that man still had by him the list of suggested investments shown in the scheme I drew up for him. The first item had gone down the drain—total loss. It happens even with a deal you feel sure of, though I had marked it 'Speculative.' But the rest showed a return for that year of grace as near £17,000 per annum as makes no difference. I admit that was partly because the other item I had marked 'Speculative' had turned up trumps—much better than I expected, though I thought it good. That happens, too. It was bringing in more that year than the whole of the poor devil's actual income—and then some. Not so bad, eh? I agree it was a gold-mine, and therefore a wasting asset. But, all the same, good for another twenty years in full yield and for another twenty tailing off. Besides the chance of another strike. 'If I had done as you advised——' he told me, looking a bit thin about the gills; and then the bus he was waiting for because he couldn't afford a taxi came along, and he jumped on. I felt a bit sorry for him—and sorry there wouldn't be any Christmas whisky turning up from him either. I own up, I do appreciate it when clients show they haven't quite forgotten."

He sighed sentimentally and lapsed into silence. Mr. Moffatt continued to stare solemnly at his glass of port, still forgetting to drink it, still forgetting to pass on the decanter. He was lost in dreams, dreams of golden streams pouring automatically into his banking account, enormous ceaseless quarterly dividends declared by benevolent directors for the benefit of their shareholders. Why not? he thought. Mr. Larson, with the regretful look at the motionless decanter of one who finally abandons hope, took a pencil and card from his pocket and began to write in his small, precise hand. Mr. Pegley watched him sideways, scowling a little. Mr. Moffatt woke suddenly from his abstraction.

"Shall we go into the drawing-room?" he said. "I expect Ena's got the coffee waiting for us."

They all three rose, Mr. Moffatt still forgetful of his port he left untouched in its glass on the table—a circumstance that made the pale, thin, softly moving butler, a man named Reeves who had not been long in his present situation, lift his eyebrows in surprise before he drank it off himself, and another to keep it company.

In the drawing-room, Mr. Moffatt's daughter, Ena, was sitting alone, waiting for them. She was small, slim, with small, attractive, well-shaped features, solemn eyes, about her a general look of health and the outdoors that went oddly enough with her reddened lips of an unnatural crimson, her painted finger-nails, the plucked ugliness of her eyebrows whereby she claimed her right to share in all the bored sophistication of modern youth. She was dividing her attention between her own thoughts, a Persian kitten—named Gwendolene—a cigarette she had allowed to go out because really she hated the things, a new novel, a magazine that told how to knit jumpers of incredible fascination, and a small table on which stood a coffee-pot, a spirit-lamp, a kettle, cups, and so on. In another part of the room stood a bridge-table, with cards and scoring-pads all ready. Mr. Moffatt was, somewhat unexpectedly, a keen and successful bridge-player who had even taken part in tournaments. Remarkable to see how neatly and swiftly those big, rather clumsy-looking hands of his could shuffle and deal the cards.

The coffee was already brewed, and Ena began to pour it out as the three men came in.

"Where's Noll?" her father said to her.

"Messing about with the snaps he's been taking," Ena answered. "Wants to develop some of 'em."

" Better tell him the coffee's ready," suggested Mr. Moffatt.

" He can come for it when he wants to," replied Ena with sisterly indifference.

Mr. Pegley, sipping his coffee, began to praise it. Ena listened indifferently. She knew she could make coffee as it should be made and so seldom is. Now, if anyone had praised a cocktail of her mixing—but, then, no one ever did, nor even drank it if that extremity could be avoided.

" There's a legend," Mr. Pegley was saying, " that you only get good coffee in Turkey, the States, and France. In France it's half chicory, in Turkey it's just mud, and in the States it's all cream. Now this is the real thing."

Then he began to talk about a coffee-making machine about to be put on the market, for which, he said, he was providing the finance.

" Speculative side-line," he explained; " not the sort of thing I could recommend to the clients who do me the honour to consult me about their list of investments."

Apparently with this machine you put the raw beans in at one end, touched a button, and in a minute or two a stream of perfect coffee poured into the waiting cups at the other end.

Ena listened, polite but bored. She hated machines. She felt they had a secret grudge against her. Whenever she went near one, it always refused to work, while her brother, Noll, had only to touch the wretched things and at once they would purr away contentedly. Ena felt it was hardly fair. She said :

" How lovely, Mr. Pegley, but it wouldn't do for us. We haven't electricity. Dad says he can't afford to install it."

" Ah, yes, of course," Mr. Pegley agreed. " Unfortunately, there is that." He paused. " So unnecessary," he murmured, as if to himself; " so very unnecessary."

Mr. Larson strolled over, his coffee in his hand, to Mr. Moffatt, and dropped before him the card he had written in the dining-room. It bore the words:

" Share Pusher."

Mr. Moffatt looked very startled. His eyes and mouth opened to their widest. His face, red with an outdoor life, went redder still. Before he could speak the door opened and there appeared the pale, soft-moving butler, a little more pale, more softly moving even than usual.

" Colonel Warden to see you, sir," he said. " In the library, sir. On business. I was to say he wouldn't keep you more than a minute or two."

" Colonel Warden ? " repeated Mr. Moffatt, surprised. " Our chief constable," he explained to the two men.

" Oh, dear," exclaimed Ena, turning quite pale. " I do hope Noll hasn't been speeding again or anything."

" Warden wouldn't come himself about that," her father said. " Is Colonel Warden alone ? " he asked the butler.

" No, sir," Reeves answered, glancing uneasily over his shoulder. " A Scotland Yard man's with him—a detective-sergeant. Bobby Owen his name is."

CHAPTER II

FIRST INQUIRIES

MR. MOFFATT put down his cup and rose to his feet. Mr. Pegley looked startled and uneasy. Mr. Larson was staring straight at him, and Mr. Pegley, catching his eye, looked more uneasy still. Ena, too, continued to look a little frightened, for she had a well-founded mistrust of her brother, once he got into that sports car of his that seemed to go to his head as cocktails went to her own. With a word of apology to his guests, Mr. Moffatt left the room.

The library was at the back of the house, a pleasant, comfortable apartment overlooking the rose-garden and the tennis-court and containing, too, some really fine old eighteenth-century furniture and one incongruously new roll-top desk in fumed oak. Mr. Moffatt had seen it advertised as necessary to all aiming at modern efficiency, and had reduced Ena nearly to tears by insisting upon installing it in the library, which served also as his business room and general sanctum and defence against all domestic worries and intrusions. It was here Ena came once a month with her housekeeping books, and here that she extracted with difficulty the sums necessary to settle the amounts owing, for Mr. Moffatt had a firm conviction that houses could easily be run without cash. An appeal for money for another new frock or for an extra visit to town met as a rule with a generous response, but a greengrocer's bill or the coal-merchant's account came always as a fresh surprise and a fresh imposition. Thither, too, came Noll Moffatt to be informed stormily that that sort of thing had got to be stopped, that when he, Mr. Moffatt, was his, Noll's age, etc., etc., and finally to depart with sufficient to cover all pressing liabilities, since Mr. Moffatt's worst roarings were the more tolerable in that they generally ended in the production of a cheque-book. Noll Moffatt, by the way, was supposed to be reading for the Bar. In actual fact his chief interest was photography and his one ambition was to become a camera-man in a film studio. But there Mr. Moffatt drew a very thick, black line, seeing, as he did, little difference between a camera-man in a film studio and a seaside photographer touting on the beach. The Church, the Army, or the Bar—the Stock Exchange at a pinch—for a Moffatt of Sevens, on the Berkshire boundary; no other profession existed.

As up to the present the film companies seemed to share Mr. Moffatt's objections to Noll's securing work with them, the young man spent most of his time at home, exploring the possibilities of novel " shots " and producing occasionally results of some interest. There was, for instance, one sequence in colour of chickens, hatching out, taken on a small poultry farm near—the Towers Farm—that had induced the Super Production Picture Company to show a gleam of interest in his work.

In this room, then, there now waited Colonel Warden, the county chief constable, a tall, strongly built, military-looking man, standing with his back to the fire. At a respectful distance stood his companion, Detective-

Sergeant Bobby Owen, of the C.I.D., Scotland Yard, studying with interest a map of the surrounding country and looking rather puzzled over it.

The door opened and Mr. Moffatt came in. The colonel apologised for troubling him at so late an hour. Mr. Moffatt said that was all right; always pleased to see the colonel; at least, unless it was any fresh performance of his young hopeful in the sports car rashly presented to him on his twenty-first birthday; and the colonel said, oh, no, nothing like that: the young man had of late been more careful to confine his exploits to the unrestricted roads where you could break your own neck or your neighbour's within the four corners of the law.

"It's really," explained the colonel, "about that bad smash there was yesterday near Battling Copse on your west boundary. You've heard of it?"

Bobby, putting a finger on Battling Copse as shown in his map, looked up to hear the reply. At first, when the duty inspector at the Yard had packed him off down here at a moment's notice to see, at the request of the local police, if he could identify the unknown victim of a motor accident, he had been inclined to suppose his mission meant no more than an agreeable interlude in serious work; a pleasant country trip, in fact.

But it was beginning now to look as if it might turn out very differently.

"I heard something about it," Mr. Moffatt answered. "No one I know, is it? Battling Copse? I didn't know it had happened near there. Something about a chalk-pit, I heard, and you couldn't run a car into that one near Battling Copse unless you tried."

"Exactly," said Golonel Warden.

"Eh?" said Mr. Moffatt, startled by the other's tone.

Battling Copse was nearly three miles distant from Sevens, forming, in fact, the further boundary of an outlying portion of the Sevens estate. It had its name from a tradition that there a Roman legion, marching to the relief of London, had been cut off and utterly destroyed by a British force during the Boadicea rising. Tradition declared that the ground had been reddened with the blood of the defeated and that the clash of spear on shield, as the Roman soldiers died where they stood, could yet be heard once every twelvemonth in the stilly winter nights. Oddly enough, though there was historical proof, confirmed by entries in the parish registers, that the copse had been the scene in the civil wars of a hot skirmish between the Parliamentary and the Royalist cavalry, no local memory thereof seemed to have survived. Apparently the earlier tale had swallowed the later one, though of the truth of the first story there was no proof whatever; and Mr. Moffatt was never quite sure whether to regret such forgetfulness of historic incident, or to be thankful for it, in view of the fact that the Roundhead force had been commanded by the Moffatt of Sevens of that time. Regrettable in the extreme, undoubtedly a sad blot upon the family escutcheon, and yet highly satisfactory proof that the escutcheon had been there to be blotted three hundred years ago. Mr. Moffatt could only hope that eight generations of unbending Toryism served for atonement, even though ever since then the eldest son of the family had always been christened "Oliver," and known as "Noll," in memory of the great Protector. Even Mr. Moffatt's father, a Tory of the Tories, had respected that tradition, though he had tacked on an "Albert" in honour of the Prince Consort, and had hoped that in time the "Albert" might displace the "Oliver."

" Do you mean you think it was suicide ? " Mr. Moffatt asked.

" It's a possibility," agreed the colonel, " but some rather odd facts have turned up. One thing is that yesterday afternoon a car was noticed by our man here—Norris his name is."

Mr. Moffatt nodded. He knew Norris well enough, the constable stationed in the village, a civil, intelligent fellow, though less active against poaching than one could have wished, and reported, though one hoped untruly, to have been seen reading the *Daily Herald*—a bad sign.

" It was standing in the lane that turns out of the road just beyond your entrance gates," Colonel Warden continued, " going west, that is."

" The lane leading to Markham's farm ? "

" Yes, and nowhere else," said the colonel. " Apparently, however, it did not go there, for there are no tracks higher up the lane, and no one at Markham's knows anything about it. Norris thought it an odd place to park a car. He took a note of the number, and it is the same as that of the car found in the Battling Copse chalk-pit. More curious still, when Norris went on, towards Sevens, he saw a man standing on the bank behind the hedge just before the Sevens entrance, watching the house through a pair of field-glasses."

" What on earth for ? " exclaimed Mr. Moffatt.

" That," said the colonel, " is what Norris asked. The fellow seemed confused. Norris had come up quietly on his bicycle and had taken him by surprise. He said something about Sevens being a fine old house and he was interested in architecture. Then he made off. Got into his car and drove away, or seemed to. Must have come back again. Nothing Norris could do, of course. Bad manners, but no legal offence in watching people through field-glasses. But Norris says he is certain the dead man found in the car in the chalk-pit is the man he saw."

"Don't understand it," said Mr. Moffatt. "If he wanted to see the house, nothing to stop him coming and asking."

In point of fact, Sevens was not a fine old house. The original building had been burnt down in mid-Victorian days and re-erected in a sham and inappropriate Gothic that always made Ena feel she loved her birthplace less than she should have done. Once, under a misapprehension born of old prints, a representative of *Country Life* had arrived, full of enthusiasm and belief that the ancient building survived. Ena had never forgotten his expression as he gazed upon the actual edifice. It had even battlements.

"Norris," continued the colonel, "says the car went on up the road. Now you know that way leads nowhere once it is past Sevens except to Mr. Hayes's place, to the Towers, and to two or three cottages and then back to the main road again in a long circuit. So what was he after?"

"Excuse me, sir," said Bobby, looking up in rather a puzzled way from the large-scale map he was studying, "is the Towers Mr. Hayes's place? I thought that was Way Side. That's marked here, but I can't see any Towers."

"Poultry farm," explained the colonel, "first place past Battling Copse—run by Miss Towers and her sister, London ladies who lost their money in some smash and are probably now on the way to lose what's left."

"Sure to, sure to," grumbled Mr. Moffatt, scowling and frowning as if he hoped as much. "I've told them so myself. Much better get back to town, much better."

He spoke with so much apparent feeling that Bobby wondered if there was any reason why these Londoners were unwelcome as neighbours, or if Mr. Moffatt merely thought it a pity people should lose money in undertakings for which probably they were quite unsuited.

" Then Way Side is Mr. Hayes's place ? " Bobby asked.

The colonel nodded, and to Mr. Moffatt he said :

" Hayes is an American, isn't he ? " To Bobby he explained, as if fearing Scotland Yard efficiency might lift an eyebrow at ignorance of any of the more prominent residents in the district : " Only been there a few months. It was empty for some time after the last owner died, and then this man took it."

" I don't think he is American," Mr. Moffatt answered. " Pleasant fellow to talk to; seems anxious to be neighbourly. Of course, I don't know him well; he's hardly got settled in yet. He's called once or twice, though, and we've been over there. He did say he had made his money in America—a place called Denver; mining town apparently."

" We found some papers in the car of the poor chap that's got himself killed," the colonel explained. " They make it seem as if he may have been in the States, too. We thought possibly he might be going to call on Mr. Hayes, especially as there is some suggestion he had been asking how to get to Way Side. We wondered if he could have confused Sevens and Way Side ? "

" Don't see how," said Mr. Moffatt, " curious, though. I've a man here to-night—came down from town to chat and talk business. A Mr. Pegley. I believe he's been in America, and I think he mentioned Denver. I asked him if he knew Hayes, but he didn't seem to. Quite a big town, he tells me—Denver."

"Interesting," said the colonel, who had known about Mr. Pegley before, but had wished Mr. Moffatt to be the first to mention him. "Perhaps he can help us. I must ask him, if I may."

"He is in the drawing-room," Mr. Moffatt explained. "If you'll come along, Ena will give you a cup of coffee and you can ask Pegley himself. Do you know his name? The dead man's, I mean."

"We think it is Bennett—Arthur Bennett," Colonel Warden answered, "but it's an odd thing again—there were no papers or letters or anything of that kind in his pocket; no personal card either; nothing in the way of name or address. The papers we found were rather tucked away—in an envelope behind a cushion. And," continued the colonel slowly, "they rather suggested Mr. Bennett—if that's his name—was engaged in—well, share-pushing, they call it."

Mr. Moffatt fairly jumped. The card Larson had so negligently dropped before him was in his waistcoat pocket and now seemed suddenly to bulk enormous there, so that he expected Colonel Warden to point at it an inquiring finger. Bewilderedly he wondered if he ought to produce it, and how doing so would conform with his duty as a host.

"That is why," Colonel Warden continued, apparently as unaware of that hidden card as though it shouted not its presence and its message to the whole world in the way Mr. Moffatt felt it must surely be doing, "we rang up Scotland Yard, as we knew they had been chasing American share-pushers lately, and asked them to send us down someone who might perhaps be able to identify the body. Detective-Sergeant Owen was good enough to come along by the next train."

He indicated Bobby as he spoke. Bobby bowed slightly. Mr. Moffatt said:

"Oh, yes—Reeves told me. Knew him, apparently."

The colonel looked surprised, even startled. Bobby looked a trifle surprised, too, and said:

"Your butler? He knew me? I didn't recognise him."

He took out his notebook and made an entry. But Mr. Moffatt was thinking of something else. He said:

"There were papers in the car but none on the body? Isn't that rather queer?"

"We thought it so," answered the colonel cautiously.

"Everyone has some sort of document in his pocket," declared Mr. Moffatt, "if it's only a notebook or an old envelope. Can they have been taken by someone—removed?"

"We thought it possible," agreed the colonel, still cautiously.

"But, then, that would mean," said Mr. Moffatt hesitatingly, "that would mean—murder?"

"We thought it possible," agreed the colonel once again.

CHAPTER III

STORY OF CARD-SHARPERS

MR. MOFFATT looked very disturbed, even uneasy, but excited and interested as well. Murder was certainly a dreadful thing, but also, in a way, impersonal. It was like a war in Spain, a famine in China, a revolution in Mexico or Brazil, tragic, deplorable, but also comfortably remote. Startling, certainly, that this time it had come even as near as Battling Copse, three miles away, on the west far boundary of the Sevens estate, but none the less utterly remote from oneself.

"Are you sure?" he asked. "I mean, what for? . . . Have you any idea?"

"Well, we haven't much to go on at present," the colonel answered. "One of Markham's men, on his way to work this morning, noticed car-tracks and broken bushes near the Battling Copse chalk-pit. He didn't think much of it—not a quick thinker, probably. Later he mentioned it to some of his mates and Mr. Markham heard of it, and went down to have a look himself. He saw at once something had gone over the edge of the pit, and there below was the car, upside-down, with the poor chap who had been driving it lying all smashed up by its side. He sent word to Norris, Norris reported, and when I heard I thought I had better come along myself. From the first I didn't think it looked like an accident. Of course, a skid at a high rate of speed might have done it. But there was no sign of that. And to get there off the road would mean a sharp turn for no apparent reason and then forcing a way through bushes that even in the middle of the night or a fog would have shown any driver he was off the road. It looks as if the car had been parked there for some time, out of the way, and then deliberately driven over the edge."

"But that would be suicide," Mr. Moffatt exclaimed.

Colonel Warden made no reply. Detective-Sergeant Owen still seemed absorbed in his map, even though at the same time he was watching and listening attentively. Mr. Moffatt was beginning to feel vaguely uncomfortable. Murder seemed somehow to be creeping near—too near. No longer did it seem merely a paragraph in the paper, something fresh to chat about, an occasion for a comfortable shiver over a comfortable glass of wine. Besides, the impression was growing upon him that these two men, the burly, elderly, soldier-like colonel, the good-looking but quite ordinary young fellow from Scotland Yard, were both watching him closely, though he could not imagine why. He said:

"You have no"—what was the word? ah—"no clues?"

"There was a woman's lipstick," the colonel answered, "picked up near where the car went over. Nothing to prove any connection, but it certainly hadn't been there long and Markham says he saw it long before, so far as is known, any woman had been near. And a fragment of the wrapper of a roll of photographic film. Someone found it and handed it to Norris, and Norris is sure no one had been taking snaps. No connection, most likely; it's not usual to take snaps of murders."

Bobby, as if in answer to the colonel's nod, opened an attaché-case he had with him and produced a small metal lipstick case and a fragment of a paper wrapper with enough printing on it to show what purpose it had served. Both were carefully preserved in cellophane envelopes, though the lipstick case had been trodden deep into the mould by the foot of its finder, and the fragment of wrapper had been handled by half a dozen persons before finally coming into Constable Norris's possession.

But routine is routine, regulations must be observed, and " Protect the evidence " remains the first standing rule of all investigation.

" Not much chance of finding anything in the way of footmarks or finger-prints," observed the colonel. " Everything was pretty thoroughly trampled over and pulled about long before Norris got there. The car had been turned right side up, the dead body carried up to one of the farm outhouses. Of course, they had no idea it was anything but an accident. There's nothing much for us to go on—except the lipstick case and the bit of Kodak film wrapper. Oh," he added carelessly, " and that odd incident Norris happened to see—the watching Sevens through field-glasses."

" Seems extraordinary," agreed Mr. Moffatt uneasily. " Not quite—well, not normal even. Why on earth should anyone . . . ? Looks to me like suicide—or accident."

" Accident we can rule out," the colonel answered. " The tracks show the car had been standing some time before being driven over the edge. Suicide is possible. People intending suicide do sometimes destroy all papers and evidence of identity. Even the tailor's tabs seem to have been removed. But, then, the papers we did find were there, and it's more likely they were overlooked by someone else than forgotten by the dead man himself—especially as they seem somewhat compromising. We may trace him through the car, of course. And we haven't the report of the doctors yet. They are doing the post-mortem, and they may find something to show one way or the other. There's another point. There's evidence two or three shots were heard close together about four o'clock, and a noise that it seems likely was the car falling. A delivery-van driver, it was. He didn't trouble to investigate; didn't think much of it, and was late on his rounds anyhow. Someone shooting rabbits, he thought. But he did mention it when he got back, so there is proof he actually heard something and he seems fairly sure about the time. Also a man working in the field beyond the chalk-pit says he saw someone leaving the copse late in the afternoon, though he's pretty vague about the exact hour. He can't give the least description of him, except that it was a man dressed in what he calls gentleman's clothes, which means, I gather, a dark lounge suit, and that he was holding a hat before his face. No hat can be found belonging to the dead man, and, though plenty of people don't wear one nowadays, especially when driving, still, Norris says the man he saw had one. Only why take away a hat of all things? It might be it was being held before the face by way of disguise," he added thoughtfully.

"Is Norris quite certain the dead man is the same as the man he saw before?" Mr. Moffatt asked.

"Oh, yes, he is quite clear about that; thought his behaviour so queer he noticed him particularly. I was wondering—most unpleasant, of course—I hate to do it—but I shall have to ask you to see if you can recognise the body. There must, one supposes, be some reason why he was watching your place."

"I can't imagine   Mr. Moffatt insisted. "Of course, if you think it necessary . . ."

"I knew we could depend on you," declared the colonel heartily. "I can't tell you how sorry I am to have to ask you. Oh, by the way, Mr. Pegley—was that his name?—have you known him long? You have another friend staying with you, too, I think?"

"Yes. A man named Larson; very nice fellow, down for the week-end. City man—finance, companies, all that sort of thing. Ena and I met him on the *Berengaria* two years ago, when we went to Boston to visit Ena's uncle there. Larson put me under a considerable obligation during the voyage."

"May I ask in what way?"

"Well, in confidence, of course. As a matter of fact, I had been playing poker a good deal. Silly, no doubt. Bridge is my game, not poker. I ought to have known better. Dropped a tidy sum. Larson looked on one night. Never said a word. He's like that. Just watched. Next day told me the play was crooked. Said it just like that. 'Crooked play last night,' like 'Nice morning, isn't it?' or 'Lunch bell gone yet?' I—well, I didn't know what to think. He offered to prove it. He joined us next night. Told me what to do. I won back all I had lost and nearly fifty more. Spoiling the Egyptians, eh?"

"And Larson?"

"Dropped a fiver. He wouldn't let me return it; said he had had more than his money's worth in fun. He watched them, saw how they stacked the cards, was able to sign to me when to back my hand, when to throw in. They didn't like it. Kept muttering and whispering to each other. Broke up the game finally, and there was no more card-playing that voyage."

Mr. Moffatt chuckled delightedly, thoroughly enjoying the memory of that past triumph. The colonel asked:

" Did you make any complaint ? "

" No. Impossible. Those fellows don't give you the chance. No proof. Larson told me they don't even use marked cards or anything. They just rely on their own smartness, palming an extra ace and so on. Besides, I had got my own back and some more, too. Not so bad to sit down with a brace of card-sharpers and get up nearly fifty to the good."

" Since then you have been friendly together ? "

" Well, I gave him my card and asked him to look me up when he was back in England. He never did, and then I ran across him in town about six months ago. He had quite forgotten me and he had lost my card. Not the only time, apparently, he has had a bit of fun with card-sharpers. I insisted on lunching him, and we've seen something of him since. But he's a very busy man. Reserved, though. Especially about business. Says it's second nature with him now; so much often depends on not letting the other fellow know what you're doing. He's in with some very big people indeed."

Bobby was making notes again. The colonel said:

" And Mr. Pegley ? Have you known him long ? "

" A few months, not more," Mr. Moffatt answered. " He wrote offering to buy a few shares I had in a West African gold-mining concern. Worth nothing at all. He offered a penny a share—they are two-shilling shares. He was quite frank about it—said there was a possibility of a new paying vein being found. One of his clients was buying up all the shares he could find—purely speculative. Pegley said I must decide for myself whether to sell out or hang on. I said I would think it over. Pegley sent me a wire next day to advise me to sell, but before I decided the bottom fell out of the whole thing and I lost the £20 I might have sold for. The shares are waste paper now."

"Do you often operate on the Stock Exchange, Mr. Moffatt?" Bobby asked, looking up from his notebook in which he had been making entries.

"Rarest thing in the world," declared Mr. Moffatt. "My money is nearly all in consols—safe two and a half; not much, but safe."

The colonel smiled to himself at the virtuous tone in which this had been said. That Mr. Moffatt was the fortunate holder of a very large block of old consols was fairly well known, for when he was not grumbling about the poor return derived from land in these days he was generally lamenting the niggardly return of two and a half per cent he derived from his invested capital. As the investment had been made a good many years before, when consols stood well over par, there really had been a considerable shrinkage in nominal capital value, even though they had recovered from those dreadful war days when they had dropped so low that Mr. Moffatt felt himself face to face with ruin.

"You have kept in touch with him though?" the colonel asked.

"Well, no, not exactly. It just happens we have run across one another once or twice—we met in the train again some time back. He got into my compartment. I was coming back from town. He was going on somewhere to see a client—he's an investment consultant."

"What's that?" inquired Colonel Warden, and Bobby, too, seemed interested as his busy pencil hovered over the pages of his notebook.

"Well," Mr. Moffatt answered slowly, "he advises

people about their investments. Has most amazing stories to tell. He tells of one client he advised to invest a trifle in Woolworths and now he draws £20,000 a year from them."

"Oh," said the colonel, with a certain touch of incredulity in his voice, for, though the tale might be true, he had heard it before.

It was the hint of scepticism in the other's voice that decided Mr. Moffatt. He drew out the card Larson had dropped before him earlier in the evening.

"Larson doesn't like him," he blurted out. "I saw there was something wrong the moment I introduced them. Larson says he's a share-pusher."

CHAPTER IV

DISCUSSION

THEY ALL THREE went down the passage and across the hall to the drawing-room, where it seemed a somewhat awkward silence prevailed; at least, awkward as far as Ena was concerned, for the mutual hostility between the two men was making itself very plain to her as Pegley fidgeted and glared, and Larson, imperturbable as ever, maintained a chilly silence that almost resembled a shouted accusation. It was to her an immense relief when the door opened and the little party from the library came in.

Mr. Moffatt introduced the colonel to his two visitors. Ena, of course, already knew him. She rang for two more coffee-cups, feeling a little sorry for the good-looking young man she understood had something to do with Scotland Yard and who stood patiently and apparently forgotten by the door, since to Mr. Moffatt of Sevens a sergeant was a sergeant and he was nothing more.

But when she looked a little more closely she was not sure that that somewhat stern mouth and the clear and direct eyes were those of one much in need of sympathy.

"There's been another of these motor accidents," Mr. Moffatt was explaining. "Poor chap killed. Colonel Warden is trying to find out who he is. Odd thing is, he was seen peeping at this house through field-glasses just before it happened—can't imagine why."

His three auditors all looked puzzled, and two of them made vague comments while Larson preserved his accustomed silence. Reeves returned with the two coffee-cups Ena had asked for. When he left the room, Bobby followed him. Mr. Moffatt noticed this and approved. Ena was a trifle disappointed. Outside, Bobby said to the butler:

"I hear you recognised me, mentioned my name to Mr. Moffatt. I don't think I remember your face."

"Oh, you wouldn't," answered Reeves quietly. "I was out of a job last year and I used to go and sit in the law courts sometimes, just to pass the time. Nowhere else to go. Cinemas cost money. So do pubs. I was there when you were giving evidence in a case and someone told me your name. Said you were a relative of the Home Secretary's."

"Well, I'm not," snapped Bobby angrily. "The lies people tell." He almost choked in his indignation. He felt this tale was one he would never, never live down. He seemed to see his tombstone with the epitaph inscribed upon it: ". . . and was a relative of the Home Secretary." He said gloomily: "I don't know the blighter from Adam. I'm a sergeant in the C.I.D., and some day perhaps I shall be an inspector if I watch my step, but not yet, because I'm not senior enough, and the High-Ups don't want any jealousy."

He went back angrily into the drawing-room. Reeves's story was probable enough. People with nothing to do often hang about the law courts for free entertainment, since these have the advantage over their equally free rivals, the big stores, the public libraries, the museums, of providing more seating accommodation than the first, more sociability than the second, more human interest than the third. All the same, Bobby did not much believe Reeves's story. The butler had certainly never been through his own hands in the way of business, but, all the same, it might be well to get a set of his finger-prints and find out if Scotland Yard was equally unaware of Mr. Reeves's past.

Bobby's reappearance Mr. Moffatt greeted with a lifted eyebrow, but did not quite know what to do about it. He had imagined Bobby, a sergeant, sitting patiently in the hall, waiting till his superiors had finished, or possibly sharing a friendly glass of beer with Reeves. Now here he was marching in again with his air of having a job to do and meaning to do it, and Ena began to fill the second cup as the colonel, sipping the contents of his, observed to Pegley and Larson:

" I understand both you gentlemen have been a good deal in America ? "

" I've lived in Denver," Pegley answered sulkily. " Business there after the war. Fine place. Business centre. Tourist centre. Health centre. It was there I picked up my knowledge of American business conditions I think my clients have found useful."

" I make occasional trips to New York on business connected with the financial group I am associated with," Larson explained. " I have never been further than New York."

" Do you know anyone of the name of Arthur Bennett ? "

Larson contented himself with a shake of the head. Pegley said:

" Don't think so. Never had a client of that name, if

that's what you mean. Of course, I should have to look up my files to be sure. I meet a lot of people; people drift in and out—sometimes business comes of it, sometimes it doesn't, sometimes a smarty just tries to pick my brains without paying my fee. They don't succeed very often. Anyhow, I can't place any Arthur Bennett? Is that the name of the man who's been killed? Was he an American?"

"We are trying to find out," answered Colonel Warden. "Sergeant Owen has been able to identify him as a man who was recently staying at a London hotel under the name of Bennett."

"A criminal?" asked Mr. Moffatt eagerly. "A burglar? Ten to one, that's what he was after with his field-glasses, trying to find out how to get in."

"There was nothing definite," Bobby explained. "I was sent to interview him in connection with an inquiry we had from New York. The suggestion was that he was one of a gang of confidence men. He wouldn't answer questions; blustered a bit and so on. He had papers to show he was a British subject and so he didn't need a passport. There was nothing we could do and we had to leave it at that. But he left the hotel in a hurry without saying where he was going, and now papers found in his car suggest he really had something to do with a share-pushing gang operating over here."

"Share-pushing?" repeated Larson, as if startled for once out of his accustomed silence. "Share-pushing?" And he turned in his chair and stared hard and pointedly at Pegley—so pointedly, indeed, that Mr. Moffatt turned and stared, too, and Ena looked rather frightened and the colonel very interested.

Only Bobby, notebook in hand, seemed unconcerned.

Pegley went first red and then white, and in his turn stared at Larson with what seemed an odd mixture of doubt, of anger, and of fear.

"What is share-pushing?" asked Ena, instinctively the hostess who sees unpleasantness brewing among her guests and wishes to divert it.

"Share-pushing," Pegley answered, still glaring at Larson, but now as if anger were getting the better of the other emotions he had at first experienced, "share-pushing, Miss Moffatt, is what it is called when an investment consultant gives advice that goes wrong. I've been called a share-pusher myself." He looked round him defiantly. "I remember placing a line of tin shares with a client. It turned out punk. He called me names. Began action—issued a writ and all that. I was able to show I had bought in the open market at the price I had sold to him, plus expenses, plus my agreed fee, and luckily I had put it in writing that I considered the investment no more than a reasonable speculation, in the hit-or-miss category. So the action never came into court—withdrawn. But I never got an apology, and the name—stung."

He wiped an indignant and protesting forehead as he finished this speech, which he had delivered with great speed and emphasis. Ena thought it was a great shame. Mr. Larson continued to look incredulous and unsympathetic, but, according to his custom, made no remark.

"I only wish," observed Colonel Warden mildly, "that as thoroughly satisfactory a reply could be made in all these cases. They are very difficult. There is always a long delay before we hear of them. Sometimes even the victim will hardly believe he has been robbed; he merely thinks it's been a bit of unexpected bad luck. He feels it wouldn't be fair to prosecute. Sometimes he's ashamed of his own folly. Then the share-pusher operates here, there, and everywhere. Sometimes a coup is prepared for years before it is brought off. They can afford to wait when the possible booty may run into the thousands."

" People should know how to look after their money," said Larson, with an air of having as little sympathy for the victim as for the swindler. " People have no right to be fools."

" Only we all are," murmured Bobby. " Some of us most of the time, and most of us some of the time."

The colonel was speaking again.

" In view of the very odd fact that the dead man was seen watching this house through field-glasses," he said, " and that he is believed to have recently landed from America and that you have all been over there, I shall have to ask you—Mr. Moffatt has already been kind enough to consent—to see if you can identify the body. If you can, it may be the greatest help."

" Oh, how awful," exclaimed Ena. " Oh, daddy, must you ? "

The colonel turned to her with a little bow.

" I'm afraid it's necessary, Miss Moffatt," he said. " Public duty and all that. Things like this have got to be cleared up. I'll do my best to make the ordeal as little disagreeable as possible for you."

He stressed the last word, and Ena noticed it and looked more disturbed than ever.

" You don't mean you want me to ? " she cried. " Oh, I couldn't."

" Surely that's not necessary," interposed her father.

" I'm afraid so," the colonel answered. " We can't afford to miss any chance, however small. Oh, and your boy, Oliver. I suppose he won't mind. He is at home ?"

" Playing about in his studio, as he calls it," grumbled Mr. Moffatt.

" Developing some new films he has been trying," Ena explained. " Oh, Colonel Warden, I am sure I can't possibly ever——"

" I know, I know," he interrupted her, " but you understand there must be some reason why this man was displaying so much interest in Sevens, and we can't afford to neglect any possibility——"

" Have you found his field-glasses ? Were they in the car, I mean ? " Larson asked.

Warden shook his head.

" Nothing was in the car," he answered, " or on the body; no personal possessions, nothing to show who he was or where he came from, except the papers we found under the cushion of one of the seats."

" Does look like murder," muttered Mr. Moffatt.

He rang the bell, and, when Reeves appeared once more, told him to find Mr. Oliver and tell him he was wanted.

" He'll be in the studio, Reeves," Ena said.

Reeves withdrew, and Mr. Larson said:

" You suspect murder, then ? "

" It is a possibility," Colonel Warden answered cautiously. " A post-mortem is being held. That may make it certain one way or another. I can't say I see how any man could get into that chalk-pit by accident, and suicide seems unlikely. I should like to thank you all for being so ready to help by seeing if you can identify the body." None of them had expressed any such readiness, but the colonel beamed gratefully upon them all the same. " Such a difference," he explained, " in police work when we get readiness to help instead of hostility—not that hostility means consciousness of guilt. It may be just a dislike to getting mixed up in such things. But this case may have developments. The American police are inquiring about a man they believe to be over here. He is said to be an Englishman, but he has been mixed up with New York gangsters—got away with a good deal of coin, apparently."

"You think this Bennett—if that is his name—may turn out to be him?" asked Mr. Larson.

"Possibly," agreed the colonel, "or—again possibly—he may be an associate come over to renew acquaintance and not very welcome. Or there may be no connection at all. We've got to dig all that up."

In the background, Bobby shut his notebook with a sigh. He had a sudden vision of very long, dull, tedious work, all very likely ending as it began—in doubt and questioning.

"Well, I don't suppose any of us will be able to help," grumbled Mr. Moffatt. "Annoying business altogether. Plenty of people have visited America; nothing in that. Hayes, for instance, at Way Side. He made his money over there. And his housekeeper is American, I think."

"No, she comes from Liverpool," Ena interposed. "She told me so. Besides, she's left."

The colonel looked interested and Bobby opened his notebook again.

"Do you know her name?" he asked.

"Mrs. O'Brien," Ena answered. "Laddy, Mr. Hayes calls her—I don't know what her first name is really."

"What makes you say she's left?" Mr. Moffatt asked.

"It's all over the village," Ena answered, beginning to laugh a little. "She got a lovely new hat down from one of the London shops yesterday, and she was so pleased with it she made the maids admire it and then she put it on to call at the Vicarage. It was one of those smart new three-cornered pointed hats—awfully stylish—but she's a big woman, and quite old, and a big face, and I expect it did look a bit odd. When Mr. Hayes saw it he began to laugh, and she was wild and tore it off and jumped on it, and he laughed more than ever, so she boxed his ears or something, and then he was furious, too—I expect it hurt—and he turned her out of the house then and there. She caught the last train to London."

"When was all this?" Colonel Warden asked.

"Last night. It was all they were talking about in the village this morning; the servants had been telling everyone," Ena explained. "I expect they're all talking about —about this poor man now."

"Very likely," agreed the colonel, and Reeves came back into the room.

"Beg pardon, sir," he said. "Mr. Oliver's not in the studio and we can't find him in the house. I think he must have gone out."

CHAPTER V

THE MISSING AUTOMATIC

IT WAS A CLEAR, BRIGHT NIGHT, moon and stars shining from an unclouded sky, and, as Colonel Warden and Bobby walked down the Sevens drive to where their car waited, the chief constable said slowly:

" Well, now, what do you think of all that ? "

" Nothing much to go on yet, sir," Bobby answered cautiously.

" All seem tied up with the U.S.," observed the colonel discontentedly.

" Yes, sir," agreed Bobby. " That's one line connecting the dead man with Sevens. It seems Mr. Hayes has been in business over there, too."

" We had better go on to his place now," the colonel decided, " and see if he can tell us anything. He had better see the body, too. He may know it."

Bobby thought to himself that between knowledge and acknowledgment there is often a vast difference. Aloud he remarked:

" I gathered that young Mr. Moffatt is interested in photography."

The colonel stopped dead.

" What's that? Why not? " he asked. " You don't mean . . . ? " He paused. Bobby said nothing. The colonel rapped out: " Oh, nonsense. You're not thinking of that bit of Kodak film wrapper ? "

" Very likely there's no connection," Bobby agreed. He added: " The young lady seemed rather to run to crimson nails and that sort of thing—including lipstick."

This time the colonel plunged angrily forward.

" You mean one of the things was found there ? " he said over his shoulder.

" Very likely there's no connection," Bobby answered, following meekly.

The colonel said:

" Miss Moffatt had her lipstick. I happened to notice. I saw her take it out of her handbag."

" Yes, sir," agreed Bobby. " So she did. I dare say most ladies have one or two—different shades for different frocks, I've been told. One gets to notice all kinds of irrelevant things," he sighed, " like film wrapper and lipsticks. I suppose they are quite well known locally ? "

" The young Moffatts ? " Warden asked irritably. " Of course, nice boy and girl—bit rackety, perhaps, like most young people to-day. Boy been fined once or twice for exceeding the speed limit—last time they endorsed his licence; couldn't think of any special circumstance, I suppose. And once or twice he's come back from town by the late train not quite—well, cocktails and all that."

" Yes, sir," said Bobby, wondering a little what the " all that " might mean.

" Some night-club," the colonel explained. " I know that—it came out because the boy was fined in London for leaving his car outside it and the local paper reported the case to spite Mr. Moffatt they had had a row with."

" Did it give the name of the night-club ? " Bobby asked.

"Cut and Come Again, somewhere near Mayfair Square. You know it?"

"We all do," Bobby answered grimly. "A good deal of drinking and some pretty high play goes on there—at least, not there so much. A fresh place every time. We've never been able to get enough evidence to act on. They're as cunning as a bagful of foxes and know the licensing laws inside out. We shall catch them out some day, of course, and then they'll wind up—and start again somewhere else." He paused and added slowly: "The Cut and Come Again is where I first got track of Bennett."

Once again the colonel came to a full stop. He swore softly and below his breath. Bobby went on:

"It establishes another possible link between Bennett and Sevens. Only a possibility, of course. Bennett may not have been sure of young Moffatt's identity and been watching Sevens to make certain—or even for a chance of a private talk."

"I can't believe," grumbled the colonel, "that young Moffatt could be mixed up in a thing like this."

"Well, sir, if I may say so," Bobby answered, "we aren't anywhere near that so far." Perhaps he laid a slight unconscious emphasis on those last two words, for the colonel gave an uncomfortable kind of wriggle on hearing them. Bobby continued: "All it means is we know now there's a possibility the two of them met at the Cut and Come Again, and that's a place with two reputations—one for keeping just inside the law; one for hatching more rascality than any place in London, which is saying something. Easy to invent a theory, of course. Young man. Night-club. Drinking. Gambling. Borrows money. Faced with exposure. I O U perhaps. Post-dated cheque, possibly. Might be father's name forged. Boy faced with exposure. Boy loses his head. Pistol goes off. And all papers taken to make sure no I O U left or anything of the kind. No evidence whatever and all mere theory. No need to give it serious consideration—as yet," he added.

The colonel swore again and walked on. He said crossly:

"Do you think young Moffatt left the lipstick behind as well?"

"Couldn't say, sir, if that's likely," answered Bobby. "I've never seen him. It might be true of some at the Cut and Come Again."

"Well, he's not that sort anyhow, that's definite," declared the colonel. "And Ena Moffatt's as straight as you make 'em," he added.

"Yes, sir," agreed Bobby. "She gave me that idea—only you never know. An honest look is a rogue's stock-in-trade. You know that, sir. Besides, a sister often knows a lot about her brother, and often it's the straight woman runs the crookedest when there's a father or a brother in the case."

"Oh, hell," said the colonel.

"Yes, sir," said Bobby. "Our job, sir." He added, though more to himself than to his companion: "That's what murder is—hell."

"You know nothing to show young Moffatt and Bennett ever met at this what-d'ye-call it club?"

"No, and I shan't be told anything if I ask. That's their speciality at the Cut and Come Again—tell nothing and deny everything. But there's the chance young Mr. Moffatt may recognise the body—and say so. It will be important to know if any of them can identify it. And important, too, to know where they all were round about four yesterday afternoon."

" They'll have had plenty of time to think that up, if they want to," observed the colonel.

" Yes, sir," said Bobby. " Checking an alibi is always useful. If it's sound—well, that's that. If it's faked—well, that's useful, too. Thank goodness, a sound faked alibi is impossible—a contradiction in terms, nature having arranged that a thing can't be in two places at once."

They had reached the entrance to the drive now, where their car waited in the charge of a constable chauffeur. He was talking to another constable who had just ridden up on a bicycle. In the light of the headlamps he showed himself as Norris, the officer from the village. It seemed he had a message just received from county headquarters over the phone with instructions to find the chief constable and repeat it to him. It was to the effect that the post-mortem had established that the unfortunate Bennett had been shot three times. Two bullets were still in the body: one had passed through. The wounds inflicted were fatal, though the injured man might have been still alive when his car plunged over the brink of the chalk-pit. The immediate cause of death might have been the very severe injuries resulting from that fall. The shots had all been fired at close quarters, and the bullets had probably come from a ·32 Colt automatic.

The colonel listened gloomily. Bobby could see that he was a good deal disturbed but could not guess why, since the report was one they had both been prepared for. Norris continued. Inquiries had been made at garages and road-houses along the route from London, and had established that a car bearing the registered number of that found in the chalk-pit had stopped the day before at the Oakley Road House, where its driver had lunched. He had asked about the best and quickest way of reaching

Way Side, the residence of Mr. Hayes, and had been shown the road on a map.

" Way Side, eh ? " Bobby muttered. " Not Sevens. Bit curious, that. Looks as if Mr. Hayes may have something to tell us."

He had made this remark to Colonel Warden, who, however, he saw, was not listening. The chief constable drew a step aside and nodded to Bobby to follow, as if he wished to say something the two policemen were not to hear. In gloomy and resigned tones he said:

" It's in my mind—I'm not sure, but I have an idea that a year or two back Mr. Moffatt took out a licence for a ·32 Colt automatic—bad burglar scare at the time."

Bobby looked a little startled. He had hardly anticipated that. But it seemed to fit in. The colonel glanced at his watch.

" It's not very late. There'll be time to run round and have a look at the Firearms Register and make sure. Then we'll go on to Way Side and see if Hayes has anything to tell us, and if he knows why Bennett should have been visiting him."

" Very good, sir," said Bobby, realising that the colonel was actually quite sure about the Colt automatic and yet would be restless and uneasy till he had confirmed the fact. " Of course, if they have found two bullets they ought to be able to identify them with the pistol, if we can get hold of it."

" Yes, you had better go back to the house and do that. Say you want it for—for——"

" For purposes of comparison," suggested Bobby.

" Quite so," said the colonel. " Be—er—we know nothing yet, and we don't want to worry people for nothing. Er—be——"

" Tactful," suggested Bobby.

" Quite so," said the colonel, relieved. " Take Norris with you. Let's see now. It won't take a minute to look up the Firearms Register, and if we speed a bit—clear night, luckily—yes, I can be at Way Side by ten easy—ample margin. That won't be too late. Hayes isn't an early bird by all accounts. If you borrow Norris's cycle you'll have plenty of time to meet me there by then. Norris can tell you the way; it's quite simple."

" I looked it up on the map," Bobby explained. " I think I can find my way all right. Straight on as far as Battling Copse. Is anyone on duty there ? "

" No. Withdrawn. Not necessary after the thorough combing we've given the place; and, Lord knows, I'm short enough of men as it is—can't afford to put one where it's not absolutely necessary. The Watch Committee," complained the colonel, even at this moment unable to refrain from uttering his perennial and bitter grievance, " seem to think I can take on unlimited extra duties but never need any extra men."

He was still grumbling as he drove away, and Bobby and Norris went on up the drive to the house again.

" The old man don't like it, not half he don't," Norris confided to Bobby as they walked along, " him and Mr. Moffatt being friendly like. That's why he's shoved it on to us, him knowing well enough about the pistol; everyone does. Why, I've seen the young gentleman myself using it to pot at rats and vermin and such-like."

" Have you, though ? " Bobby asked. " You mean Mr. Moffatt's son ? Oliver, didn't they call him ? "

" That's right. And well the colonel knows it. That's why he's gone off; didn't like the job. Don't know that I blame him, either," added Norris generously. " Duty's duty, and same must be done, but I take it hard myself when I'm playing darts with a man one day and have to run him in the next."

"It's a thing we all have to face," Bobby said absently, his mind busy with the coincidence of the pistol and the missing young man. "Only thing is to remember it's not us, but the law."

"Ah," said Norris, musing upon this. Presently he added: "You can't be tactful like, asking to look at a pistol when a bloke's just been done in with one round the corner, so to say."

"Ah," said Bobby in his turn.

They went on to the house, and not all the tact Bobby could muster sufficed to dispel, or even much to alleviate, the evident uneasiness with which his request was greeted —or the still greater uneasiness when the pistol could nowhere be found.

Mr. Moffatt, who had made no effort to deny possession of such a weapon, believed it had been in a drawer in the library but he was not sure. After the burglar scare died down, he never thought of it again. A packet of ammunition was discovered, unopened. But that was all, though Mr. Moffatt agreed at once that his son sometimes used the pistol, sometimes merely for target practice, sometimes, as Norris had said, on rats and other vermin.

"Most likely Noll will know where it is," Mr. Moffatt said. "I'll ask him as soon as he comes in." And the scowl he gave the clock as he glanced at it suggested that the whereabouts of the missing automatic would not be the only subject discussed when the young man did make his appearance.

It was growing late now, so, leaving Norris to await the return of Noll Moffatt, and the possible production of the missing weapon, Bobby started off on the constable's cycle. He knew, from his careful reading of the map, that he had to go straight on, avoiding all turnings, till he came to Battling Copse, whose dark and heavy shadows it would be impossible to miss. A little further on he would come to the Towers Poultry Farm—" Teas " as well—and then, leaving that on the left, to where the road forked by a small pond. Keeping to the right, and taking the first turning on the right again, he would reach the entrance of the lane that led to Way Side. Half an hour's brisk cycling in the clear moonlight, or perhaps a little more, sufficed to cover the whole distance, and then, as he drew near the copse, he became aware that not only the moonlight shining through the close-growing branches upon the dense and heavy undergrowth accounted for the light that seemed to lie in a pool at the foot of the trees. He slowed down. There came clearly to his ear a trampling of feet, a sound of blows, and for a moment he remembered the tale of how here victorious Briton and stubborn Roman fought out once again each year their ancient conflict.

The moment passed. He jumped down and leaned the cycle against the nearest tree. He heard a voice say loudly:

" Like to chuck me into the chalk-pit too, wouldn't you ? "

CHAPTER VI

FISTICUFFS

BOBBY RAN FORWARD QUICKLY. In a kind of bay or inlet of open sward, surrounded on three sides by the dense growth of tree and bush that was Battling Copse, the clear moonshine, reinforced by the beam from the headlamp of a motor-cycle, showed two young men standing facing each other.

One, his back to Bobby, was tall, heavy, somewhat clumsily built; the other was of a smaller, more slender build, and, as he soon showed, very quick and active in his movements.

For, as Bobby came in sight of them, the taller of the two flung out at his opponent a heavy, somewhat ponderous right-hand punch. But the other adroitly side-stepped, and then retaliated with a quick left and right that brought from the onlooking Bobby a spontaneous and appreciative:

"Oh, pretty, very pretty."

Indeed, had those punches had a little more weight behind them they might have brought the fight to an immediate end. Both got well home, but the big man merely grunted, shook himself rather with the air of a duck shaking off raindrops, and then rushed forward. At once they were hard at it, for the smaller man stood his ground. Blow after blow the bigger of the two sent crashing in, and all of them his antagonist either took on the retreat with diminishing force or else avoided altogether. Once or twice indeed, as Bobby noticed with enthusiasm, he succeeded in avoiding devastating punches by simply moving his head an inch or two to one side, so that the other's ponderous fist missed by inches only, but missed all the same. Almost as clever was the speed with which he flung back in answer his own quick blows that only needed just a little more weight behind to make them as quickly effective.

He seemed to realise this, however, and that at close quarters he was no match for his antagonist. He began to give ground, making the big man use his energy in pursuit and taking advantage of his own greater agility to leap in with swift flashing hits that in the end must tell and then back again before the other could retaliate with effect.

A very evenly matched couple, Bobby thought; skill and speed against strength and weight; and then he reminded himself dolefully that a breach of the peace was being committed and that he was an officer of police.

"Just my luck," he thought sadly, and nearly cheered aloud as the big man made one of his bull rushes that would probably have been more effective in the ring, with ropes against which an opponent could be pinned. Had anything of the sort been possible in this open glade, or had the big man succeeded, or the other consented, in continuing in-fighting, the battle would probably not have lasted long. At close quarters greater height and weight have their full effect. But this time, when the big man made his charge, the other dodged with an astonishing speed and the agility of a tennis champion on the central court at Wimbledon. Then, as his opponent lumbered by, he hit him two or three times with a magnificence of speed and accuracy that not only fully justified Bobby's instinct to cheer, but sent the big man crashing to the ground.

He fell heavily enough, but almost instantly was on his feet again, showing a nimbleness his previous somewhat heavy movements had hardly promised. He turned, and was about to rush again at his antagonist, who had stood back to allow him to recover his feet, when Bobby resolutely roused himself from the trance of admiration and delight in which he had been lost. Paying to stern duty the tribute of a sigh, he stepped forward from the shadows in which hitherto he had been standing.

" Now then," he said sternly, " what's all this about ? "

Startled, they both turned and stared at him.

" Go to hell," said the first man.

" Get to blazes and quick about it," advised the second.

" Two minds with but a single thought," observed Bobby. " No, no," he added, getting between them as they were about to start again after their brief replies to him. " Apologies and all that, you know, but there it is. Got to stop, I'm afraid. Awful shame, of course."

" Who in thunder do you think you are ? " demanded the smaller man.

" Mind your own business if you don't want your head knocked off," said his erstwhile enemy.

Side by side, sudden allies, they stood and glared at him. Bobby beamed on them with all the friendliness he felt. This seemed to annoy them both still more.

" Chuck him in the chalk-pit," suggested the bigger and more truculent of the two, " and then I can get on with that hiding I'm going to give you."

" Take a better man than you," retorted the other, and instantly, forgetting their momentary alliance, forgetting, too, all about Bobby, they were at it again as fiercely as before.

But now Bobby took a hand—or, more accurately, a foot—by dexterously and unexpectedly tripping up the big man as he was making one of his bull rushes, and then the other as he dodged away, so that the two astonished combatants found themselves unexpectedly supine, gazing with some bewilderment at the calm moon above.

" Sorry," said Bobby contritely. " Awfully sorry. Let me answer your questions. As to who I think I am, I have reason to believe I'm a policeman. And I don't want my head knocked off, and you mustn't try, because you simply can't imagine the fuss there is if you hit a policeman. We might all be made of glass and liable to break. So it's not done. Never. Unconstitutional. Oh, and I am minding my business, because it is my business to see the King's peace is not broken, as seemed to be happening just now—very prettily, of course, but that doesn't count. The law cares nothing for art."

They were both on their feet again by now and were both gazing at Bobby in complete bewilderment as he delivered this long speech, which was, of course, intended to puzzle them and give them something else to think about than their apparent desire to annihilate each other.

" I don't see——" began one of them hesitatingly.

" I don't see either," agreed Bobby, " but there you are. Why not a gym, six-ounce gloves each, and an invite for me to look on ? What about it ? "

They both made sulky noises. Apparently the suggested delay did not appeal to them.

"It's all rot," said the bigger man. "Come on," he invited his opponent.

"You mustn't," said Bobby earnestly. "Really. Or I shall have to arrest you both. I should hate to do that."

He was one and they were two, and, as they had shown, both sufficiently vigorous and able-bodied. But he spoke with all the weight of authority, with all the majesty of the law, behind him. They were evidently impressed. The smaller of the two said:

"How do we know you are a policeman?"

Bobby produced his warrant card.

"Detective-Sergeant. Criminal Investigation Department. Scotland Yard," he recited. "At present detailed for duty with the county police."

They looked at each other. The police are always the police, but, all the same, the village constable is one thing and an emissary from Scotland Yard another. They began to put on their coats, though reluctantly and still looking sideways at each other.

"Sorry to be a spoil-sport," said Bobby, still apologetic. "Think over that gym idea—jolly good, if you ask me, though I shall call it a dirty trick if you don't let me know the date. By the way, I've been sent down over that affair that happened near here—dead man found at the bottom of the chalk-pit. Know anything about it? I heard something about chucking someone down the chalk-pit too."

He put a slight emphasis on the last word, and the smaller of the two men started and turned a little away, so that his profile showed clearly, caught in the beam from the motor-cycle headlamp. It reminded Bobby of another he had seen that evening, and he remembered also that Oliver Moffatt had not been found at his home.

"Are you Mr. Oliver Moffatt?" he asked.

" How do you know ? " the young man exclaimed, surprised.

" Oh, police, C.I.D., and all that," Bobby explained airily. " Hullo, where's your pal ? " he added.

For the big man had seized the opportunity to disappear, wheeling the motor-cycle before him, and now they heard its engine starting on the path that ran by one end of the copse.

" I'm going too," said Oliver Moffatt, and began to walk away.

" Half a minute," Bobby protested. " There are just one or two questions I want to ask. Your friend's name, please, for one thing."

" Ask him," snapped Oliver.

" You don't wish to give it ? " Bobby inquired.

Oliver only glared.

" Oh, well," said Bobby, producing his inevitable notebook. " Objection duly noted. Any objection to telling me what the row was about ? "

" Yes. Every possible objection."

" I wonder why ? "

" Wonder away."

" Bad mistake, if I may say so," remarked Bobby, " to set the police wondering. Never know where their wonders may not end. That affair in the chalk-pit here—you knew that was murder ? "

" Murder ? " repeated Oliver. " Murder ? " he said again.

Bobby waited, hoping for further comment. The young man was clearly troubled, but he said nothing for a time. Then he asked :

" How do you know ? Are you sure ? "

" Our information," Bobby said slowly, " is that the dead man had been shot. The pistol used was probably a

Colt automatic, ·32. We also have information that you are, or have been recently, in possession of a pistol of that make and calibre."

"Good Lord!" gasped Oliver. "You don't mean you think I did the chap in, do you?"

He was plainly startled and alarmed, even more so than seemed quite natural in one conscious of complete innocence. Bobby waited again, hoping more might be said. But after a moment or two of troubled silence all that came from the young man was an angry exclamation:

"You've no right to say things like that!"

"All I've said," Bobby pointed out, "is that you are reported to have had in your possession a pistol similar to that with which it is believed a man was shot close to this spot yesterday afternoon. Do you care to say if that is correct?"

"Dad has a Colt automatic," Noll admitted. "I haven't seen it for months."

"You have often used it?"

"I did a bit of potting at rats and so on at one time."

"Not lately?"

"No. It got a bit damaged; a spanner or something fell on it in the garage; dented the barrel and knocked the foresight crooked. You could fire it all right, but not much good for taking aim. It'll be in the house somewhere."

"It's been looked for but can't be found," Bobby said. "Any objection to my making sure you haven't it on you?"

Without waiting for any such objection to be made, he ran his hand lightly over the other's clothing, making sure Noll had on his person nothing large, hard, and heavy, like an automatic, and at the same time keeping a wary eye open for any sudden punch that might come his way, for he had acquired a considerable respect for the young man's gift for rapid hitting. However, nothing happened. Noll, taken entirely by surprise, submitted meekly, and Bobby stepped back, out of fistic range.

"That's all right," he said, and added warmly: "Thanks so much for letting me make sure."

"I didn't," snapped Noll with some truth. "And look here, I've had enough of this. I'm not going to answer any more of your damn' questions."

He turned his back and marched resolutely away. Bobby made no attempt to follow. He felt it would be useless to ask any more questions just then, and he had at any rate assured himself that Noll was not carrying the missing automatic on his person. Besides, a few hours' reflection often made people much more willing to talk than they had seemed at first. Opening his notebook, Bobby jotted down the number of the motor-cycle he had been careful to memorise.

"Won't be difficult to trace that young man," he told himself, and then went back to where he had left his cycle and rode on towards Way Side.

In spite of the delay, it still wanted a few minutes to ten when he reached his destination, and, as there was no sign of any car standing in front of the house, he concluded the chief constable had not yet arrived. He hesitated for a moment and then went round to find the back entrance. He had an idea that a little information about Mr. Hayes, who had made his money in America, and for directions to reach whose house the dead man had inquired, might be of interest, and might be gleaned better than by direct questioning through a little quiet gossip with the domestic staff.

CHAPTER VII

WAY SIDE GOSSIP

WAY SIDE was a comparatively small, modern house. The servants' entrance was at the side, opposite a small detached building Bobby guessed was the garage. Here, leaning against the wall, was a motor-cycle, and Bobby, turning the lamp of his own cycle upon it, saw at once that the registration number was that of the machine on which the big and truculent young man of Battling Copse had ridden away.

Bobby stood for a moment or two wondering what that could mean. It could hardly have been Mr. Hayes himself, he supposed. But Mr. Hayes might have a son, perhaps, or it might be merely a visitor. He would have to try to find out.

He knocked at the back door. An elderly woman appeared; and Bobby explained that he was a sergeant of police, and asked if he could wait there for the arrival of Colonel Warden, the chief constable, who was on his way to call on Mr. Hayes. Bobby did not mention Scotland Yard. He felt that if he could be accepted as a member of the local force his visit would cause less excitement, and the Way Side staff be less impressed and perhaps more willing to gossip.

He was at once invited in and hospitably conducted to

a small sitting-room he gathered was that set aside for the use of the servants. He was also offered a glass of sherry, but this, with many thanks, he begged to be allowed to decline, on the ostensible grounds that he was on duty, discipline was strict, and the chief constable ferocious in enforcing it. He regretted his devotion to discipline the less as a whisper he overheard made him darkly suspect that it was the cooking sherry he was to have been offered, since all other wine, apparently, was in the cellar and " master took care to put the keys in his pocket, the old screw, when he cleared her out."

Bobby guessed that the " her " referred to Mrs. O'Brien, the former housekeeper, of whose quarrel with Mr. Hayes, and subsequent dismissal, Ena Moffatt had spoken. A judicious inquiry or two confirmed this, and confirmed, too, the tale Ena had told. Evidently there had been a first-class row between Mr. Hayes and Mrs. O'Brien, ending in a slap across the face for him and a not unnatural dismissal on the spot for her. All this had happened the day before, between tea and dinner, and Mrs. O'Brien had departed accordingly in a whirl of tears and indignation, breathing, too, many dark threats of vengeance.

The elderly woman who had admitted Bobby, and whom he now knew to be Mrs. Marshall, the cook, added cryptically:

" If she hadn't gone when she did, she'd have stayed."

" That's right," said a brisk, good-looking young woman who had now joined them, and who it was had suggested the cooking sherry as a way out of the impasse caused by Mr. Hayes's having impounded the late housekeeper's keys.

She had been introduced as Miss Edwards, the house-parlourmaid, and was addressed as " Aggie " by Mrs.

Marshall. The only other resident member of the staff was apparently a young man named Ned Thoms, the " chauffeur-gardener," the establishment running much to hyphens and Mrs. Marshall having already tacked " housekeeper " on to her former title of cook, so that she was provisionally " cook-housekeeper." In addition, a woman came in every day from a cottage about a mile distant to help in the rougher work.

Both women, Aggie and Mrs. Marshall, would have been more willing to talk about Mrs. O'Brien's sensational exit from their midst but for their curiosity to know the purpose of the chief constable's approaching visit they were already associating with the chalk-pit tragedy every visiting tradesman or van-driver all day had been eager to tell them about. But, before the conversation changed, Bobby learned that Mrs. Marshall's cryptic remark that if Mrs. O'Brien had not gone when she did she would have stayed was less a truism and a platitude than an expression of a firm belief that Mrs. O'Brien had meant marriage, that the new hat, the ostensible cause of the quarrel, had been intended to clinch the matter, that Mr. Hayes's ridicule of it had been a symbolic refusal, and the slap across the face an acknowledgment of defeat.

" Meant he knew what she was up to and he wasn't having any, and so she let him have it," explained Mrs. Marshall, still inclining to the cryptic.

Miss Edwards had been punctuating Mrs. Marshall's observations with knowing little giggles that Bobby was sure meant there was more to the story than had yet come out. But Mrs. Marshall discouraged them with answering frowns; and Bobby thought it best to let that lie for the time, and to confirm their expressed supposition that the chief constable's coming visit was in connection with the death of the unknown motorist whose body had been found in the chalk-pit not far away.

" It's possible he was on his way to visit someone in the neighbourhood," Bobby told them, " so the colonel wants to find out if any of the residents knew him. We've been round by Sevens already, because we heard Mr. Moffatt had two American gentlemen staying with him."

" Did they know him ? " Mrs. Marshall asked.

" Didn't seem to, but they are to have a look at the body to-morrow in case they do."

" Oo-ooo," said Aggie, shuddering. " How awful like."

" The colonel seems to have an idea Mr. Bennett—that's his name, we think; the motorist's, I mean—was either an American or else had been over there," observed Bobby. " Mr. Hayes is an American gentleman, too, isn't he ? "

" Oh, no, he's a Londoner, he is," Mrs. Marshall answered.

" America's where he made his money," interposed Aggie. " He often talks about it. I've heard him at table. He says it's a lovely country; he says America for making money, England for spending it. That's why he's come home, he says."

" He'll be pleased to see your gentleman," Mrs. Marshall said to Bobby—this expression he gathered, and thought it a very nice one, referring to Colonel Warden. " He's always saying how good the English police are, and you know you can trust them, and not like them over there where anyone can be kidnapped in their beds any night almost."

" Oo-ooo," said Aggie tremulously, but all the same a little as if she felt the experience might not be without its interesting side.

"As all can see for theirselves on the pictures," added Mrs. Marshall. "I don't know how they ever dare go to bed."

"I'm sure I don't either, Mrs. Marshall," said Aggie, but again a little as if she would have risked it all the same.

"Very nice Mr. Hayes feels like that; means a lot on both sides when people are friendly to the police and feel they can trust them," observed Bobby. "Mr. Hayes isn't scared of burglars, then?"

Mrs. Marshall went pale at the thought of burglars, and said the very idea of such gave her quite a turn. Aggie opined that it would take a good deal to scare Mr. Hayes.

"Look at the way he stood up to Mrs. O'Brien," she said in tones that suggested that for her part she would far rather meet half a dozen burglars than one Mrs. O'Brien.

"Formidable lady, Mrs. O'Brien?" Bobby suggested.

Mrs. Marshall admitted it. Miss Aggie mentioned that Mrs. O'Brien stood near six feet. Mrs. Marshall remarked reminiscently that once a carter delivering goods had tried to be cheeky. It had been a fair treat to see Mrs. O'Brien reach for the rolling-pin and see him go off down the drive in such a scare as never was.

"He's little and thin and quiet, Mr. Hayes," said Aggie, "and she would have made twice him and to spare, but after she lost her temper and slapped him—well, all in a twitter, she was, and glad no worse happened to her than told to get out. There's a way he has of looking at times makes you go all crawly up and down the back, like when you see you've just nearly gone and been and trod on one of them big spiders or there's a rat about might run up under your dress if you didn't mind—Oo-ooo."

"Be quiet, Aggie. I don't know how you can think of such horrors," exclaimed Mrs. Marshall, and poked the fire for protection.

" Oh, I don't mean it isn't all right if you do what he says," protested Aggie.

" Well, he's the master, and good wages, too, if distrustful like, and keeps things locked up the way a real gentleman wouldn't; but, then, likely that comes from living in foreign parts," said Mrs. Marshall, for whom evidently foreign parts excused much.

" Just as well not to be nervous when you live so far in the country," Bobby said. " He's not like Mr. Moffatt, over at Sevens. He doesn't keep a pistol by him, just in case ? "

" Oh, no," said Mrs. Marshall.

" Yes, he does, Mrs. Marshall," said Aggie. " There's two in a drawer in his bedroom. I saw them when I was tidying up one morning. Gave me quite a turn. It's a drawer he generally keeps locked, but that morning it wasn't."

" Well, you didn't ought to have opened it," said Mrs. Marshall. " Mrs. O'Brien would have given you fair what for if she had known."

Aggie tossed her head, and pouted, and Bobby guessed that fear of a rebuke from the formidable but departed Mrs. O'Brien had probably been her reason for not mentioning her discovery before. Bobby observed that gentlemen living in the country often liked to have a pistol by them in case of emergency, and tried to find out if the two Aggie had seen had been revolvers or automatics. But she had no idea of the difference, and could give no description of the weapons. She had, she explained, shut the drawer again in a hurry, since you never knew " when them things mightn't go off and kill someone."

Bobby agreed with this pronouncement, and thought to himself that another inspection of the Firearms Register was indicated. One pistol in a lonely country house was not very exceptional, nor a licence for it very difficult to secure. Two of them seemed, however, to require explanation, nor would it be so easy to procure a second licence. But the two women, leaving again the subject of the departure of Mrs. O'Brien—for that, exciting and absorbing as it was, and fit topic for many a chat to come, was none the less eclipsed for the time by the newer thrill of the chalk-pit tragedy—began to question Bobby afresh about this latter event. With a great appearance of frankness he told them nearly as much as they knew already from the gossip they had heard, though they were almost as thrilled to hear it all again, only this time, as it were, from officialdom itself, as if it had all been new. On one or two points of entire insignificance Bobby corrected what they had heard; and on his side he was interested to find that already there was current a vague idea that what had happened had not been wholly accidental. He slipped in an inquiry as to whether anyone had mentioned having seen or heard of any strange motorist in the district. Strangers were rare at this time of year, when touring was out of season, and the roads seldom used by other than the inhabitants of the district. None, however, had been mentioned, and Mrs. Marshall and Aggie explained that neither of them that day had been beyond the Way Side grounds.

"And Mr. Hayes?" Bobby asked. "Did he stay in all day?"

This question set Aggie off giggling again in the same way as before. Mrs. Marshall told her sternly there was nothing to laugh at, and Aggie said she wasn't, and anyhow Mrs. O'Brien wasn't there any more, so what did it matter? And, after various other mysterious allusions, it began to appear that Mr. Hayes was in the habit of strolling over to the Towers Poultry Farm somewhat frequently, even occasionally of having tea there in preference to returning home for it; that this practice had been for some time concealed from Mrs. O'Brien, and that, when she had discovered it, it had been the underlying cause of the arrival of the new hat from London and of the subsequent events, including the famous slap on the face and the subsequent swift departure.

" Knew her nose was out of joint," said Aggie.

" Now, now, Aggie," said Mrs. Marshall.

" Knew she hadn't an earthly," declared Aggie.

" When it gets to face-slapping," mused Mrs. Marshall, " it means you've come to the parting of the ways."

" So it does," agreed Bobby.

" And the eggs he orders, and the prices charged as would make a West End tradesman blush, or as near as he could get," said Mrs. Marshall.

" I don't blame her for trying," said Aggie. " Why not ? "

" Chicken, too, till I'm tired of the sight of 'em," said Mrs. Marshall. " And beats me how to use the eggs, useful as eggs is and in most places hard to get the half of what you need. I gave Mr. Thoms four for his breakfast with his bacon this morning and he wanted to know if I thought he was an incubator, and me old enough to be his mother—or very near."

" Mr. Thoms ? " repeated Bobby. " Is that the chauffeur ? "

" Yes. Very respectable young man," said Mrs. Marshall, with a stern eye on Aggie, who was tossing her head again and giving other signs of disapproval, " even if he do like to keep himself to himself, and hours he spends in that garage on his own——"

" And welcome," interposed Aggie, but not as if she meant it.

" And had a nasty fall to-night," Mrs. Marshall went on. " Went off on the motor-bike to get some cigarettes at the post-office and come back with his poor face all swelled up, and such a black eye as you never saw."

" Dear me, must have been a nasty fall," said Bobby with keen sympathy—and even keener interest.

" Skidded," explained Mrs. Marshall, " and went right flat on his poor face."

" Made it," explained Aggie, " even uglier than it was before. He'll have to wash it now, though."

" Now, now, Aggie," protested Mrs. Marshall. " As smart a young man as ever donned a chauffeur's uniform," she told Bobby.

" Happened somewhere near Battling Copse, didn't it ? " Bobby asked.

" He didn't say," Mrs. Marshall answered.

" Worst of these country roads—the risk of skidding, I mean," Bobby said sympathetically, wondering, too, what cause of dispute could have arisen between Mr. Moffatt's son and Mr. Hayes's chauffeur.

Hardly a police matter perhaps, and yet one that might bear investigation. He was beginning to feel, too, that a visit to the Towers Poultry Farm—" Teas " as well—seemed to be indicated, and was it mere coincidence that a quarrel between Mr. Hayes and his housekeeper had broken out so fiercely on the very day and within an hour or two of the stranger motorist's mysterious death ? He tried to establish the exact times. There was evidence that the car had gone over the edge of the pit a minute or two after four in the afternoon. Mr. Hayes, it seemed, had gone out some time before that; had returned between five and six, saying he had had tea.

"Towers Poultry Farm," interposed Aggie with a fresh giggle.

"That's as may be," said Mrs. Marshall sternly, "and no concern of anyone's."

Aggie looked disposed to make a pert reply, so Bobby interposed with an inquiry as to whether Mr. Hayes was fond of the country, as he had come to live in such a quiet, out-of-the-way spot, and Mrs. Marshall expressed an opinion that it bored him to death and Aggie that he hated it. Aggie had known him stand at the dining-room window and curse the whole landscape in terms that had both shocked and thrilled her, though she had hardly understood a word, in spite of an extensive film education and a considerable knowledge of current literature. Mrs. Marshall said that the poor soul never seemed to know what to do. He went up to town two or three times a week, and on those mornings he would be quite cheerful. Other mornings he generally spent most of his time yawning and grumbling, cursing the paper because there was nothing in it or the wireless because there was nothing worth listening to.

"Cheers up, though," added Aggie, "when it's time to go and order a couple more chickens or another dozen new laid."

"Now, Aggie, no gossip," said Mrs. Marshall sternly. "Gossip's a thing I never could abide."

Bobby applauded, and said he couldn't either, and, by way of diversion, Mrs. Marshall got up and produced from a cupboard the very identical hat that had been the apparent, if not the real, cause of the parting between Mrs. O'Brien and her employer.

" Looks funny now it's been jumped on," Mrs. Marshall confessed, " but cost five guineas——"

" Oo-ooo," said Aggie.

" —as the ticket shows, from the Blue Jay in Middle Bond Street."

" Oo-ooo," said Aggie again, for the fame of the Blue Jay was widespread and the name appeared on most theatrical programmes—" Hats by Blue Jay "—and on the screen as well, " Hats, by Blue Jay," being a frequent feature of Topical Budgets.

" But, queer as it looks now, not beyond——" mused Mrs. Marshall.

" It just needs——" said Aggie.

" If you just——" said Mrs. Marshall.

" You could easily——" Aggie pointed out.

" A new ribbon there——" Mrs. Marshall suggested.

Bobby, Mrs. O'Brien's departure, the chalk-pit, all were forgotten till a ring at the front door called them back to their surroundings. Bobby said it was probably his chief, and time, too, for now it was nearly half past the hour. Aggie went to answer the summons. Bobby said he would come with her, as the colonel would be sure to want him, and in the passage outside, that lay between the servants' sitting-room and the kitchen, they came face to face with a big, sullen-looking young man whose somewhat damaged countenance Bobby had no difficulty in recognising, as he in his turn was also recognised, to judge by the other's start and grumbled and uncomplimentary comment.

" We meet again," Bobby said to him amiably, " and not perhaps for the last time."

" Go to blazes ! " snapped the other, and passed on his way.

CHAPTER VIII

MR. HAYES

MR. HAYES was, as his house-parlourmaid had described him, a small, thin, meagre little man. But Aggie had not mentioned his voice, which, especially as issuing from so narrow a chest, had an unexpectedly rich, deep note, a voice, indeed, that could emulate the lion's roar or the cooing of the dove. Nor had she spoken of his eyes, large, dark, languorous—eyes, indeed, almost feminine in their appeal, and as oddly discordant with his shrivelled and mean little personality as were the organ-like notes of his voice.

He seemed quite pleased to see his visitors, welcomed the colonel warmly, was genial to Bobby, tried to insist on their both joining him in a whisky-and-soda—Bobby noticed that the whisky bottle was nearly empty, and so did Mr. Hayes, for he promptly told Aggie to bring a new one and did not seem to regret the necessity. Colonel Warden at first declined the invitation, but Mr. Hayes would hear of no refusal and poured out a drink to whose seduction, after his long drive and hard day, the chief constable yielded. Bobby, however, turned teetotaller for the occasion, so Mr. Hayes offered him sherry instead, and seemed quite surprised to find that teetotalism covered sherry as well, though Bobby regretted the fact the more that this time the sherry offered was emphatically not o the cooking variety.

The formalities of hospitality concluded, Mr. Hayes began to talk at once, and without asking the business of his visitors, about the recent tragedy.

"Can't think," he declared, "how any man could contrive to get into that chalk-pit. Of course, on a dark night, and a bit over the nine, you might manage it. I don't see how else. I expect you know there's a lot of talk going. I drop in sometimes at the Red Lion for a pint. You get all the news there," said Mr. Hayes, chuckling, "as well as the little bit that others haven't heard."

The colonel smiled, said he supposed there was sure to be talk, and had Mr. Hayes heard anything definite?

"Bless you, yes," answered Mr. Hayes. "Lots, all contradicting all the rest. Knife found in the poor devil's heart; his throat cut from ear to ear; a pool of blood ankle deep, sometimes at the bottom of the chalk-pit and sometimes on top; full and precise particulars of sinister-looking strangers—when the beer's in, the tongue wags. I don't suppose much of it would be repeated to you folk, though. One thing to spin a yarn in a pub to make the other chaps gape, quite another to repeat it for taking down in a notebook, eh?"

And Bobby noticed that those soft, languorous eyes rested for one brief moment on the bulge in his pocket that showed where his substantial notebook was stored and then flickered swiftly away. Bobby told himself that it looked as though those soft, gazelle-like eyes missed little; he even wondered if they were always so soft and gazelle-like as they now appeared.

"I've got men out," observed the colonel, "trying to

pick up any local gossip that might give us a pointer. You can't tell us anything likely to be useful ? "

" I don't think so," answered Hayes, considering the point. " I didn't pay an awful lot of attention, and all it came to was that none of them believed it was an accident. What do you think ? That is, if it's a fair question. Of course, if it's an official secret . . . "

" Hardly that," said the colonel. " It will have to come out at the inquest, anyhow. The post-mortem shows shots through the heart."

Mr. Hayes whistled. Also he emptied his glass and thoughtfully filled it again.

" Funny," he said, " how often there's truth behind these pub stories. All the details wrong, of course, but the essential fact there all the same. I'm certain none of the Red Lion crowd knew there had been shooting, and yet they were all sure as hell there had been dirty work. Well, well. No idea who the chap was, I suppose ? But perhaps that's not a fair question either. The Red Lion seemed sure he was a stranger here."

Without waiting for a reply to his question, Mr. Hayes began to remember the claims of hospitality again, produced a box of what seemed excellent cigars, urged the colonel to let his glass be filled again, offered to have a cup of cocoa made for Bobby.

" Or anything else ; coffee, anything," he boomed in his rich, deep tones. " Very wise of you young fellows to be T.T. I'm not myself," he explained unnecessarily, for he was now at his third drink since the arrival of his visitors, and he had certainly been imbibing before—not that it appeared to have had the least effect on him ; he might have been emulating the night-club hostesses who remain sober all evening on the cold tea that is whisky's innocuous twin looker. " But I do advise it for all young chaps. I do indeed. Isn't there anything I can offer you, inspector ? " he asked, his voice so coaxing, so winning, so full of sympathy and true friendship, that Bobby felt his refusal ought to have been accompanied by a tribute of regretful tears. " Nothing at all ? Too bad. I'm sorry," said Mr. Hayes, making the words sound like a lament over the heroic dead. " You know," he continued, turning to the colonel again. " I never saw how it could be an accident. I know the place quite well. If I go for a country stroll—I love a country stroll," he interposed, his voice vibrant with emotion; " peaceful, beautiful, a lovely calm; to one who has had to spend his life in crowded towns, inexpressibly attractive. I often go by the copse. The blue-bells in the spring "—and now his voice was like a song—" remind you of a carpet with the spotlight turned on it. And too well hidden for London trippers to get at, fortunately. I was by there yesterday just about the time the thing must have happened."

" You didn't see or hear anything ? " the colonel asked.

" Nothing. Not a sound; not a sign," declared Mr. Hayes, the regret of all the ages in his sadly lingering tones. " No. I wasn't hurrying either. Just strolling along, enjoying the air, on my way to Miss Towers's place. You know it ? She and her sister run a poultry farm. There's an old mother, too. Lost all their money in some City smash, I'm told. Took it on the chin, though, and started this poultry idea. I get a lot of stuff from them, just by way of helping a bit; more eggs than cook knows what to do with, I believe. I have tea there sometimes, too. Nice, pleasant people, all three, and I'm afraid they have a hard time of it; very few customers, which is why I'm one more. Got to do what you can to help, you know."

" Had you tea there yesterday ? " the colonel asked.

" Yes. I expect I was eating my muffins while—well, while whatever happened did happen. About four, wasn't it ? At least, that's the Red Lion story. Someone heard the crash and noticed the time but didn't stop to look—thought it was someone playing marbles, I suppose. Nice friendly folk about here, but dumb; no imagination, no pep. I know it was about four when I got to Miss Towers's place, because I couldn't make them hear at first. They were all in one of the sheds, packing eggs or something. I remember thinking they couldn't be far away as it was tea-time. It was just the quarter past when one of them appeared. I remember looking at my watch and saying something about the time. Sort of mild hint I had been waiting. I had come straight by Battling Copse on my way, and I certainly didn't see or hear anything unusual. I expect I had gone some distance past before the thing actually happened. Anyhow, I heard nothing."

" You didn't actually come through the copse ? " asked the colonel.

" Oh, no; just passed by; the path skirts it but doesn't go through."

" There may have been someone there ? "

" Oh, yes, certainly; might have been as full as hell for all I know. If they had kept quiet and out of sight, no reason why I should know. Don't understand, though, why anyone should drive a car in there—rough ground, undergrowth, bushes, so on. Even if he wanted to go inside the copse himself, you would think he would park his car outside. Cook's persuaded it was burglars—she's got burglars on the brain. I suppose you don't put any stock in that idea ? Burglars having a preliminary look-see; car parked ready for a quick get-away; row over something, and one of them croaked?"

"We have no ideas as yet," the colonel answered slowly. "We think the dead man's name was Bennett."

"Yes?" said Mr. Hayes, the name apparently meaning nothing to him. "Nothing to identify him? No cards, no papers, letters?"

"Everything like that seems to have been carefully removed," the colonel explained.

"Everything? No bag? No valise?"

"No, nothing; even the tabs from the clothing had been cut out.

"Very odd."

"Evidently the murderer wished to destroy all possibility of identification," the colonel said.

"What about the car number?"

"Hired. Name Arthur Bennett and address a West End hotel Bennett left without saying where he was going. The address he gave at the hotel was in New York, but he claimed to be a British subject, and there hasn't been time yet to make inquiries in New York. But we did find some papers in the car, apparently overlooked by the murderer, and they suggest he was engaged in trying to sell American shares over here."

Mr. Hayes fairly jumped on his chair.

"Share-pushing?" he cried. "Good Lord, can the fellow have been after me?"

"After you?"

"Well, I just thought——" said Mr. Hayes apologetically. "Nothing in it, I dare say. But I made my bit over there—catering business, some, but more by speculating. Not difficult if you keep your head. Most don't. And if you aren't too greedy. Most are. Anyhow, once your name gets on brokers' lists you're apt to be marked down as a possible mug. I get offers through the post sometimes—the W.P.B. is where they go. Two or three times I've had visitors. I show 'em the door. Plausible beggars, too. Talk the gold filling out of your teeth, some of them. I remember one. Little man, round face, all one smile. ' Ted ' or some such name—wanted to be on ' Ted ' and ' Jack ' terms at once. My name's John, you know. I don't think I ever got his surname; don't remember it, anyhow. I let him talk. Then I rang for the salt. ' What's this for ? ' he says, looking at it sort of puzzled. ' To put on the tail of the next bird,' I said. So he grinned. Saw I was on his game and went off. Curious business. I suppose they do find mugs at times and then it pays all right."

" I understand there's an American gentleman interested in finance staying with Mr. Moffatt at Sevens," the colonel remarked.

Mr. Hayes whistled again.

" Then Moffatt had better see the red light," he declared. " But I think Moffatt's wide enough, isn't he ? Goes across the pond pretty often, he says, so I dare say he knows how to bat."

" It does seem," remarked the colonel, firmly removing his now empty glass beyond the reach of Mr. Hayes, plainly itching to refill it, " a little odd the dead man came from New York and——"

" And so many round about here have been there, or still go ? " interposed Hayes. " Like me to see the body ? I met a hell of a lot of folk over there, one way and another. There's just a chance I might know him."

" If you're sure you wouldn't mind," said the colonel gratefully, accepting a voluntary proposal where otherwise he would have had to make a formal request.

" Delighted," declared Mr. Hayes warmly. " At least, delighted's hardly the word, eh ? Poor devil. Delighted if I can help you, I mean."

" It's possible you may know him," observed the colonel. " We have information he asked about Way Side—asked how to get here, in fact."

" How to get here ? " exclaimed Hayes, his rich voice running up the scale to a superb crescendo of utterly bewildered astonishment. " Well, if that don't beat Finnigan, and Finnigan beat the band. That all ? Did he ask about me ? Or anyone here ? "

" Not that we know of."

" Sounds as if it must be someone who knew me over that side," declared Mr. Hayes. " Anyway, I shall be interested to see. Might be someone on the share-pushing stunt. Or someone I knew. You say he was shot ? Found the weapon ? "

" No," said the colonel. " No trace of it."

" It was probably a ·32 Colt automatic," observed Bobby, speaking for almost the first time.

" Plenty about," observed Mr. Hayes. " I've got one myself. In the good old States, they're just one of the necessities of life, like cough-lozenges over here. Don't need them this side, but I've kept mine all the same."

" I suppose you've a licence ? " observed the colonel.

" Licence ? No. I thought that was only for sporting guns—if you go potting rabbits and so on. I don't. I'm a fisherman. Never cared for shooting."

" A licence is required for a pistol also, Mr. Hayes," the colonel explained. " I'm afraid you're liable to a fine and confiscation of the weapon."

" Well, now, if that isn't just too bad," declared Mr. Hayes, his voice now a deep and tragic murmur. " What do I do about it? Pay my little fine, I suppose. Ought I to see a lawyer? I would like to keep the gun, I think, out here in the country. But I'm more than sorry if I've been breaking the law. Shall I hand it over right now? Do I get it back?"

"Well, perhaps, if you would let me have it, it might be as well," agreed the colonel. "I dare say in the circumstances you might be allowed to keep it, but you must make formal application."

"Right. I'll get it at once. It's upstairs. I keep it locked up in a drawer in my room."

Bobby had produced his notebook. He was making a quite unnecessary entry. Looking up, he said:

"Have you any other firearms in the house, Mr. Hayes? A second pistol, for example?"

Mr. Hayes shot at Bobby a look from eyes that had ceased to be soft and languorous, that had grown hard, keen, searching instead. Eyelids, half lowered, screened them almost immediately, and it was perhaps only Bobby's fancy that made him think he detected a note of menace in the other's soft, slow, alluring tones as he answered:

"Why, no, sure, one automatic's enough for me. I'm no two-gun man."

CHAPTER IX

SHARE-PUSHERS' "M.O."

MR. HAYES duly produced his automatic. Colonel Warden gave a formal receipt for it, noticed it was loaded, withdrew the clip, observed that the bullet had been extracted from the first cartridge—a not unusual precaution against an accidental discharge—and also observed that the weapon was in good condition, clean and oiled, and showed no sign of recent use. There had, of course, been ample time for cleaning and reloading, but the chief constable supposed that a firearms expert would be able to tell whether or no the bullets found came from this pistol.

But that the colonel did not think probable. Had Mr. Hayes been the murderer, and this the weapon used, it would hardly, he supposed, have been handed over so complacently.

When they had taken their leave and were again in their car, he said to Bobby:

"Well, sergeant, what do you think of all that?"

Without replying directly, Bobby told of the bout of fisticuffs by Battling Copse his sense of duty had so unfortunately obliged him to stop, and he repeated also the pieces of information given in the gossip of cook and maid.

" If Hayes has two pistols and has only turned up one, looks rather bad, eh ? " remarked the colonel, who had listened to all this with close attention. " We ought to get hold of the second one as well."

" Yes, sir," agreed Bobby, who did not see how this was to be accomplished, since they had no authority to search the house, and in any case Hayes had had plenty of time to conceal, if he so wished, any second pistol he did in fact possess.

" Awkward to do it, though," muttered the colonel, who saw as clearly as Bobby the difficulties in the way. " Very awkward."

" Of course, sir," Bobby pointed out, " it's possible the maid was mistaken. She was a bit scared, evidently, and shut the drawer in a hurry. I asked her one or two questions and she wasn't at all clear in what she said. She may be wrong in thinking there were two of them; she may have mistaken something else for the second pistol. I'm inclined to accept her story myself, but it's not much to go on. In cross-examination, a clever counsel would make her contradict herself every minute."

" Hardly good enough to apply for a search-warrant on," agreed the colonel.

" No, sir, especially as it may have been got rid of by now," Bobby said. " I would like to know, though, what the fight was about. I thought possibly young Moffatt might be more willing to tell you."

" I'll ask him," declared the colonel. " Moffatt's son and Hayes's chauffeur ? Curious. A lot of curious things about this business."

" There's the row between Hayes and his former housekeeper, too," Bobby said. " From what the other servants say, she expected to marry Hayes. He may have forced

FH

the quarrel simply to get rid of her. A little odd, though, its happening just now."

"What did you think of Hayes himself?"

"Very friendly gentleman; very frank and open," Bobby answered. "He told us everything we wanted to know before we asked, almost as if he had expected our questions. And he went out of his way to provide himself with an excellent alibi."

"He made no attempt to hide his having an automatic," the colonel remarked.

"He may have suspected the servants knew and were likely to tell," Bobby pointed out. "I couldn't help feeling, when he was talking about Miss Towers, he was answering any gossip he thought we might have heard. Unreasonable to complain of people being too free with their information when generally the trouble is to get anything out of them, but there it is; he struck me as all prepared to tell us just what he wanted us to know—too innocent to be true. Of course, if his alibi stands, he can't be mixed up in the actual murder. But he may know something about it all that frankness and openness of his is meant to hide."

"Have to interview Miss Towers, see what she has to say," the colonel decided. "Bit late to-night," he added, glancing at his wrist-watch, for, indeed, by now it was not far from midnight, "and I shan't have time in the morning. I think you had better see to that, sergeant, first thing to-morrow. You'll know better than anyone else what to ask and what to look out for."

"Very good, sir," Bobby answered. "Do you know if what Miss Towers says can be trusted? She and he have had time to fix up a story if they want to."

Colonel Warden had, however, never heard of the

Towers Poultry Farm or its occupants till now. He supposed some information about them might probably be obtained from Norris, the local constable.

" Seems," observed Bobby thoughtfully, " there are three women just outside the case—Mrs. O'Brien, Miss Moffatt, Miss Towers. And I suppose they all use lipstick, because I suppose all women do, and they are all apparently friendly with Mr. Hayes."

" I think we can leave Miss Moffatt out of it," the colonel said stiffly.

" You see," explained Bobby apologetically, " I keep wondering what her brother and Hayes's chauffeur were fighting about—one would hardly expect a youngster in Mr. Oliver Moffatt's position to be on fighting terms with a neighbour's chauffeur. Very likely nothing to do with our case, but one never knows. You noticed, sir, that Hayes rather went out of his way to tell us the older Moffatt went across to the States every year. Do you know if that is so?"

" No, I don't. Don't believe it either. I've known Moffatt long enough to feel sure I should know if there was anything in that story. Why should he take a trip like that every year? He has no business over there. If he does go, he must be deliberately keeping quiet about it. He does," added the colonel, with a touch of uneasiness in his voice, " take rather a long holiday every autumn, and never seems to have much to say about it."

" Inquiries," hinted Bobby, " could be made at the steamship offices."

" I'll see to it," said the colonel briefly, " though I'm sure there's nothing in it."

" Mr. Hayes," Bobby went on, " seemed quite enthusiastic about the country and country life. I never heard anyone quite so—well, almost lyrical."

" I suppose it's why he came here," the colonel said.

" The servants gave rather a different impression," Bobby pointed out. " They seemed to think it bored him to death; said he was only cheerful the days he was running up to town."

" Different moods, perhaps," suggested the colonel, and then he chuckled. " I must say," he went on, " Hayes can put away the drink all right, and I do like a man with a good head. He had had some before we got there, he had three or four stiff glasses while we were talking, and it hadn't the least effect. Sometimes the way, though, with these dried-up little men; they lap it up like so many sponges. The New York police didn't give you any description of the man they are inquiring about, did they ? Hayes was quite open about that, too. Knew all about the share-pushing game, evidently. Possibly he may be able to identify the body."

" Great help if he does," said Bobby, though he thought few things less likely. " It wasn't the New York police we heard from though. It was the F.B.I."

" F.B.I. ? " repeated the colonel, puzzled, thinking of the Federation of British Industries, for which he had a great respect as the bulwark of the world's prosperity, peace, and general well-being. " How do you mean ? How do they come into it ? "

" I don't quite know," answered Bobby, for whom the initials stood for the United States Federal Board of Investigation. " Some question of a Federal Bank having been let in, I think. The U.S. police system is a bit complicated. There are ten or twenty different bodies apparently, besides the State police and the local men as well, not to mention the recognised private detective forces. If a burglar sends a post-card arranging for a pal to meet him, then the post-office inspectors come in—unlawful use of mails. If he crosses a State border going to or from a job, then that makes it a Federal offence, and the F.B.I., the Federal Board of Investigation, comes in—the "G-men," as they call them on the films. If he doesn't make a correct income-tax return of his profits from burgling, then the Treasury agents follow it up. Any suspicion that he uses cocaine to buck him up before going burgling, and the Narcotic Board is on his trail. And so on. If he is very, very careful, he may have only the State police to deal with, but that seems exceptional. I suppose it works out all right, but it sounds more like a crossword puzzle than a police system. Anyhow, the F.B.I. people seem to be the ones interested this time. And they seemed to think we should know at once whom they meant without any details from them—seemed to have an idea England was such a small country, we would know all our crooks the way a village policeman knows all the bad characters on his round."

"But surely they gave some indication?"

"Well, what it came to wasn't much more than that they thought he was an Englishman by birth, and probably a Londoner, very quiet and self-possessed and unassuming, cool as hell——"

"Cool as—what?" asked the colonel, slightly startled by this metaphor.

"Cool as hell," Bobby answered gravely, "but I think over there they use 'hell' merely as a general adverb of emphasis. Liable to shoot to kill when in a fix—a 'killer,' they called him—and probably middle-aged. And that's about all."

"What about the M.O.?" asked the colonel, M.O. being the usual abbreviation for that method of procedure

—the *modus operandi*—which it is the general police experience all over the world very few criminals ever vary, those who do being those who are really dangerous, at the very head of their profession.

" The general idea, from what they say, but it seems largely guesswork," Bobby answered, " is that this unknown Britisher—Mr. X—picks up rich Americans over here, gets friendly with them, gets to know a lot about them, goes out of his way to put them under some obligation if he can, is very careful to do nothing in any way suspicious. If cards are played, for instance, he never wins. On this side that's all there's to it. All as innocent and above-board as you please. A year or two later—it's all carefully worked out; months between each move sometimes; they can afford to wait, with cash winnings in the thousands in prospect—Mr. X turns up on the other side and meets his former American friend once again, apparently by accident. At first even he will hardly remember him, then, of course, he does remember and is delighted. But he is a stranger in a strange country, and he grows confidential presently. He wants advice. He wants a helping hand. The American is interested, and good-naturedly willing to do what he can. Mr. X explains he is over on a big deal—too big for him, he is afraid. Big profits in view, certainly, but a big risk, especially for a stranger who doesn't know his way about too well. Sometimes it's a big arms deal, and he daren't touch it because, if his Government got to know, he would lose big contracts. Or he hasn't enough capital. Or he is called back to England over a still bigger deal—telegram from the Rothschilds, perhaps, anyone can send a cable and sign Rothschild. Anyhow, on one excuse or another he fades out. His American friend takes his place, goes on with the deal, and, when finally he is a good fat sum out of pocket, he may be inclined to regard it as an ordinary business loss. Even if he has suspicions, he may prefer to say nothing for fear of being shown up to his business friends as a 'mug.' And he never associates his nice, frank, straightforward, pleasant English friend Mr. X with the gaping hole in his bank account. Why, the F.B.I. say they have heard of one case in which the victim finally settled up a loss of a hundred thousand dollars and on the same day wrote a letter of introduction to Mr. X, recommending a friend of his, visiting England and also a rich man, to Mr. X's kind attentions. Probably he received them, but names are not known, so we can't tell what happened. But the F.B.I. say they have reason to believe something like a hundred thousand sterling has been extracted from American business men by our Mr. X, and they also seemed to think that on that information we could do him up in a brown paper parcel and pack him off to them by return of post. Another thing they say is Mr. X is careful never to operate on two men from the same town. If he gets hold of a St. Louis man one year, then St. Louis men are safe from him for ever after. America's a big place; the big business man from Pittsburg and his opposite numbers from St. Paul or New Orleans may never meet. But people from the same town might meet and might compare notes."

"Nothing much in all that to go on," commented the colonel.

"No, sir, except the fact that we suspect Bennett had something to do with some such swindle. And it's more than a little curious that one of Mr. Moffatt's friends should have given him a warning against the other gentleman dining there—Pegley, I think his name was.

It did strike me that the description Hayes gave of the man he said called on him to try to push off some rotten shares was a bit like Mr. Pegley."

" I noticed that," agreed the colonel. " Seems more promising trail to follow. I happen to know—he grumbles about having so much tied up on such low interest—that Moffatt has a very large sum in old consols. He hinted once that it was in six figures."

" Sort of thing the share-pusher goes for," Bobby remarked. " ' What's the good of leaving all that money at two and a half when with a little enterprise you can get five or ten, double or quadruple your income ? ' That's their line of country. It succeeds, too, very often. Of course, that means Mr. Moffatt is more likely to be a share-pusher's victim than in the game himself, as Hayes's story of secret visits to America seemed to hint. I suppose you know, sir, if the six figures in consols is a fact ? There's no chance it's imaginary ? "

" How should I know ? " snapped the colonel irritably. " We were talking about investments one day, and Moffatt happened to say that. That's all."

CHAPTER X

THE POULTRY FARM

IT WAS EARLY, then, the next morning when Bobby presented himself at the Towers Poultry Farm. At least, he thought it was early, but on the farm it was merely the pause in the daily routine when the necessary morning work was over, the afternoon toil not yet begun, and so there was opportunity for attention to odd jobs always clamouring to be seen to.

Bobby was not much of an agriculturist, but even to his inexpert eyes sundry signs suggested a certain lack of ready cash; nor was he sufficiently accustomed to poultry farms to know that such signs are their almost necessary and inevitable characteristic. A girl appeared from behind one of the outhouses and, seeing him, came towards him. She was of tall and vigorous build, dressed in rough country attire, with heavy boots and gaiters and with her hair closely cropped. No one could have called her even moderately good-looking, for her features were large and irregular, there was a small birthmark on one cheek, the Eton crop she affected as little suited her as any style of hairdressing she could possibly have chosen. One had the idea, indeed, that she wished to emphasise her lack of any claim to prettiness or charm. None the less, the direct look in her wide, straight-gazing eyes, the whole healthy vigour of her appearance, gave her an attractiveness of her own.

"A real Amazon," Bobby thought, as she strode towards him, her heavy boots crunching the gravel of the path, in her hands a long-handled hoe and a basket she managed somehow to hold as though they were spear and shield.

"Oh, good morning," he said, lifting his hat as she came striding up. "Miss Towers, I think? I'm so sorry to trouble you." He produced his card. "I am inquiring into the accident at Battling Copse near here," he explained.

"Oh, yes," she said, looking at him steadily. "Was it an accident?" she asked. "There's a lot of talk."

"Yes?" he said. "You have heard something?"

"I've heard nothing else," she answered. She added: "There was a policeman here yesterday. He wanted to know if we had seen any strangers and if we had had anyone for tea. We provide teas. We couldn't tell him anything."

"You had seen no one?"

"Only neighbours. No strangers."

"No one for tea?"

"No. Mr. Hayes came over from Way Side, but no one else. We don't often, at this time of year."

"Oh, yes," said Bobby, thinking to himself that this tall, direct, well-built girl might easily exercise a strong attraction on the little, dried-up Hayes, even if only by force of contrast. "Mr. Hayes is a friend of yours?"

She did not answer that at once. Her frank and direct gaze was full upon him. Quite plainly she was thinking: "What does 'friend' mean?" Bobby told himself that she was one of those people who are inclined to take words in their exact and literal meaning, whose very simplicity of thought and outlook can at times be more baffling than any subtlety.

"Why do you want to know?" she asked abruptly. "Does it matter?"

"All depends," Bobby answered. "You said just now there was a lot of talk going on. Well, it will be no secret soon; it will have to be said publicly at the inquest. The dead man was not killed by any fall; he had been shot. So naturally we have to make all kinds of inquiries, most of them entirely useless and pointless, no doubt, but we can't tell that till we've made them. We have nothing to go on but what people can tell us. Even the smallest detail, quite unconnected you would think, might prove the very pointer we need."

She considered this with the grave straightforwardness that seemed a characteristic of hers.

"You mean it may be murder?" she said, and paused. "I don't see what I can tell you," she went on, "beyond what I told the other policeman. But if you want to ask any questions you had better come into the house. It's cold here."

Bobby thanked her, for in fact the wind was blowing chillingly by the corner where he was standing. He followed her towards the house—a small country cottage, low-roofed, creeper-clad, picturesque, damp, inconvenient. Its utter destruction and replacement by the most repulsive of modern bungalows would have drawn passionate protests from any lover of the old English countryside, but none from its inhabitants.

Bobby's introduction to it was by way of bumping his head hard against the lintel through failing to heed his guide's curt warning: "Duck—low doorway." He was still rubbing his head and feeling slightly dazed when there appeared coming down the path to the cottage another, younger girl—one in every way an entire, almost comically complete contrast to Miss Towers, and yet bearing so strong a resemblance to her it was evident at once they must be sisters.

But where one was tall, large-limbed, vigorous, the other was small, slender, slightly built; where the one was straightforward and direct in her bearing, carrying basket and hoe like spear and shield, the other had a lost and wondering look, as though caught up into a strange land, carrying a sketch-book she held in her hand as though it were a scroll of magic spells. Where the one strode along the gravel path with purpose in every movement, the other seemed to wander in a dream; where the one had made him think of an Amazon armed for battle, the other reminded him of a little child far distant from her home. And where the elder girl's attire and whole appearance had been severely workmanlike and practical, this other younger one was all one dainty loveliness that seemed to have but small relation to the common tasks of everyday life. Her features, too, in spite of the strong family resemblance the two girls bore to each other, were somehow in her case transmuted to a grace and a perfection that gave her some claim to be called even beautiful. Her hair, for instance, was not Eton cropped, but a mass of soft and lovely curls that seemed to hold the sunlight imprisoned and yet to radiate it, too. She gave Bobby a glance as she came up that was not exactly uninterested, but seemed more to pass him over as though he were not there at all, as you might pass over a broom standing in a scullery corner, and she said very earnestly to his companion:

" Henrietta, this time I've got those beeches almost as they are."

"Then," said Miss Towers promptly, "you had better give it me before you burn it."

The girl shook her head.

"No, Henrietta," she said sternly. "You are so weak. If I let you, you would keep things of mine that are really —bad." She shot out this last word with an unexpected, tremulous vigour that made Bobby think of some criminal confessing such guilt as human ears had never heard before. "I must look at it again later on to see if it is worth keeping." She paused, and then, now like a child whispering its love to its mother, she said: "But I do think perhaps this time it's—good."

The last word was murmured like both a benediction and a prayer; and it was as in the light of another world that she drifted away from them. The girl she had called Henrietta said to Bobby in a voice full of a tender and affectionate pride:

"Molly's always sketching and painting. Nobody will buy her work, though. They say it's like nothing they ever saw. That's because they haven't her eyes, so how can they? Come inside."

Bobby followed her into what was evidently the kitchen. Something was cooking in the oven, to judge by the extremely pleasant smell pervading the room. The kitchen was plainly also the general sitting-room, and on one wall hung a series of water-colours, chiefly sketches of flowers, sometimes just of a bird on a bough in blossom. Bobby, looking at them hurriedly—he had a certain talent for drawing himself, though a comparatively poor feeling for colour—thought at first they were quite commonplace, just ordinary little drawings with a vague, indeterminate colouring. He paid them no more attention, having, indeed, other things to think of, and it was only when he was in bed that night, and on the verge of dropping off to sleep, that he seemed suddenly to remember in those slight water-colour sketches a quality as though upon them, too, had shone the light that never was on land or sea.

At the moment he was very much more interested in some photographs standing on the broad window-ledge. They seemed to him to be exceedingly good and striking work. Two, in separate frames, represented the two girls he had already seen. In another frame, intended for three photographs, but now with only the central space occupied, the two side spaces holding only pen-and-ink sketches of fruit blossom, was a photograph of a much older woman—probably, Bobby thought, from the resemblance she bore them both, the mother of the two girls, even though that resemblance included neither the direct vigour of the one, the elfin loveliness of the other. Looking at them, two thoughts occurred to Bobby: firstly, that young Noll Moffatt had been spoken of as an enthusiastic and highly skilled amateur photographer, and, secondly, that the Molly girl was really extremely pretty, and that, when two lads start fighting, a pretty lass is as likely an explanation as any.

Keeping these two ideas at the back of his mind, he began to ask a few vague questions. He learned that the occupants of the farm were Miss Henrietta Towers, to whom he was talking; Miss Molly, whom he had just seen; and their mother, who was out at the moment. Henrietta, it was plain, was the working partner. The mother, whom, Bobby noticed, Henrietta referred to once as Mrs. Oulton, looked after the house, and prepared teas for such visitors as the better weather chanced to bring. Molly, Bobby gathered, helped when she remembered, but was generally absorbed in her painting.

Occasionally she made a sale, but very seldom, her earnings not very much more than paying for the materials she used.

" Of course, she helps, too; she's very useful in the farm work," declared Henrietta. " Only sometimes she forgets." She gave a little sudden laugh, a bubbling laugh that came unexpectedly from her grave, impressive presence, as though some solemn flowing river began all at once to sparkle like a running brook. " Molly," she explained, " was helping pack eggs the other day, and what she did was to make a symphony of the brown, the speckled, and the white. It was awfully nice as a colour-scheme, but we weren't ready when the egg-gatherer got here and he wasn't a bit pleased at being kept waiting."

Occasionally, too, they hired a little outside assistance. But the bulk of the work was done by Henrietta; and she intimated quite plainly that there was lots of it—too much, anyhow, for her to spend time on idle converse with Bobby.

" I'm awfully sorry," he apologised. " I'm trying to make a complete picture in my mind of the district and everyone living in it. We think the dead man knew someone round here. It seems as if he must have had some object in coming here."

Henrietta made no comment. She did not seem interested.

" You know Mr. Moffatt, of Sevens," Bobby went on. " They may be customers of yours? "

" Yes," she answered. " Why? "

" Did young Mr. Moffatt take those photographs on the window-ledge? " Bobby asked. " I am told he is a first-class photographer."

"Yes, he did," she answered, and then asked again: "Why?"

"I think," Bobby continued, "Mr. Hayes at Way Side is a customer of yours, too?"

"Well?"

"He employs a chauffeur, doesn't he? Young fellow named Thoms?"

For the first time he had the feeling that a question had embarrassed and troubled her. Her gaze was as direct as ever, but now her clear, far-seeing eyes seemed to show a troubled look.

"You are asking a great many questions," she said suddenly. "You seem to know the answer to them all."

"I am investigating a murder," he reminded her.

"Well," she said, with an air of admitting his answer.

"Last night," he went on, "I happened to come across young Moffatt and Thoms fighting each other."

"Fighting?" she repeated, this time with a very startled air.

"By Battling Copse," he added.

She made no comment, but sat staring straight in front of her.

"Breach of the peace," Bobby went on. "I'm a police officer. So I had to interfere. I asked what the trouble was. They wouldn't say. Can you guess?"

Again she did not answer, but her expression remained moody and troubled.

"This may be a case of—murder," he reminded her.

"It can't have anything to do with the murder," she told him with an emphasis that made him wonder whether she did not in fact either guess or fear that some such connection might exist.

"Are you sure of that?" he asked.

"Of course I am; it can't, how could it?" she replied, again very emphatically and again a little as if it were as much to herself as to him that she gave the assurance.

He left the point, feeling it would be useless to press her just then. He said:

"I want to be as frank with you as possible. There is your sister, Miss Molly. Anyone can see she is an exceedingly pretty and attractive young lady."

He paused, and she gave him a look strongly reminiscent of a tigress suspecting interference with her cubs.

It was very clear that anyone who touched Molly, or Molly's interests, or Molly's happiness, would have an exceedingly determined and formidable guardian to reckon with.

"Sorry," said Bobby. "You see what I mean? If two boys quarrel about a girl they both want to please—well, it's nothing much to do with the police, though we have to stop it if we actually see them trying to punch each other's heads. But if they were fighting for any other reason . . ."

He left the sentence unfinished. For the first time she was no longer looking directly at him. She got up and went to stand by the window, looking out of it. She said over her shoulder:

"Who was winning?"

This question was so unexpected that Bobby could only gape. She did not follow it up. After another pause, she said, still throwing the words at him over her shoulder:

"Boys fight about anything. I'm sure it had nothing to do with the poor man who has been killed."

"We are groping in the dark," Bobby said. "We must, if people won't tell us what they know."

"There's nothing I can tell you," she said moodily,

and came back to her seat. " I don't think I want to answer any more questions."

" Miss Towers," Bobby said earnestly, " refusing to answer is itself an answer. I don't want to press you, of course. I have no right to. I am merely asking for help. A man has been murdered."

" There are things worse than murder," she muttered.

" Why do you say that ? " he asked.

" Well, there are, aren't there ? " she retorted gloomily.

" No," he answered then. " There may be worse criminals than murderers; there is no worse crime."

She did not seem to be listening to this. She said:

" They were saying here his name was Bennett. Is that true ? "

" Yes. Why ? "

" I knew a Bennett once," she said. " Or, rather, father did. In business. It can't be the same, though."

" Why not ? "

" Well, why should it be ? It's a common enough name. Besides, that Bennett was a tall, big man. Six feet. They say this man was small, with small hands and feet."

" Yes, that's true," Bobby agreed. " You have heard a good many details."

" We have heard nothing else all day," she answered.

" Has young Mr. Moffatt been here to-day ? "

" No."

" Or Thoms ? "

" Why do you ask about him ? I don't think he has ever been here. Why do you ask ? "

" Well, Mr. Hayes is a customer of yours, and so I thought perhaps his chauffeur "

" He has never been here, never," she repeated, with what he felt again was unnecessary emphasis.

" But Mr. Hayes buys a good deal of stuff from you, I understand ? Eggs, chickens, and so on ? "

" Yes, he does. But he always comes himself for what he wants. He is the best customer I have. He buys a lot, and I always charge him double."

" Oh," said Bobby, faintly surprised. " How's that ? "

" He's trying to seduce me," she explained.

CHAPTER XI

HENRIETTA'S STORY

BOBBY DID NOT QUITE KNOW what to make of this somewhat embarrassing declaration, made, as it had been, in the most matter-of-fact way conceivable. He was not even sure at first that it had been made quite seriously. He wondered vaguely what the somewhat conventional-looking elderly woman—to judge from her photograph—who was Henrietta's mother, would have thought of the remark. Glancing again at her photograph where it stood on the window-ledge in that frame intended to hold three pictures but in which her own was now solitary, he was more struck this time by the quality of the sketches flanking it. For a moment he thought he saw in them a curiously vivid and exceptional quality, and then he looked again and thought they were quite simple and ordinary little things, such as almost anyone could produce, with a certain fancifulness in their manner that made them unlike anything he ever remembered seeing in nature. He jerked his mind back from them to what Henrietta had just told him and said:

" You don't mean——"

He paused, uncertain how to complete his sentence, and she answered:

" I just thought you ought to know, perhaps. There's

a lot of gossip going on. I expect you are sure to hear. Mrs. O'Brien was very upset. Only she would think it was Molly. She couldn't believe it was only me. Molly always makes him uncomfortable. She often does—his sort, I mean. If it had been Molly——" She paused, and again that look of the tigress defending her young burned for a moment in her eyes. Bobby had the impression that she would have sent the whole world crashing to its doom rather than see her sister threatened by the smallest danger. " I can look after myself," she said abruptly. " It amuses me to charge him threepence for a three-ha'penny egg."

" I see," murmured Bobby, thinking that she looked fully capable of putting the withered-up little Mr. Hayes across her knee and administering the required chastisement. But then he remembered a certain veiled menace he had thought he detected in Hayes's half-closed and peeping eyes, and he was not sure of what might happen after. A little worried by thoughts he felt could have no connection with the inquiry it was his duty to pursue, he put them out of his mind and said: " You know Mrs. O'Brien has left Way Side ? "

" I heard there had been a row," she answered. " Everyone was talking about it till this other thing happened."

" It's not often," he remarked, " that there are two such exciting pieces of news in a quiet place like this, I suppose ? "

" You mean there may be some connection," she said in her frank, direct way, looking full at him. " I don't see why you should think so."

" I don't either," he agreed. " Coincidence, that's all, I suppose, like your having known a Mr. Bennett and that being also the dead man's name."

"Well, they can't be the same," she repeated. "There are lots of Bennetts."

He asked one or two more questions, trying to find out something more about the Mr. Bennett she had known. But she said again he had been a purely business acquaintance of her father's, and that neither she nor her mother had ever seen him. In speaking of her mother she again referred to her as Mrs. Oulton, and, seeing that he noticed this, she said:

"Mother has been twice married. My own father died before I was born. When I was ten, mother married Mr. Oulton. I always called him father; he was like my own father. No one could ever have told there was any difference between any of us."

Bobby noticed, too, the expression, "any of us." He said:

"Were there other children?"

She did not answer for a moment or two. He had the idea that this question had been singularly unwelcome; it was even something like a momentary fear that seemed to flash for an instant across the placid depths of those direct and open eyes of hers. Then, as if reflecting that there was no point in attempting to withhold from him information he could easily obtain elsewhere, she said:

"Yes. A boy. Two years older than Molly."

"Does he live with you?"

"No."

"Can you give me his address?"

"I could," she answered, "but I don't see why I should, and I don't think he would want me to."

"May I ask why?"

"Not everyone enjoys being cross-examined by the

police about things they know nothing of," she answered deliberately.

"Very well," Bobby said. He never, if he could possibly help it, pressed a reluctant witness. Pressure was apt to produce lies for one thing, and lies were a nuisance, misleading and also embarrassing to the liar, who often then had to tell more lies to bolster up the first, till finally he himself grew confused between lie and truth. And an interval for quiet thought and reflection was often much more effective in producing a readiness to give the required information. It was his general experience that one thing told willingly was worth half a dozen resulting from what are called "third degree" methods.

"There's mother," she said abruptly. "Excuse me a moment, I must tell her you are here."

An elderly woman, whom Bobby took to be Mrs. Oulton, had just come in by the garden gate. Henrietta got up quickly and left the kitchen. Bobby thought it was like her direct methods to have said outright that she wished to tell her mother of his presence instead of making some excuse or another. He got up and went across to look at the tiny water-colours hanging on the wall—almost a schoolgirl's work in their extreme simplicity and yet with a haunting quality about them that was difficult to appreciate. And how had she been able to imagine that effect of light on the dew-drops caught upon a spider's web spun between the twigs of a rose-bush? Sentimental, he decided, only that it was austere as well; and then Henrietta came back into the kitchen, looking very cross.

"Molly's just too trying," she declared. "She's torn up the thing she'd just done of the beeches, and it was lovely."

"She is a severe critic of her own work," Bobby

remarked, making up his mind now that the one he had been looking at of the dew upon the spider's web was, after all, quite ordinary—anyone could have done it who had happened to see it like that.

" I could shake her," declared Henrietta formidably. " Molly's wonderful, but no one understands. Mrs. O'Brien did."

" Did she ? " exclaimed Bobby, interested.

" She said Molly was a genius," Henrietta said, a little as if challenging him to deny it, and, if he did, then he would get the shaking Miss Molly merited. " She gave her an introduction to an agent—someone she knew—Fisher, his name was, off Fleet Street somewhere. He has got Molly one commission. Twenty pounds. She goes up to town once a week to see him now and to try other places as well. Mrs. O'Brien wanted us to go back and live in town; she said you had to be on the spot; she said Molly was wasted here. Of course, she wanted to get Molly away ; away from Mr. Hayes, I mean."

" Mr. Hayes goes up to town pretty regularly, too, doesn't he ? " Bobby remarked.

" Yes. He hates the country really. I can't think why he ever came to live in it," she answered.

Bobby couldn't either. But, then, Hayes might have thought he would enjoy country life before coming to experience it; expectation so often outruns reality. He went on:

" You said Mr. Hayes was here for tea the day before yesterday ? "

" Yes," she answered, looking at him again in her grave, direct way. " He got here about ten past four. Is it true that—that whatever happened at Battling Copse happened at four exactly ? "

"We have evidence," he told her, "that shots were heard at four o'clock and further evidence that almost immediately afterwards a noise was heard coming from the copse of something heavy falling. Presumably that was the car going over into the chalk-pit. Also a man, in what the witness calls gentleman's clothes—which seems to mean an ordinary lounge suit with a bowler hat—was seen leaving the copse somewhere about four. Unluckily, that's all the description we have of him, but all of it together fixes the time pretty accurately. You are sure of the time Mr. Hayes got here?"

"Oh, quite sure," she answered, smiling a little. "He happened to say it was a quarter past. We were in the egg-shed, and he said he had been waiting so long without seeing anyone he thought we must all have gone off for the afternoon and there was no chance of tea. It struck the quarter"—she glanced as she spoke at the clock above the mantelpiece that Bobby had already noticed possessed a loud strike, and chimed both the hours and quarters—"and Mr. Hayes looked at his watch and said we were just right." She smiled again. "It's a good quarter of an hour from Battling Copse here," she said, "even hurrying. Mr. Hayes hadn't been hurrying, and he had been here some minutes."

"Has there been any talk about him?" Bobby asked.

"There's been a lot of talk about everyone," she retorted. "I don't think I heard anything about him specially, though, only you were rather anxious to know the exact time he was here."

"Well, it's always a help," Bobby admitted, smiling, "to know the exact whereabouts of everyone in the neighbourhood."

But to himself he thought that the alibi she had thus

provided depended a good deal upon clock and watch being both correct, and that it is by no means difficult to alter clock or watch when necessary. For that matter, apparently no one else had been present, so that the Hayes alibi depended solely upon Henrietta's word—as hers presumably would do upon his. Not completely satisfactory, he thought.

" I am sorry to have asked you so many questions," he said presently. " I am afraid you thought a lot of them very stupid and boring. It's just routine. We have to go on worrying and worrying till perhaps we do—or we don't—get hold of something. There's just one other thing, and after that I shan't have to worry you any more, I hope. You said your father—Mr. Oulton—had business dealings with a Mr. Bennett. Very likely the coincidence means nothing. But you said he was unusually tall, and yet you also said you had never seen him."

" It was what father said once," she explained. " Molly found a pair of gloves in his car. We knew they weren't dad's, because they were too big. Dad said he and Mr. Bennett had been making business calls together and Mr. Bennett must have forgotten them. Molly laughed about their being so big. She tried them on and we all laughed—her hand would have gone into the thumb nearly—and dad said Mr. Bennett was a very big man, over six feet. That's all."

A memory had been stirring faintly in Bobby's mind.

" I don't want to distress you," he said, " but the name—Oulton. Was there not—two or three years ago or more . . . ? "

" He was found shot," she answered steadily. " They said it was suicide. We never believed it. But that was the verdict."

" At the seaside, wasn't it ? " Bobby asked.

" Yes. They found him in the car. He had lost all his money. He had always been very well off. We lived like that—I mean a big house and so on. When he died there wasn't anything. Even mother's bonds had gone. They said that was why—why they believed he shot himself. But dad wasn't like that."

" No," said Bobby, who knew, however, that sometimes those who are not " like that " break down before the threat of poverty and the imagined shame of failure. He added :

" I think I remember vaguely something about bonds."

" We were sure they had been stolen," she told him. " They said dad must have sold them, but we knew he wouldn't do that because they weren't his; they were mother's, her very own."

" Couldn't they be traced ? "

" They were bearer bonds," she explained. " It was about the income-tax."

" Income-tax ? " he repeated, puzzled.

" Mother thought it was such a shame she had to pay such a lot after she married again," Henrietta explained. " Before, with the allowances and so on, the tax wasn't so very much. But after she got married she had to pay super-tax as well. It took more than half her income. Dad said he would manage it for her. He told her to take her money out of consols and buy bearer bonds from America and put them in a safe in a bank in Paris. Twice every year they went to Paris—they made a little holiday of it—and mother cut off the coupons and dad got them cashed for her, and it was all right. Money invested in America and cashed in France had nothing to do with the Government here, had it ? "

"I don't think I can give an opinion on that," Bobby answered, a little stiffly.

"It was quite all right," she insisted, in tones that suggested very strongly she was not quite comfortable about it. "I asked father once, but he showed me what Dean Inge said about under a purely predatory Government it was not clear there was any duty to make a true declaration of income. And he said of course that meant the Labour Government, and, anyhow, he and mother were making a true declaration of their income, only what they got in France was different. Besides, the bonds have all gone now."

"We needn't discuss that, fortunately," Bobby said. "You mean these bonds disappeared?"

"Yes. After father's death, mother and I went to Paris to get them and the safe was empty. There was nothing to show what had become of them. Mother didn't even know what they were for; she had never noticed. She says she would know them again, because they were all stained with ink she upset over them once in Paris when she was cutting off the coupons. But you can't trace them by that. You see, everything was done privately."

Bobby nodded. Precautions had plainly been taken to cover up even the cashing of the coupons so as to avoid any risk of difficulty with the British revenue authorities. Quite possibly they had not been stolen at all, but Mr. Oulton, hard pressed, had disposed of them, even if they were his wife's property, hoping, as people will, to be able to replace them quickly. All the same, the story seemed to him curious and interesting, and he wondered a little if she had any purpose in relating it to him in such full detail.

"Couldn't they help you at the bank where the bonds had been kept?" he asked.

She shook her head.

" They wouldn't help much," she said. " They were afraid of being sued for negligence. We did hear that a little, shabbily dressed man had shown the bank a note from father, authorising him to open the safe to obtain some papers from it. But we couldn't prove it, and the bank would admit nothing. We don't know ourselves if that's true, but we are sure, if there was such a letter, it was a forgery. Because there was nothing in the safe ever, except mother's bonds. There was one thing. The bank had one of father's cards. It was one of some new ones he had just had done, in a different type. We knew he hadn't been in France since they had been printed. So how did that card get there? We thought perhaps the bank had accepted the card as proof of identity or as authority. Someone might have got hold of it and shown it at the bank, and a careless or stupid clerk or porter or someone might have thought it was all right. Or there might have been bribery. But they denied it, and we had no proof, and, anyhow, the bonds were gone. It seemed hopeless to think of getting them back. Our lawyers said, both in France and England, there was nothing to be done. Mother always said it was Mr. Bennett."

" Was he asked? "

" No. We couldn't trace him. We heard he had gone to America but we couldn't find out. It seemed very—well, funny."

" So it does," agreed Bobby. " How did Mr. Oulton meet Mr. Bennett? "

" That was in Paris once, when he and mother were over there to get the coupons. He saved father from a bad accident—pulled him out of the way of a car that was skidding or something. Father was knocked down but he wasn't hurt. He told mother, but when they went to Mr. Bennett's hotel to thank him, he had left. Then they happened to meet by chance in London, at Charing Cross. Father used to joke about always meeting everyone at Charing Cross if only you waited long enough. Father said Mr. Bennett didn't know him at first, and didn't like being recognised, because he was meeting some Americans on important business. It was confidential, and he thought at first father knew something and was trying to force his way in. After that they got very friendly, and mother was always wanting father to bring him to dinner, and he was always coming and then he couldn't because of business—he had a lot of business abroad. Then he had to rush off to America—he had a cable asking him to go at once; it was about two big banks that were joining up." She paused and then went on slowly: " After that, father invested a lot of money in America and everything went wrong. And after they found him in the car at High Beech, near Deal, there wasn't anything left at all. When we found the bonds had vanished as well, none of us had a penny except our clothes and a few hundred pounds an aunt left me when she died. So we bought this farm with that and came here to try to make a living."

Bobby, who had been watching the clock, rose to go. It was fully time he was off, but before he went, after he had thanked her again for having spoken so freely, he added:

" Do you think you could let me have a photograph of Mr. Oulton? It might be useful if we came across any trace of this Mr. Bennett."

The request evidently both surprised and disturbed her. She glanced, as it were involuntarily, towards the frame made for three photographs but now holding only that of her mother, flanked by Molly's two sketches, and Bobby was very sure it was again a momentary uneasiness that flickered and passed in those deep, wide-set eyes of hers. Then she faced him resolutely.

" No," she said. " I do not wish to do that."

" It is, of course, for you to say," he agreed, and took his leave, and he was aware that as long as he was still in sight she stood there, watching him.

CHAPTER XII

IDENTIFICATION PARADE

IN ALL THAT DISTRICT there was nothing in the shape either of a mortuary or a coroner's court. Any available shed or barn had to serve for the one, any convenient room for the other. In this case the inquest was to be held in one of the rooms of the Red Lion. In a barn near by the post-mortem had been performed and the body still remained, waiting there till it had been seen by the jury. To-day the Sevens party was to view it in the hope that one or other of them might be able to identify it, and when Bobby arrived after his long talk with Henrietta Towers this ceremony was already over.

Bobby asked one of the police present to report his arrival to Colonel Warden, and so was soon summoned to that gentleman's presence. He had established himself in the small room that served as an office for the landlord of the inn, and he listened with a somewhat worried attention to the very full report Bobby made of his talk with Miss Towers.

" I don't see what all this about stolen bonds has to do with us," he complained irritably when Bobby had finished. " Most likely they were simply sold by Mr. Oulton, only his family prefer to think of him as a victim of theft and murder rather than as an embezzler of his wife's money and a suicide."

" I couldn't help feeling, sir," Bobby said, " that Miss Towers had some reason for saying what she did "; and, when the colonel grunted impatiently and looked more impatient still, Bobby thought it as well to change the subject by asking: " No one identified the body, I understand ? "

The colonel continued to look worried.

" I'm not satisfied," he declared. " I'm not at all satisfied." He referred to some papers at his side. " Mr. Moffatt," he said, " was very emphatic; he had never seen him before or anyone like him. I've known Moffatt a long time," the colonel added. " I think he can be trusted. For that matter, I don't think he would make a good liar."

" No, sir," agreed Bobby, who knew, however, only too well that the really good liar is precisely the man who gives the impression that he is nothing of the sort.

" Mr. Larson," continued the chief constable, " —he is still staying on at Sevens for the time; quiet, reserved sort, he seems—appears willing to help, though. He hesitated; wasn't perfectly sure; thought the face familiar but he couldn't place it. Probably some chance resemblance, he said. But he said if we could let him have a photo he would show it to some of his business associates. Very good of him."

" Make our work a good deal easier if everyone was as willing to help," observed Bobby with some feeling.

The colonel agreed.

" Then there's Mr. Pegley," he went on. " Seemed nervous, uneasy, I thought. Asked for some brandy afterwards. Bit of an ordeal, no doubt, for some people. Quite clear it was a perfect stranger, but they could hardly get him to look. Seemed to think if he looked too long he might be the same way himself."

"Is he staying on at Sevens, too?" Bobby asked.

"No. He drove down from town," answered the colonel, continuing to stare at the papers before him as though he found them extremely distasteful. "Oh," he said, a little like one clutching at a respite, "yes. Hayes was there, too. Said the same thing—perfect stranger. Quite interested, though. Asked a lot of questions. A cool customer; all in the day's work, so to say. Might be used to viewing dead men every day."

"Yes," agreed Bobby slowly. "I should think Hayes was a man not easily taken off his guard. Did Reeves, the butler at Sevens, come, too?"

"No. Why? Why should he? He wouldn't be likely to recognise the body if Mr. Moffatt didn't."

Bobby said nothing. It was not for him to direct the investigation. His duty was merely to collect and to submit facts. But he did not quite like the way in which Mr. Moffatt seemed to be accepted as above suspicion—not, of course, that there were any grounds for suspicion beyond the vague and probably inaccurate suggestion that he went frequently to the States and kept that fact private to himself. All the same, Bobby felt that in every investigation an open mind was essential, and the chief constable's seemed closed as regarded Mr. Moffatt. Less closed, though, than Bobby had supposed, for abruptly the colonel said:

"I'll phone Moffatt to send Reeves along—waste of time." Then he looked angrily at Bobby and added: "I've asked your people at the Yard to make some inquiries at the shipping offices; may as well check up on this story of Moffatt's going to America every autumn."

"Just as well," agreed Bobby warmly, "to get that story out of the way. Help to check up on Hayes, too."

"Yes, I thought that," the colonel agreed, continuing to poke uneasily at his papers.

To help him—for Bobby guessed what this unease meant—he said:

"I suppose the two young people couldn't help?"

"Both denied knowing anything, and stuck to it," the colonel answered, looking as if he would like to resign on the spot and go away to Bournemouth, there to sit on the front all day and play bridge all night. Bobby waited, sure there was more to come. "Miss Moffatt fainted," said the colonel slowly.

"While viewing the body?"

"No," the other answered, "that would have been—well, natural enough." He had an air of approving of a woman fainting in such circumstances. Very right and proper, he seemed to be saying to himself. He went on: "It was after. I pressed her a little. I had an idea somehow. She seemed nervous. I tried to persuade her that if she had any doubt, hesitation whatever—then she fainted. If she did——"

"If?" repeated Bobby, puzzled for the moment.

"I wasn't quite sure," admitted the colonel reluctantly. "The modern girl doesn't faint. Ena is very modern. It did just cross my mind that possibly she wished to avoid further questioning."

Bobby's mind flew quickly back to the lipstick case found on the scene of the tragedy. A faint and slender clue, he thought. Not one that could be built upon, yet not one to be forgotten either. He waited. The chief constable continued:

"Young Moffatt was very emphatic. Very emphatic

indeed. Positive he had never seen anyone with the least resemblance. I noticed he hardly looked, though. He didn't seem to want to, I thought. I remembered you had said something about him and a London night-club—the Cut and Come Again. I mentioned it. He was a good deal startled. Very startled. Finally he admitted that perhaps he had seen there someone like the dead man. Stuck to it he wasn't sure, and, anyhow, quite certain it was no one he knew. He tried to bluster at times. I had to take rather a sharp tone. He left me strongly under the impression that he had recognised the body and didn't want to say so." The colonel sighed heavily. "My experience," he said, "is that girls are much better liars than boys."

"Yes, sir," said Bobby, in full agreement with this great truth. "Anyhow, if anyone says he doesn't recognise someone else, you can never prove he did; question of memory. And then a dead body has a different look. You can't be sure it wasn't a genuine mistake."

His mind flickered back to that fragment of Kodak wrapper found in Battling Copse. A faint and slender clue, he thought, and one it would never be safe to build on. Yet again not one to be forgotten.

"Plenty to do," said the colonel abruptly and a little as if "doing" would be a welcome relief from thinking. "Have to get the inquest adjourned, for one thing. The fellow must have had some reason for being here, some reason for watching Sevens. Oh, well, there's this Miss Towers's story, too. What do you make of it?"

"Not much, sir," admitted Bobby. "She gave Hayes an alibi, but, then, in doing so she provided herself with one."

"Eh? What?" exclaimed the chief constable. "I never thought of her. You mean——?"

"Oh, no, sir," protested Bobby, hastening to disclaim

any meaning. " She seemed very frank and straightforward—almost embarrassingly so. Of course, frank and straightforward is often a good card to play to throw you off the scent. She's quick, too; she wasn't long in seeing we were interested in Hayes."

" But what possible, conceivable motive—— ? "

" Well, sir, of course," Bobby answered, " I must say I was a little—well, it's not quite usual for a young lady to announce that someone is trying to seduce her. And it's quite plain there was an underlying motive for Hayes's quarrel with Mrs. O'Brien—the hat business and the face-slapping had something else behind it—' not the sort to go so easy,' was the way one of the maids put it. Miss Henrietta said herself Mrs. O'Brien was jealous of her sister, Miss Molly. It did just strike me as possible that Miss Henrietta—I am sure she would do anything for her sister—knew it was Molly by whom Hayes was attracted, and wanted to keep her out of it." He added slowly: " I think I should not care to be any man Miss Henrietta suspected of trying to harm Miss Molly."

" Getting rather away from realities, aren't we ? " the colonel suggested.

" I dare say I am," agreed Bobby. " It's a puzzling case, though, and I feel Miss Henrietta does come in somewhere. There's that row between young Moffatt and Mr. Hayes's chauffeur. Miss Molly does water-colours, Moffatt is keen on photography, and he has done what I thought looked very fine photos of both the Towers girls. It is just possible Moffatt knew Hayes was worrying them—that the chauffeur had been carrying messages or something like that—and that was what the trouble was about. Moffatt started questioning the chauffeur and a row developed. I know that's all just guessing."

"What sort of man is this chauffeur? Do you know his name?"

"Thoms. Edward Thoms. He seemed quite young, big, clumsy, talks as if he had some education; sulky, angry sort of air; keeps very much to himself, the maids said; not much liked by them apparently. Of course, I only saw him during the row with Moffatt and afterwards when he had a black eye that didn't improve his appearance."

"Better be questioned, perhaps. Better ask Hayes about him, too," the colonel remarked. "I'll ring Hayes up and ask him to send the fellow along—I can say it's just occurred to me there's a chance he may have seen the dead man hanging about."

"It struck me," Bobby continued, "as just a little curious that, while Miss Henrietta was very frank about most things, she wouldn't give me her brother's address. She said he had nothing to do with the case and he wouldn't like being questioned by us. It's true enough that people hate the idea; they all seem to think a harmless question or two means an arrest next minute."

"One of our biggest handicaps," agreed the colonel.

"So I didn't think much of that," Bobby continued, "but she was rather emphatic, too, about refusing to give me a photograph of her stepfather. I don't see why she should object. It's long enough ago."

"Well, I—well, anyhow," the colonel said, "there can't be any connection between a death—suicide or murder either—years ago and this business."

"It doesn't seem probable," agreed Bobby, "only why did she tell me all that long story? That's what's worrying me. Another thing I noticed. Most likely it doesn't mean anything. There were a lot of Miss Molly's water-colours in the kitchen—and some photos. There was one frame meant to hold three photos. In the centre was one of the girls' mother—Mrs. Oulton—and on each side it was flanked by a small drawing of Miss Molly's."

"What about it?" asked the colonel, puzzled.

"It did just occur to me," said Bobby, "that possibly that frame had held photos of Mrs. Oulton's late husband and of her son."

"You mean they had been removed to prevent anyone seeing them?" asked the colonel. "But why? What for?"

"I haven't the least idea," Bobby answered.

"You don't mean," demanded the colonel, staring at him, "you think this dead man can be the missing brother—or the father come back to life if the suicide tale was a fake?"

"I don't think so, sir," Bobby answered. "For the brother, the age doesn't agree. But the suicide story might be a fake. The identification of the family might have been accepted too easily. It's an idea."

"Better," said the colonel, with sudden determination, "go up to London. We can look after this end. Ask your people to try to find out if there is any possibility of the suicide yarn having been faked. Good God, if it was a fake, there must have been a dead man all the same. And you had better go round to this club you mentioned—the Cut and Come Again. There is just the chance they might be able to tell you something there."

"Very good, sir," Bobby answered, and thought to himself that, with the Cut and Come Again, what they might tell and what they would tell were as different as anything well could be.

CHAPTER XIII

BLACKLISTED

BOBBY ACCORDINGLY RETURNED to London, though, as there had been one or two other matters connected with the case needing his attention, it was late in the evening before he reached town.

He put off further action till the next morning, therefore, since, though night was when the activities of the Cut and Come Again blossomed to their full, also at night the merest glimpse of a " busy "—a C.I.D. man—would be enough to reduce the club to a silence deep as death, with the boldest holding their breath for the rest of the evening.

In the daytime, however, all would be calm, peaceful, law-abiding as a suburban tea-party, and there might possibly be a chance of getting a few questions answered. Not too early, of course, for till noon the club premises were inhabited by charwomen alone.

So, as there was an hour or two to spare before it would be any good visiting the Cut and Come Again, Bobby took a bus to Fleet Street and there presented himself at the office of Mr. Fisher, the agent Henrietta had mentioned as having dealt with some of her half-sister's drawings. He discovered it in one of those odd, narrow alleys winding between Fleet Street and New Oxford Street that serve to show us what most London streets were like in past centuries.

Up a dark and twisted staircase Bobby made his way to a smart modern office whereof the chief features seemed chromium and lipstick—the chromium appertaining to the furniture, the lipstick to three maidens busy with typewriter and phone.

Bobby produced his card—his private card, not his official—and explained that he was interested in the work of Miss Molly Oulton, for whom he understood Mr. Fisher acted as agent.

The first maiden had never heard of Miss Molly Oulton; the second said: "Oh, yes! Wishy-washy stuff. No pep, No punch, No push"; the third said: "Well, we clicked once. Twenty pounds. You never know what stuff will go and what won't."

Bobby asked if he could see Mr. Fisher. The first maiden disappeared into an adjoining room and returned and said Mr. Fisher was disengaged. So Bobby was ushered into an inner office, with even more chromium but with the lipstick *motif* replaced by a general impression of whisky and cigars.

Mr. Fisher himself was a young man with black hair as straight and shiny as brilliantine could make it, and a general air of having devoted considerable time and thought to the choice of his tie and his socks and to his personal appearance in general, though, unfortunately, he had forgotten his finger-nails. However, he greeted Bobby warmly, called him "old chap" on the spot, instantly produced the whisky and soda he appeared to consider the necessary accompaniments to conversation, and said:

"Oh, yes, you're *Daily Peeps*, aren't you?" He made

a dive at a drawer of his desk and produced some photos.

" 'Lady Whats in her new swim suit.' Not bad, eh? 'Debutante Joan tries on her Chinese pyjamas.' Pretty hot, but not," declared Mr. Fisher judicially, "not too hot. What about it?"

Bobby modestly disclaimed being *Daily Peeps*, thought the two photographs equally remarkable though penny automatics on seaside piers gave you, so to speak, more—or even less—for your money, and said he was interested in the work of Miss Molly Oulton.

Mr. Fisher made another dive at another drawer, and produced a folder with some of Molly's water-colours in it which he scattered on his modern "executive's desk."

"Not my line; more a Bond Street stunt," he pronounced. "Connected once for her. Twenty pounds. No repeat. Not my line at all. I told her so. Legs, I said. That's what the demand's for. Legs."

"Dear me," said Bobby, surprised. "I thought legs were a back number, what with cars and buses and tubes."

"In art," pronounced Mr. Fisher, "legs hold their own—art and the stage. Now this kind of stuff." He turned over Molly's unlucky sketches, and Bobby noticed that on the back of one or two of them was written in a large, bold hand: "Introduced by Laddy O'Brien," followed by the Way Side address. "You know," said Mr. Fisher unexpectedly, "I like 'em. But what's the good of liking stuff that don't sell?"

"There's that, isn't there?" agreed Bobby.

"Look at this one—caterpillar swaying on the top of a blade of grass. Almost see it sway, can't you? Not that I've ever seen anything like it myself, but somehow it gives you the idea that some day you might. Not my line, though. I thought I would try; struck me *Daily Peeps* might run 'em—hidden secrets of nature stunt or something like that. No good. They said if the artist would put in some human interest, they might think about it. She said only a fool would want human interest in nature studies. Got a way of saying 'fool,' too—not loud, but signed, sealed, and delivered, and no appeal allowed. But what's the sense of calling *Daily Peeps* a fool when they've a circulation of two millions? I ask you."

"There's that, isn't there?" agreed Bobby again. "Mrs. O'Brien a friend of yours?"

"No; never set eyes on her. One of the staff, Janey Briggs—smart girl; senior here—has an evening job at the Dukeries Restaurant. Gets her dinner free—and commission. Sort of dinner hostess. She pals in with anyone looking lonely and puts in spare time telling all the rest what a swell place it is. Mind you," added Mr. Fisher, suddenly severe, "everything perfectly straight or she wouldn't stop here."

"Of course," agreed Bobby.

"Met Mrs. O'Brien there," continued Mr. Fisher. "She was pulling her usual stuff about what a swell joint the Dukeries was, and how she had just recognised the Prince of This or the Duke of That. No flies on Mrs. O'Brien, though, and she tumbled to the game. After that they got quite pals. I expect Janey—she's Veronica Orsini at the Dukeries; slap-up Italian name—let herself go a bit. I'm really Press, General, and Advertising, but Mrs. O'Brien got the idea we were in the hunk-a-dory, high art, Bond Street line. Maybe some day, but not yet. Bond Street pays O.K., but it takes some digging in to get there. I took these Oulton things round to the Cut and Come Again, a club I know."

"Oh, yes," said Bobby, more interested than he showed.

"Wanted to get a line on them," explained Mr. Fisher. "A lot of queer birds there, but some of them know what's what in high art. I thought I could get an opinion. No good. The stuff was pulled to bits. One chap said it would have done all right for the *Keepsakes* a hundred years ago. Widgett turned 'em all down at once. He said they looked as if they had been done by someone who had never even heard of the surrealist movement. A chap named Bennett seemed interested, but he wasn't a buyer, so that was no good."

Bobby asked a few more questions. But Mr. Fisher knew nothing of Mr. Bennett. He had only heard of Mr. Bennett's interest at second hand. He had left the sketches at the club for the opinion of Mr. Widgett, recently down from Oxford and a great authority on modern art; his proof that the Elgin Marbles were merely rejected workshop fragments put together by an incompetent workman having recently made a great sensation and given rise to many admiring articles in the more advanced periodicals. Mr. Bennett had chanced to see the drawings and had admired them, and that was all, though Mr. Fisher had heard that Miss Oulton had visited the Cut and Come Again several times in recent weeks.

"Hoping to make a sale, very likely," said Mr. Fisher, winking, "though whether it's her drawings or a kiss or two—ha, ha!"

Bobby's disciplined existence helped him to repress his natural instinct to cut Mr. Fisher's chuckles short by throwing him out of the window. But he reflected that probably Fisher meant no harm, and so he thanked him for the information so freely given and after lunch proceeded to the Cut and Come Again, where his welcome was less cordial than wary.

Finch, the porter, who held the doors of the club against all unauthorised intruders—not provided with a search-warrant—observed untruthfully that any visitor from the Yard was always welcome, and agreed that the secretary, Mr. Dillon, was in his room. Mr. Dillon, declared Finch without batting an eyelid, was never happier than when receiving a visit from his good friends at the Yard; and, anyhow, was it likely there would be anything going on at that early hour when many of the club *habitués* would hardly be out of bed? Bobby agreed that it wasn't, assured Finch his business had nothing to do with the club as a club, and so proceeded to the presence of the wizened little Irishman who directed all the activities of the establishment, knew the Licensing Acts backwards, looked as harmless as a rabbit, and was in fact as vicious as a weasel. For him whisky seemed to take the place of food and sleep, since apparently he never either ate or went to bed. Bobby was not surprised to find him filling a glass with what he called " the best," and he seemed a good deal relieved to hear that it was only about Miss Oulton Bobby wished to inquire.

" Not a member; a visitor," Mr. Dillon explained, giving the information with a readiness he did not always show in answering police inquiries. " Pretty little drawings she does. I told her she ought to try the Christmas card manufacturers."

" What did she say? " asked Bobby.

" Oh, she had. Or Fisher had for her. Turned down. Not up to their standard. Unreal, I expect. I thought that myself."

Bobby mused for a moment on unreality as an objection

to a design for a Christmas card and then asked about Mr. Bennett.

Mr. Dillon, for once startled, sat upright with a jerk. Then he filled his glass again.

" See here," he said, " my job is to keep order in this club. Fighting don't go here. I don't deny Finch handled him rough. He asked for it. If he wants a summons for assault, all right. We'll defend."

" I wish you would tell me exactly what happened," Bobby said.

" I expect he had had one over," Mr. Dillon explained. " Not here. He wasn't served here. Refused. Put his dander up, most likely. Next thing we knew he was on the floor, with Thoms trying to strangle him."

" Thoms, did you say ? " asked Bobby, his voice unmoved though something in him had leaped at the name. " Who's he ? "

" Young fellow. One of the members," answered Mr. Dillon. " Don't know anything about him. I forget who proposed him. It'll be in the book. Quiet, well-behaved young chap as a rule. Didn't often come. I don't think I had ever seen him since the day he signed the members' book. Quite a job to haul him off Bennett. Two minutes more and Bennett would have been done in. But was Bennett grateful ? All he did was to go for Finch. A foul. So Finch threw him down the stairs into the street. Bad breach of instructions."

" What was ? " asked Bobby.

" The stairs," explained Mr. Dillon. " Finch's instructions—and well he knows it—are to put 'em to sleep with a tap on the nob and then carry 'em out quiet and peaceful, as far away as convenient. It doesn't look respectable," said Mr. Dillon earnestly, " when people see members being thrown into the street; doesn't set a good tone, if you see what I mean."

"I think I do," agreed Bobby.

"After a dirty foul like the one Bennett pulled, I can't blame Finch so much," Mr. Dillon admitted. "Lost his temper. Bit scared, too. If we hadn't hauled Thoms off in time, Bennett would have passed out for keeps most likely."

Bobby asked a few more questions but got little more information. Mr. Dillon had no idea, evidently, that Bennett had in grim earnest "passed out for keeps," to use the little Irishman's own phrase. He read, it seemed, no paper but the *Cork Examiner*, and that journal had been too full of the more recent local political excitements and assassinations to have space to spare for an obscure, uninteresting murder near London. Nor had he any idea what the quarrel had been about; about nothing, most likely, both disputants having probably had more than was good for them, though neither, he earnestly assured the quite unimpressed Bobby, had been served on the club premises. One point did emerge. Before his ejection, and during that process, Mr. Bennett had uttered violent threats against Thoms, but addressing him by some other name which, however, in the general excitement had not been noted and could not now be remembered. But Thoms was not the only member of the club possessing a name other than that derived from birth.

Bobby asked some further questions about Molly Oulton. But Mr. Dillon, who had been unusually communicative in the belief that Mr. Bennett had so far forgotten the etiquette and custom of the club as to lodge a complaint about his treatment there, now returned to his usual tactics of a comprehensive ignorance. He repeated that though she had come to the club sometimes, it was as a visitor only. He could not be sure how often, but he would inquire. He knew nothing about her sketches, but aspiring artists often brought work to show at the club in the hope it might win recognition from some of the prominent and influential people who made the Cut and Come Again their home from home, so to say. As Sergeant Owen well knew, the Cut and Come Again was practically modern art headquarters in town.

Another question or two brought the admission that two other members were Mr. Oliver Moffatt and his sister, Miss Ena Moffatt. They often came; whenever they were in town, in fact. Miss Moffatt had recently, indeed, been receiving lessons from the barman in the art and craft of mixing cocktails, but these were the less effective on account of her inclination to substitute lemonade for gin, as being a so much more agreeable beverage. This tendency the barman, in unaccustomed fatherly mood, had duly encouraged. Young Mr. Moffatt was interested in films. As the Cut and Come Again was, as Sergeant Owen well knew, practically the London headquarters of the film industry, it was natural he should be a frequent visitor.

Bobby turned the conversation back to Mr. Bennett. He felt if he could only get some information about Bennett's earlier life, trace his friends, acquaintances, business connections, and so on, probably a long step would be taken towards solving the mystery of his death. But Mr. Dillon had, as usual, little to tell. Nor did he think any of the other members knew Bennett at all well, or anything about his past career. That, Bobby was obliged to admit to himself, was probable enough. Past careers tended to be taboo at the Cut and Come Again, where the accepted principle was: " Ask no questions and be told no—or at any rate, fewer—lies." Bennett had been, it appeared, a member since the foundation of the club, but did not often come. Unfortunately, said Mr. Dillon, most of the books and records of the club had been destroyed in a small and otherwise harmless fire that had broken out on the club premises a year or two previously. Sergeant Owen might remember the incident.

Bobby knew all about that fire. It had been, he was well convinced, ingeniously engineered for the sole purpose of destroying the club records and so providing a reasonable excuse for inability to answer the embarrassing inquiries too often posed by Scotland Yard emissaries. Bobby asked to see the new members' book, kept so far with a meticulous care but probably destined to disappear some day in some strange, mysterious fashion. However, he found in it nothing of interest, and so departed for the Yard, whence he rang up Colonel Warden's office to report the incident of the quarrel and fight between Thoms and the murdered man. Colonel Warden was not there, but the sergeant who took the message promised to see he had it as soon as possible. Afterwards Bobby reported to his own officers, and Inspector Ferris said to him:

" We sent round as requested to check up on Mr. Moffatt of Sevens at the steamship offices. He's blacklisted."

" Blacklisted ? " repeated Bobby, very surprised.

" Yes. Complaint of card-sharping. Complaint made by two big pots——" He gave their names, one of them that of the chairman of the National Universal Bank, the other almost equally awe-inspiring. " Poker," explained Ferris. " The steamship people were very surprised.

They knew Moffatt well enough as a regular passenger, but this was the first time there had been any complaint. But of course, coming from the nobs it did, something had to be done. So now, when Mr. Moffatt wants to cross, all berths are taken."

CHAPTER XIV

REEVES'S RECORD

BOBBY RETURNED THE SAME NIGHT, by the last train, to make his report to Colonel Warden, but arrived too late for an immediate interview. And the next day was Sunday, when in England all things must endure the universal pause.

It gave Bobby, however, an opportunity to go over carefully the evidence so far collected and to consider the various implications involved. Then, on the Monday, as early as might be, he secured an interview with Colonel Warden, who had by now heard direct from Scotland Yard of the blacklisting of Mr. Moffatt by the steamship companies. He was almost equally disturbed by that and by Bobby's report of the quarrel at the Cut and Come Again between the chauffeur, Thoms, and the dead man.

"The more that comes out," he complained, "the further it seems to lead us away from the facts. Thoms will have to be questioned, but why should a quarrel with Thoms in London bring Bennett down here to spy on Moffatt's place through field-glasses?"

Bobby had no comment to make, so he held his tongue and tried to look less puzzled than he felt.

"There must be some mistake or misunderstanding about Moffatt," continued the colonel moodily. "I know he has a name for being lucky at cards, but I've never heard of even a breath of suspicion about his play. One of those people with a natural instinct for the best call and the right lead. I simply can't believe it."

"Well, sir, the complaint was laid by——" and Bobby mentioned again, and with proper reverence, the name of that awe-inspiring magnate, the chairman of the National Universal Bank. The other party to the complaint had been an almost equally semi-divine potentate of finance—one of those to whose piping nations dance and to whom the peoples of the earth lift songs. They had been travelling under assumed names to a conference summoned in New York to consider, and find a remedy for, the disastrous price of meat, which had sunk so low that almost anyone could have as much as he wanted. Consequently even the captain of the ship had not known their identity till they had felt it their duty to speak to him, and only respect for their wish to remain unknown had saved Mr. Moffatt from extremely unpleasant consequences.

"Amazing," repeated Colonel Warden, who had given Bobby some of these further details from the more complete written report received from London. He added, with an air of relief at being able to put aside a distressing and unwelcome problem: "Our job isn't to find out whether Moffatt cheats at cards, but who killed Bennett. And if it's Thoms, why did Bennett, who seems to have been the threatened party, follow him down here, and why was he peeping at Sevens? Amazing, too, that following up Mrs. O'Brien's interest in Miss Oulton's drawings should lead to your hearing about this other affair. Curious, again, how everything seems to lead back to this Cut and Come Again place."

" Well, sir, I don't know that that's so very curious," Bobby answered. " Half the rascality in London is planned there, though half the members don't know anything about all that. They think it's just a jolly, unconventional, Bohemian sort of show. But if we want to pick up any well-known rogue, that's where we look first."

" I'll have to go over to Way Side and talk to Thoms," the colonel decided. " I'll look in at Sevens on the way, too. It's likely enough, if Bennett and young Moffatt were both members of the Cut and Come Again, they met there, and Moffatt recognised the body but didn't want to say. You had better come with me, sergeant. It'll have to be after the inquest, though. No time before."

" I wish we had the finger-prints of the whole Sevens party," Bobby observed. " We may have some of them on file."

" Can't suggest taking them at this stage," decided the colonel. " And even if we had them, would that help to identify the murderer ? Because that's our job. Nothing else."

" No, sir," agreed Bobby. " I think Thoms and Reeves have seen the body ? "

" Yes," answered the colonel. " Both denied all knowledge. I questioned them afterwards. Thoms seems a sulky, suspicious young fellow. He gave me a bad impression. And then, of course, now there's this affair with Bennett shows he was lying when he said he didn't know him. We shall have him there, anyhow."

" He'll probably plead he actually didn't recognise the body," Bobby suggested. " I've known that happen. And you can't prove anything. Death does make a difference."

" Not that much," grumbled the colonel. " I pressed

him about his fight with Noll Moffatt. Most insolent tone he adopted. Told me it was no business of ours. He denied ever having been at the Towers Poultry Farm. I said that was curious, as his master made so many purchases there. He only mumbled something about not being the housekeeper. I didn't feel at all satisfied. I must find out how Hayes came to employ him."

"That might be a useful line to follow up," agreed Bobby.

"Reeves," continued the colonel, "was quite cool and collected. Positive he had never seen Bennett. Both he and Thoms refused to have their finger-prints taken. I couldn't insist. But Reeves left his all the same. He went into the Red Lion bar and had some beer. One of my men was smart enough to have his glass collected, and there were quite good prints on it. Now there's a phone call through to say they've been identified, and he's well known."

"Is he, though?" Bobby exclaimed. "I wondered if that was just a tale about recognising me because he had seen me in court."

"Served two sentences for burglary, three years and five years," said the colonel. "Interesting, eh?"

Bobby agreed that it was.

"Had a good character till about ten years ago," the colonel continued. "Then he was discharged without references. A diamond ring had disappeared and he was suspected. Apparently he was innocent of that, for the ring was found afterwards down a wash-basin waste-pipe. I suppose he might have put it there to avoid discovery. Anyhow, by that time he had been caught red-handed and was serving a three-year sentence. After his release he was caught again and got five years, half a dozen other cases being taken into consideration. His time was up about eighteen months ago, and since then nothing has been heard of him till now. During his ticket-of-leave period he worked as a waiter in a small Brighton café and seems to have been quite satisfactory. Odd to have him turning up here and now, but can there be any connection with the Bennett murder? I don't see what myself."

Bobby didn't either. A coincidence, perhaps, and nothing more. But Bobby had grown to dislike coincidence nearly as much as a modern poet dislikes rhyme, rhythm, and sense. He said

"I was wondering, sir, if it might be as well to try to trace Mrs. O'Brien. I don't know if that's been thought of. It's just possible she might have something to tell us."

The colonel nodded, a little pleased to show Scotland Yard they too, in the county constabulary, could think of things, even though murder cases were so rare in their well-ordered, law-abiding neighbourhoods.

"I rang up Hayes to ask for her address," he said. "He said he hadn't got it, and didn't know that of any of her friends. But he thought she was sure to write soon, either for a reference or to ask for some of her things she had left behind to be sent on. He promised to let us know as soon as he heard. They say at the station that she booked to London, so I've asked your people to make inquiries at the hotels."

"There's the Dukeries Restaurant, too, near Leicester Square. Mr. Fisher's young woman saw her there, and she might go again."

"Yes, that could be followed up," agreed the colonel, making a note of it, and, after a little more talk, Bobby retired.

The inquest had been called for noon and did not take

long, only formal evidence being offered and then an adjournment being ordered to allow, in the customary phrase, "the police to complete their inquiries."

But then there had to be time taken for luncheon, and various other matters had to receive attention, so that it was late, and darkness had set in, before the colonel and Bobby were able to present themselves at Sevens, where they were admitted by Reeves, the ex-burglar—if he was an "ex"—and ushered into the library. There they were a little surprised to find not only Mr. Moffatt, but Mr. Pegley, who had ventured to call, it seemed, to hear the result of the inquest and any further developments.

"Interested, you know," he explained; "on the spot at the time."

It struck Bobby as a frank remark, and frankness is the natural use of innocence and therefore often used by guilt as well.

The colonel was asking about the other members of the Sevens party. Ena, it seemed, was out, but would be back soon. Noll Moffatt was in his studio, as he called it; that "damn' dark hole of his," as his father generally referred to it; his "cubby-hole," as his sister named it. He would be sent for. Mr. Larson had gone back to London. His address was Royal Chambers, the enormous and well-known block of buildings in Park Lane that had some claim to be considered the ugliest ever erected. It seemed he had no office, as he conducted all his business from his flat there.

"Saves overhead, staff, and rent and all that," observed Mr. Pegley enviously. "Where you score doing underground work for the swells—hearing at luncheon at the Ritz that one big nob wants to sell a railway or a mine, and at dinner at the Savoy that another wants to buy, bringing them both to meet at the Carlton for cocktails, and pocketing a fat cheque for commission. Enough to make you turn Labour when you think how you have to sweat yourself to earn a decent living. Believe it or not, I know the Stock Exchange list almost by heart, and that takes some doing."

"We must get in touch with him," the colonel remarked, and explained they were trying to place the exact position of everyone in the neighbourhood at the actual moment of the murder; at, that is, four o'clock in the afternoon.

"Well, I can tell you where I was," Mr. Moffatt answered promptly. "I like forty winks sometimes. So after lunch that day I came in here, wrote a letter or two, had a look at *The Times*, and then I expect I dozed off. I often do."

"Did anyone else come into the room during the afternoon?" the colonel asked.

"No one; they know better," Mr. Moffatt answered with a grim smile, apparently quite unaware of the implications of this question. "They all know I don't like being bothered in the afternoon. No one would unless it was something special."

"I see. Thank you," murmured the colonel, and, glancing up, saw that Bobby was looking at the French windows, and guessed he, too, was reflecting how easy it would be to open those windows and slip out unperceived, to return the same way equally unnoticed.

Not that there was anything to show that that had actually happened. But the possibility had to be remembered, and Colonel Warden looked more worried than ever as he asked one or two more questions about Mr. Moffatt's trips to America.

It amused Bobby a little, when he remembered the chief constable's opinion that Mr. Moffatt would not make a good liar, to note with what a calm assurance that gentleman put forward the trip on which he had met Larson as his first visit to the States. The evidence that he had gone there pretty regularly every year for some time before that was, however, conclusive. To Colonel Warden's inquiry whether he intended to go again soon, he replied by a shake of the head.

" I might, of course," he said. " Ena enjoyed it. It's her uncle, my brother-in-law, we went to see. He's living in Boston now; used to be Hawaii, and that was a bit too far. There was some talk of it last year, but when I wrote for a berth they were full up, and so was the next boat, and then I got a touch of influenza and we gave it up. Might go next year."

Either he was ignorant of the blacklisting or he possessed a remarkable self-control, Bobby thought. He wondered which was the correct explanation.

The colonel looked a little disconcerted, too, as he turned to Mr. Pegley.

" We have to make our record as complete as possible." he said, " so perhaps you wouldn't mind telling us where you were about four that afternoon."

Mr. Pegley had no objection in the world, but could not undertake to be accurate to a half-hour or so. He said slowly, plainly trying to remember:

" I left town in my car early and had lunch at the Oakley Road House. After that I made a call on a client. I wanted to advise her rather strongly against taking money out of war loan to put it in a concern I have confidential information isn't too good. Then I came on here for my chat with Mr. Moffatt, who had very kindly suggested my staying to dinner. I should imagine I got here somewhere about five. At four I would be somewhere on the Bath Road, but Lord knows where exactly; I don't. Anyhow, I wasn't anywhere near the place where this poor cove of yours got done in," he added cheerfully.

But for that, it seemed, there was no evidence save his own.

"Could you give me your client's name?" the colonel asked.

Mr. Pegley shook his head smilingly.

"Confidential," he declared. "One of my rules—never give a client's name. Special reason in this case, too, as the lady doesn't want hubby to know she dabbles. Besides, what would be the good? She could only say I was there, and didn't stop to tea as she wanted me to. She wouldn't get any nearer than that; very vague about time, ladies often are."

Ena had come into the room now. She had listened to all this; and her own account of her movements that afternoon was that after lunch she read a little and then went out for a solitary walk—towards Winders Green, however, not towards Battling Copse, so she had neither seen nor heard anything of what had happened. She did not remember having seen or spoken to anyone during her walk except Mrs. Markham, the wife of Mr. Markham, the farmer on whose land Battling Copse bordered, and Mr. Larson, who had passed, coming from the Winders Green direction by the path crossing the fields and skirting Higham Wood. It was growing dark; probably it was about half past four, but of the exact time she could not be sure. Anyhow, she was back in the house pouring out the tea at five. She was sure it was Mr. Larson, because at first in the dusk they had both thought it was one of

Mr. Markham's labourers till he had lifted his hat in passing, as no labourer would have done. Later a comparison of time and place had made certain it was Mr. Larson. He explained he had not stopped to speak as he had seen she was talking to a friend. He had lost a gold cigarette-case on that walk, Ena added. Apparently he had seated himself somewhere for a rest and a cigarette, had put the case down, and had then forgotten it when he went on. Luckily it had been found by probably the first person using the path when it was light next morning, still lying on the stile where Mr. Larson had left it. He had been very pleased to get it back, and had liberally rewarded the lucky finder.

Then Reeves was summoned, and appeared, pale, thin, and noiseless as ever, but with a certain lurking apprehension, Bobby thought, visible in his uneasy eyes. At the colonel's suggestion, Reeves was questioned in private, so that he might not be embarrassed by his employer's presence. But he had little to say. He had spent the afternoon carrying out his usual duties, and then reading the paper in his pantry and possibly snoozing at times. He confirmed as far as he could the stories told by the others. Mr. Moffatt was never disturbed in the afternoon, and did occasionally—this in answer to a casual question of Bobby's—sometimes stroll out into the grounds by the French windows. He might or might not have done so that particular day. Mr. Pegley had arrived about half past five or six, or possibly a little later—in ample time, anyhow, for a wash and a chat before dinner. Miss Ena and Mr. Larson had been out for walks, and he had heard of the discovery of Mr. Larson's gold cigarette-case left lying on a stile for the first person passing to pick up, and lucky it had been someone honest, though Mr. Larson had come down handsomely with a pound note. Reeves added gloomily that it was easy enough to see what all these questions were getting at. He supposed he himself could have slipped out easily enough without anyone knowing, got to Battling Copse, committed the murder, and returned without being seen.

" Only I didn't, and why should I ? " he grumbled. " Never having set eyes on the chap."

" There's no question of that, my man," the colonel told him. " Preliminary inquiries do not indicate suspicion."

" Oh, yes, they do," retorted Reeves, a little less than usual now the well-trained and deferential servant, " when it's the likes of me. There's Mr. Noll coming in now," he added, as they heard the front door open and shut. " Take a lot to make you suspect him, wouldn't it ? "

" Why should we suspect him ? " Bobby asked quickly, and Reeves looked at him sideways and said:

" Everyone's talking about the bit of photographic film that was found, and about Mr. Moffatt's pistol being missing."

" If everyone's talking, you had better tell them not to," snapped the colonel, " or they'll be getting into trouble."

" Yes, sir; certainly, sir," answered Reeves, at once the smooth, deferential butler again.

CHAPTER XV

MR. HAYES HAS SUSPICIONS

THE INTERVIEW with Noll Moffatt did not prove very satisfactory. The young man seemed in an angry and suspicious mood; he answered questions as briefly as he could and would evidently have liked to refuse to answer at all. He did refuse once again to give any explanation of his quarrel with Thoms. It had nothing to do with the police. Scowling at Bobby, he wanted to know why Bobby had been so anxious to save Thoms from the jolly good thrashing he, Noll Moffatt, had been about to administer.

To Bobby this seemed an optimistic view. Thoms was probably a stone or two the heavier of the pair, certainly he was three or four inches taller, and it is an old and true saying in the boxing world that a "good big 'un will always beat a good little 'un."

"I think," Bobby remarked, "I heard you say something to Thoms about his wanting to throw you down the chalk-pit—too?"

"Well, what about it?" snarled Noll. "Eavesdropping, too, were you? One chap had been thrown down there, hadn't he?"

He stuck to it that what he had said had been no more than a passing reference to the recent tragedy, and had had no other meaning. To further inquiries he answered defiantly that he had no idea where exactly he might have been at four o'clock in the afternoon on the day of the murder. He didn't go about with a stop-watch and a time-table. He had been out all afternoon with his camera. Probably he had been quite near Battling Copse most of the time. But he had neither seen nor heard anything unusual. Asked what photographs he had taken that afternoon, he got rather red in the face—unnecessarily so, it seemed—and said he had only taken one or two. A bull under a beech-tree had offered a fairly good subject, and he had snapped it and that was about all. They could see the snap if they liked, but it wouldn't be any good; it was neither signed nor dated. Nor had he seen anyone during the afternoon who could confirm his statements. He added with some violence that if they thought he had murdered Bennett they could jolly well go on thinking so. He didn't care.

The colonel observed mildly that an inquiry did not necessarily imply a suspicion; and Bobby observed in his most mournful tones that it was always like that: if you asked some people if it had stopped raining, they would be quite capable of interpreting the remark as a subtle attempt to trap them into an admission of guilt; and Noll told them heatedly to " come off it."

" Think I don't know what that fellow's digging bullets out of trees for ? " he asked hotly.

Bobby and the colonel both looked and felt a little disconcerted. They had hoped that the activities of the police emissary trying to recover the bullets fired from Mr. Moffatt's missing automatic by Noll when amusing himself with target practice would go unremarked, or at any rate with their significance not realised.

" It is necessary," the colonel said mildly, " for us to

ascertain if possible what pistol was used. Probably we shall test all we can trace. It is a pity Mr. Moffatt's can't be found."

"I haven't seen the thing for months," Noll declared. "It was in a drawer in dad's room. Anyone could have got at it."

Noll also denied stoutly that he had recognised Bennett. If Bennett had been a member of the Cut and Come Again he might very likely have seen him there; he might even have exchanged a word or two with him. If so, that might account for a vague feeling he had had on his first sight of the body that he had somewhere seen someone like the dead man. But emphatically he had not recognised him or associated him with the Cut and Come Again. One met heaps of people. He noticed people's looks and whether they would "take" well, but he couldn't often put names and dates and places to them.

From that position there was no moving him. He agreed that of course he had met Miss Molly at the club. He spoke of her as Miss Towers, though he appeared to know that her real name was Oulton, but, then, Henrietta Towers had mentioned that her mother and her half-sister were generally known as Mrs. and Miss Towers, as the farm itself was known as the Towers Poultry Farm and Tea Garden.

"She went there to try to hear of an opening for her stuff," Noll explained, "just as I went there to meet the film crowd. What about it?"

There was no reply to be made to this demand, truculent though the tone was in which it was uttered. The colonel said he hoped all at Sevens would do their best to find out what had become of the missing automatic, and now they must be going, as there were plenty of other inquiries to be made, but they would like to say good-bye to Mr. Moffatt first. That gentleman accordingly appeared, and the colonel took the opportunity to ask how long Reeves had been in his employ.

"About six or eight months, I think," Mr. Moffatt answered. "Ena could tell you exactly. Not easy to get a good, competent man. They like places in town, and they can pick and choose nowadays. We were without one for nearly a year."

"How did you come to hear of Reeves?" the colonel asked.

"Oh, he applied. He heard somehow I needed a man and he wrote. He has been quite satisfactory."

"I suppose you had references?"

"Oh, yes; he had been in his last place for a good many years; since he was a boy, in fact. Went there as boot-boy and stayed on till there was a death and the establishment was broken up. Mrs. Oulton gave him a most excellent reference."

"Mrs. Oulton?" repeated the colonel sharply, and Bobby could not quite prevent the little start he himself gave.

"Yes. Why?" Mr. Moffatt asked, noticing their interest. "His master's widow. I thought it was good enough if he had stayed in the same place so long; not too common to-day, when all they think of is bettering themselves, as they call it."

The colonel agreed that it wasn't too easy to find any servant willing to stay long in one place. Then he and Bobby departed, and when they were in their car again, and driving towards Way Side, the colonel said moodily:

"Well, now, what do you make of all that?"

Bobby made nothing of it, and so prudently said nothing.

"Is it the same Mrs. Oulton?" asked the colonel.

Bobby thought it might be as well to try to find out.

"Anyhow," said the colonel, "we know it was faked. The reference said he had been in the one place all his life, and we know he was sacked from one job on suspicion and has spent most of the last ten years in gaol. But how does that link up with Bennett's murder?"

Evidently the colonel expected no reply, so Bobby offered none, having, in fact, none to offer. But he was a little disconcerted when the colonel gave fresh instructions to the driver to stop at the Towers Poultry Farm.

"I'm going to get to the bottom of this, anyhow," he declared, when they arrived, and, leaving Bobby in the car, he descended and knocked at the cottage door.

He was admitted, and Bobby told himself that this visit was probably a mistake. Unlikely, he thought, that Mrs. Oulton knew anything about the reference, or that anything would be gained by questioning her. And Reeves would very likely come to hear of it and take the alarm and possibly disappear, which would be another complication in an already sufficiently complicated case. The colonel, to Bobby's mind, was behaving too much like the contract player who puts down his cards on the table, and that you should only do when you are certain of winning every trick—a degree of certainty certainly not yet attained in this case.

The colonel came back soon, frowning and disturbed.

"The old lady was there alone," he said. "Gave her quite a shock when I asked her if her name was Oulton. She says she prefers to be known by her first husband's name, and she didn't know people here knew she was

Mrs. Oulton. I think she has an idea it might prejudice people against the girls if it was known their father had been a bankrupt and had committed suicide. But she says she has never given anyone a reference since Mr. Oulton's death. They had three or four menservants during his life, but none named Reeves. She has seen Reeves himself, and is quite certain she doesn't know him and that she never employed him. She gave me the names of the menservants they had, and I expect they could be traced, though it hardly seems necessary. We know Reeves is a wrong 'un, and if we want to we can charge him with presenting forged testimonials."

"Yes, sir," agreed Bobby, hoping that would not be done just yet.

They were silent for the rest of the drive, each busy with his own thoughts. When they stopped before the Way Side front door, Mr. Hayes was on the threshold before they could alight.

"I wondered if it could be you by any chance," he said, welcoming them warmly. "Do you know, I was thinking of ringing you to ask, if you had the time to spare, if you would give me an appointment for a few minutes' chat."

He ushered them indoors, established them in armchairs, produced his inevitable whisky, hoped they would stay to dinner—it would be a charity to share a meal with a lonely man, only he must let cook know, or she would be going on strike. And did they really mean it when they declined a drink, and, if they unbelievably did mean it, would they mind if he lubricated?

They did mean it; they regretted pressure of business made it impossible to accept his kind invitation to dine; they would not mind in the least how much and how often Mr. Hayes "lubricated"; and was it anything of importance Mr. Hayes had been intending to ring up about? Unnecessary to repeat that even the tiniest piece of information might be of the greatest value.

"Well, I don't know, and that's a fact," said Mr. Hayes, dallying with the soda-water syphon and then setting it aside in favour of the whisky bottle. "I should hate to think I was putting you on an innocent man. Still, you would soon find out he was innocent if he is, and that would be all right. Clear the ground, so to say."

"Always a help," observed the colonel.

"Well, there you are," said Mr. Hayes. "But it's up to you to decide what my say is worth; that's your responsibility, and mine is to say it. It's Thoms."

"Thoms?" repeated the colonel. "The fact is, we came to ask you about him. Has he been with you long?"

"A year, or a little longer. Curiously enough, it's through him I found this place. He knew I was on the look-out. He heard of it from some other chauffeur he was talking to—a gossiping lot, chauffeurs, when they get together. He passed it on to me. I ran down to have a look-see, liked it, bought it, here I am. Thanks to Thoms," he said, and laughed, and Bobby thought that laugh was not altogether natural.

The colonel asked:

"Do you know anything about him before he came to you? He had references, I suppose?"

"I never saw any," admitted Mr. Hayes. "I just took him on, just like that. I had had to fire my man. On the spot. Caught him with my wallet in his hand. Petty thieving—cigars and petrol and so on—you expect, but a wallet with a wad of notes in it I thought going a bit far. I had missed money before. So I told him to clear, and he was off in two minutes and glad it wasn't in handcuffs. I'm a pretty good driver, but I own up the innards of a car are just a bag of mystery to me, as the schoolboy said of the sausage. Before I had even started to get a fresh man—I half thought I would do without one—I got into a jam. The car stuck. Couldn't move her. Stuck for keeps, it seemed, and me late for an important appointment that meant money. I cursed some, but that was no help, and then Thoms popped up. Passing, as it happened, saw my fix, stopped to watch, and then stepped up and told me what was wrong. Like that. Seemed he was a chauffeur and out of a job. I took him on—he had saved me a goodish little pile I would have missed if he hadn't got me going in time—and he's been with me ever since."

"Wasn't it a little rash not to take up his references?" the colonel asked.

Mr. Hayes shrugged his shoulders, toyed again with the syphon, again rejected it in favour of the whisky bottle.

"I dare say it was," he admitted. "United States fashion, though. Over there you judge a man for yourself by himself, not on what someone else says about him—probably hoodlum, anyhow. If he makes good, you keep him, if not, you fire him. Seems to work well, and gives many a poor devil a chance to make a fresh start. Over here his past hangs about him like a logging chain tied to his foot."

"A man's present is his past," said the colonel sententiously. "You have found Thoms satisfactory?"

"Good driver, first-class mechanic. A bit sulky, and doesn't get on too well with the other servants. Lately, though—well, nothing serious. I know I'm a bit careless about small change, and I don't count my cigars or lock them up, either. He's given me the idea lately there was something on his mind—worried. Pressed for money, too. He's had his wages in advance once or twice—I believe he's had them up to Christmas. My own idea is he's been betting. I bet myself, for that matter, but I take good care not to get into deep water. Anyhow, to talk plain United States, I was worried about him without knowing why. You remember when you were here before ? "

" Yes," said the colonel, surprised at this sudden question.

" Well, I didn't say anything at the time. I didn't quite take it in. I've been thinking about it since. You remember ? I had to own up I had a ·32 Colt automatic ? "

" The one you gave us ? " the colonel asked.

" Yes. Well, I kept it in a drawer, and I could have sworn that drawer was locked. I kept it locked; careful, too. I would have staked my last penny it was always locked. That night it wasn't. Honestly, I couldn't believe it when I put the key in and it wouldn't turn, and then I gave it a pull and the drawer came open. At the moment I put it down to forgetfulness on my part. Everyone's liable to forget. But the more I thought of it the more I was sure I remembered locking it the last time I opened it, some days back. When I came to think, I distinctly remembered letting the key slip out of my fingers. I remembered picking it up off the floor and giving the drawer a pull to make sure it was fastened."

" What sort of lock is it ? " the colonel asked.

" A Chubb. I had it put on specially. To keep private papers in. That's why I kept the automatic there. Always locked. Another thing. When I began to feel worried after you had gone, I went to have another look. I feel sure it had been disturbed—the papers in the drawer, I mean.

The pistol was right at the back. You couldn't get at it without moving a lot of things."

"Was anything missing?"

Hayes looked at the colonel a little queerly.

"It seems too silly to mention," he said, "but I had a flashlight—electric torch made to look like a small ·22 automatic. They were rather popular in the States when I was there. The idea was, you showed it to a hold-up man and scared him off and no risk of an accident. Recommended for the use of ladies. Had quite a run for a time, and then people got tired of them. I had one. I'm sure it was in that drawer. Now it isn't there. Don't see why anyone should want it, though."

"Had you anything of value—money or jewellery—in the drawer?"

"No. Only private papers; notes of investments and so on. Valuable to me, but to no one else. Another thing. I don't believe I have touched that automatic for years. It has just been lying there. I got the impression when I handed it to you it had been recently cleaned and oiled." He paused and said gently: "As it might have been after recent use."

CHAPTER XVI

NO QUESTIONS ANSWERED

WHEN HAYES HAD SAID THIS he relapsed into silence, and neither of the other two spoke. In the quiet room it seemed there hung the menace of a direct accusation, and presently the colonel said, a little as if speaking to himself:

" Is there anything more you think you can tell us ? "

" Only," answered Hayes, " that twice—once it was Mrs. O'Brien, my housekeeper; she's left now; and once the housemaid saw him—Thoms was in my room upstairs. Both times he had some sort of excuse for being there and I didn't hear anything at the time. But it got round to me finally, and I'm beginning to wonder why a chauffeur should go wandering upstairs to ask for orders when he knew his master was out."

" What you are telling us sounds serious, Mr. Hayes," the colonel said. " You realise that ? "

" No, I don't," Hayes snapped. " It's only serious if you take it seriously. That's up to you. I'm worried. I own up to that. If you can tell me I'm worried about nothing, that goes with me. Lord knows, I don't want to think Thoms a murderer. If he is, it might be me next."

He laughed uneasily as he spoke, and filled his glass again. His capacity for absorbing whisky seemed almost to equal that of Mr. Dillon of the Cut and Come Again—almost, but not quite, since none can equal the unequalled. Bobby, watching Hayes closely, was aware of an inner conviction that the man was really afraid. Possibly that might be merely on account of the unexplained tragedy happening so near by, but fear was in him none the less.

"You don't know of any connection between Thoms and the dead man?" the colonel asked.

"Oh, no. I've told you every single last thing I know," Hayes answered, and paused, and then added abruptly: "Finger-prints—that's what you people depend on, isn't it?"

"They provide proof of identity," the colonel agreed.

"Well, you can have Thoms's, if you like," Hayes said. "A wire came from my bookie the other day—a hot tip. I gave it to Thoms to read; I was with him in the garage when it came. I told him I would put a pound on for him. He had been doing a bit of repair work on the dynamo—we make our own electricity; quite a small installation, but enough for the house and the garage. Thoms is smart at those sort of jobs; he had saved me a bill for repairs and all the bother of waiting for workmen, so I thought I would let him in on the bookie's tip. His hands were a bit oily, and I noticed his finger-prints were plain on the wire when he gave it me back. Well, I never gave it another thought, but I've got the wire still. Pushed it in my pocket and found it there only yesterday." He produced it, a finger and thumb print clearly visible. "It occurred to me that if you cared to test some of the papers I've had locked up in that drawer of mine, you could find out if Thoms has handled them at any time."

"We could do that, perhaps," agreed the colonel.

" Going a bit beyond our authority, perhaps," he added uneasily, for he had a wholesome dread of what happened in England to policemen who didn't mind their step—a question in Parliament, perhaps; and that dread thought will make any official shiver in his shoes. " You would regard all information we gave you as confidential ? "

" I'll promise that," said Hayes at once. " I'll go get them."

He left the room accordingly, and returned with papers he was holding wrapped in a handkerchief. It was a precaution Bobby admired.

" Thought I had better not confuse them with my own," he said, noticing perhaps Bobby's quick glance.

The colonel said it was always best to be careful, and Bobby took charge of the papers, placing them carefully in one of the cellophane envelopes he had with him.

" Oh, Mr. Hayes," he said suddenly, " might I see the key of the drawer ? "

" There won't be any prints on that, you know," Hayes said. He pulled from his pocket a bunch of keys on a ring secured by a light chain to a trouser-button. " Even if Thoms got hold of it some time and got an impression to have a duplicate made, I've used it too often since for his prints to be still on."

" I suppose that's so. Sorry," agreed Bobby. He gave the bunch of keys—there were twelve or fifteen of them—a casual and somewhat dispirited glance, and made no protest when Hayes slipped them back into his pocket. " You always keep the drawer key on that same bunch, I suppose ? " he asked.

" Oh, yes," Hayes answered. " I have left them lying about once or twice, I know. Thoms might have got hold of them, though I've no reason to think so. But if that drawer was opened—and it must have been—well, there's no sign it was forced, so I suppose a key was used."

The colonel asked where Thoms slept. Hayes explained that he had a room over the garage, though he took all his meals in the house. Probably he would be in his room now, but he would be coming across for his supper soon, if they wanted to talk to him. The colonel thought it would be as well, and added that he would like to ask the maids a question or two. Hayes nodded, as if he fully understood, and, ringing the bell, told the girl, Aggie, who answered it, that the gentlemen wanted a little information it was possible she or cook might be able to provide.

Much impressed, Aggie accordingly escorted them to the little sitting-room Bobby knew already. Their answers to the colonel's questions soon showed that Aggie was somewhat spitefully inclined towards the chauffeur, and that Mrs. Marshall, the cook, wanted to approve of him as a seriously minded young man who had no use for flighty girls, but, all the same, found him a little difficult.

" Never says a word he can help, and it isn't natural for a young man to sit and brood the way he does," she observed.

" Does he brood ? " Bobby asked, thinking it possible that reading, study, or some hobby might account for Thoms's apparent love of solitude.

" Well, what do you call it, sitting up there alone every evening ? " demanded Mrs. Marshall.

" And welcome," added Aggie, with a most unconvincing toss of the head.

But at least from the two of them came ample confirmation of the fact that on two or three occasions Thoms had been discovered in the upper part of the house where normally a chauffeur's duties had no occasion to call him. He had even been seen coming out of Mr. Hayes's bedroom when everyone knew Mr. Hayes was in London. However, he had always had an excuse for his presence, and at the time no one had thought much about it.

" He's been up there when no one's known," Aggie interposed. " I've smelt baccy in Mr. Hayes's room when both him and Mrs. O'Brien were in town."

The colonel asked the two women to say nothing about this questioning, dropped a hint about possible actions for slander he hoped would help them to observe their given promise of silence, and then he and Bobby went across to the garage.

" Hayes's story may prove important," the colonel remarked as they walked along, " but we'll have to find if there's any link between Thoms and Bennett. Luckily there's the Cut and Come Again affair to start from. May have been some quite casual drunken quarrel, of course. But it may mean a previous connection. As soon as we get the firearms expert's report in, we shall know if Hayes's automatic was the one used. What he said about the flashlight made to look like an automatic seemed to clear up the maid's story about the two pistols."

" Yes, sir," agreed Bobby. " Mr. Hayes has a way of clearing up doubtful points before he is even asked about them."

The colonel made no reply to this except to scratch his chin thoughtfully. Then he said:

" You asked him something about his keys? "

" Yes, sir. I noticed he said he remembered dropping the key of the drawer on the floor, as if he were speaking of a single key. Afterwards he said he kept the drawer key on the bunch he showed us, with others. Nothing in it, very likely."

The colonel looked more thoughtful still, but by now they were at the garage door and he made no comment. The door was not fastened, and opened at once to their touch. Just within was a flight of steps leading to the upper part used as Thoms's living-quarters. At the top of the stairs was a small landing and a door, beneath which showed a thread of light. Thoms had apparently heard their entrance, and, as the colonel and Bobby reached this landing, he opened the door, switched on the bulb that lighted stairs and landing, and stood there, scowling at them.

"You again," he said.

"There are just a few questions I would like to ask you, Thoms," the colonel said briskly.

Thoms went back into the room and they followed him. It was a fair sized apartment, plainly though quite comfortably furnished. Heat was provided by an electric fire, with an attachment for a kettle, so that Thoms could evidently make himself a cup of tea or warm water for washing or shaving when he wished. But there was little in the room to indicate personal habits or history. There was a row of pipes—a strong odour of tobacco in the room suggested that Thoms was a heavy smoker—and there were a few books, mostly technical, a few magazines, a pile of newspapers, motor periodicals, and catalogues, that seemed the total of his personal possessions. There was not even a photograph to give a single intimate touch to the bare apartment; and all his clothing seemed either hanging on pegs or put away in a plain deal chest of drawers opposite the window. Bobby could see no suit-case or box or trunk of any kind. If Thoms chose to walk out at any minute, there would be little he need take, nothing left behind to trace him by.

Thoms had not asked them to sit down. He stood in the middle of the room, his hands deep in his pockets, glowering at them.

" I'm answering no questions," he said abruptly and angrily. " That's final."

" Which means, I suppose," the colonel rapped out, " you have something to conceal ? "

" Suppose what you like," Thoms retorted.

" For one thing," the colonel went on, " why did you try to murder Bennett the other day at the Cut and Come Again club ? "

Thoms thrust his hands deeper still into his pocket, thrust his chin still further, still more aggressively forward.

" I'm answering no questions," he repeated.

" You prefer," the colonel asked, " that we should form our own conclusions ? "

That remark was a favourite police card ; it was a kind of general ace of trumps, bound to take the trick. No one, innocent or guilty, wished the police to form their own conclusions. Only this time Thoms did not seem to notice that the trick was taken.

" Free country," he growled. " No law against forming conclusions."

The colonel was beginning to lose his temper.

" You are making me consider your behaviour extremely suspicious," he said sternly.

" Don't let me keep you," Thoms answered. " I'm sure your time is fully occupied."

The colonel had one more shot to fire.

" Why did you lie when you said you didn't recognise Bennett ? " he asked. " We have proof you met him at the

Cut and Come Again, quarrelled with him, tried to murder him. What have you to say to that?"

"Do you want me to go on repeating that I don't mean to answer any questions?" Thoms retorted. "There's the door," he added.

"You understand," demanded the colonel, "that we are officers of police acting under authority and investigating a case of murder? You are making me take a most serious view of your behaviour."

"For which," retorted Thoms, "you are responsible, not me. And as you are officers of police you know quite well there is no authority in law to examine anyone till an actual charge has been preferred. And then no one so charged is bound to answer any questions or to give any reason for his refusal."

"You are evidently well acquainted with the law, Mr. Thoms," said the colonel grimly. "As a rule only professional lawyers—and habitual criminals—know so much. But you've forgotten one thing. The coroner has authority to ask questions. At the adjourned inquest, you will certainly be called as a witness—and questioned."

He watched for the effect of this shot. Apparently it had none.

"May I again remind you," Thoms said calmly, "that there is a door behind you? I take it you have no search-warrant? No? I thought not. And I am sure I may take it, too, that you and I would both regret it if I had to throw you out because of your obstinate refusal to go. You are trespassers here, you know."

The colonel went red—or, rather, he went a deeper red, little though that, the moment before, had seemed possible. Bobby appeared uninterested, though he watched Thoms warily, for he was not sure the truculent-looking chauffeur might not attempt to carry out his threat. With what dignity he might the colonel turned and strode out of the room and down the stairs. Bobby started to follow, and in the doorway turned and looked back.

" Oh," he said, " I wonder why young Noll Moffatt asked if you were going to throw him down the chalk-pit —too ? Think up an answer, won't you, ready for the coroner ? "

Without waiting for a reply—which in fact did not come, for Thoms took no notice—Bobby ran down the stairs after the colonel, to whom he thought it prudent not to speak just then. Indeed, the silence between them was not broken till they were back in their car and well on their way home, when at last the colonel said:

" Mere insolence, cheek, defiance. He has heard the best plan is simply to refuse to speak. But they can't keep it up. When they have a good satisfactory explanation, they can't help giving it, and, once they begin to explain, we have them."

" Yes, sir," agreed Bobby, whose experience was indeed much the same.

" Makes it pretty plain he's our man, though," pronounced the colonel. " Of course, we want more evidence, but we shall get it."

" Yes, sir," agreed Bobby once again.

CHAPTER XVII

ANALYSIS

A DAY OR TWO WENT BY with no fresh development, and, as there seemed nothing else for him to do, Bobby was sitting this morning in his room in the house where he was staying—that of one of the members of the county police force. Before him lay a blank sheet of paper at which as blankly he was staring, and now and again he scratched reflectively the end of his nose.

These were occupations in which he had been engaged ever since breakfast, and now it was nearly noon. After dinner he had to report to Colonel Warden, and he was a little afraid that this might mean he was to be taken off a case to the elucidation of which he had so far contributed but little, and sent back to more humdrum duties in town, where, however, the squad for which he, as sergeant, was primarily responsible seemed to be getting along quite nicely without him. But, then, he had an idea that some of those at headquarters were not too grieved at his continued absence.

A horrible legend was growing up there that he was a favourite, a " pet "; that he took afternoon tea regularly with Cabinet Ministers; that the Home Secretary in especial was his dearest friend; that as a consequence all the plums came naturally his way. All quite unfounded, of course; especially that hateful yarn about the Home Secretary he knew he would never be able to live down, and that was spoiling all his chances of promotion, since his superiors simply dared not risk the comment running all through the force:

"Oh, yes, the Home Sec's pet—that's the way to get on. Be in with the nobs and nothing else matters."

So there were influences more than favourable to keeping him out of the way in the country. Then, too, the county chief constable seemed willing enough for him to remain.

"Just potter round a bit and see what comes of it," Colonel Warden had said, leaving him the free hand Bobby's somewhat lonely and independent nature always made him long for and that he so seldom secured.

For the case interested him, as did the personalities concerned in it, and, if it could lead to the identification of the confidence man the American police described as a "killer," that would be a highly desirable result, and mean the removal of one who seemed a standing danger to society. Not to mention that it would be pleasing to inform the newly established, highly successful—and well aware of it—Federal Board of Investigation of the United States that the man they had inquired about, and seemed to have so little knowledge of, was now safe under arrest. Professional pride, not to say swagger, of course, but pleasing to bring off, all the same. Bobby, therefore, had been glad to accept the suggestion that he might "potter around" a bit, even though his "pottering" this morning had consisted in sitting in a chilly bedroom, inadequately warmed by a smoky oil-stove, on a hard and rickety chair, before a washstand turned for the occasion into a writing-table, staring solemnly at an entirely blank sheet of paper.

True, his landlady had somewhat hesitatingly offered him the use of the front sitting-room, but Bobby knew well that apartment was for Sundays and for company alone, and he had been tactful enough to decline her offer to light a fire for him there when she knew he meant to spend the morning writing.

" More forms, I suppose," she said. " My man's always saying that's all police work is now—just filling up forms."

Bobby agreed that that is indeed half the work of the modern world, so that to-day we live not so much by taking in each other's washing as by filling up forms about each other and ourselves.

The church clock in the distance struck twelve. Bobby started convulsively, grabbed his pen, thrust it into the inkpot, and began hurriedly to write.

He headed the paper:

THE BENNETT CASE SO FAR

He paused, frowned, took another sheet of paper, and wrote:

RE BENNETT CASE

He paused again, and surveyed this new heading with a satisfied smile. It seemed so much more official.

He continued:

A

STARTING POINTS.

A1. Inquiry from America about British-born confidence man, said to have secured large sums in the States. Described as cool, reckless, and dangerous, suspected of one or more killings. No personal description.

A2. Bennett known to have recently returned from America and believed to have been engaged in "share-pushing"; showed interest in the Sevens party and asked to be directed to Way Side.

Deductions.

A1*a*. Bennett either confidence man wanted by F.B.I. or killed by him.

A2*a*. Concentrate on trying to find out whether the Molly Oulton drawings, any member of the Sevens party, or Way Side, was chief attraction in bringing Bennett to the neighbourhood, or if they interlock in any way.

Note.—At present Colonel Warden seems inclined to suspect Thoms. The fight between Thoms and Bennett at the Cut and Come Again undoubtedly suggestive.

B

Material Clues.

B1. Lipstick.

B2. Photographic film wrapper (fragment).

B3. Bullets—found in body and recovered from trees near Sevens.

B4. Car.

B5. Body of victim.

Notes on Above Clues.

B1*a*. Lipstick common type and unidentifiable.

B2*a*. Wrapper fragment unidentifiable.

B3*a*. Report from firearms expert not yet received, but Mr. Moffatt's automatic known to be missing.

B4*a*. Car hired. Nothing known at garage. Dead end.

B5*a*. Everything likely to help identification removed from body.

Deductions from Above.

B1*a*1. Lipstick suggests presence of woman. Women connected with case: Ena Moffatt, Mrs. (Laddy) O'Brien, Henrietta Towers, Molly Oulton.

B2*a*1. Film wrapper suggests presence of photographer. Accidental or purposed? Why purposed? Probably, then, accidental. Who? Oliver Moffatt known to be keen photographer and to have been out in the neighbourhood that afternoon, taking snaps. Fellow member with Bennett of Cut and Come Again, but no proof they had ever met there. Note that many people besides Oliver Moffatt take photos. Are any of the above-mentioned women interested in photography?

B3*a*1. Wait report from expert.

B4*a*1. These taken together suggest that Bennett was alarmed on finding police inquiries were being made about him and had himself taken precaution to cover his tracks and to destroy all means of identification. This would mean that he himself—not his murderer—removed tabs from clothing and so on. This is the more probable, as the murderer would hardly have had time; the noise of the falling of the car over the edge of the chalk-pit seems to have followed almost immediately on the sound of firearms.

C

FACTS KNOWN (*as established by evidence of witnesses*).

C1. Bennett showed interest in Sevens party. Proved by evidence of Norris, who saw him watching Sevens through field-glasses. Also interested in Way Side, as he had asked what was the best road to take to get there (Oakley Road House evidence). Had also seemed interested in Molly Oulton's drawings (Cut and Come Again evidence).

C2. Time of murder established as four in the afternoon (evidence of driver of tradesman's delivery-van). Corroborated by labourer who also saw a man leaving the copse holding a hat before his face, presumably to avoid risk of recognition.

Deductions.

C1*a*. Bennett must have had something to do with someone at Sevens and with someone at Way Side, since he showed interest in both houses. Mrs. O'Brien's name was written on the back of one or two of Miss Oulton's sketches, and she may therefore be the link with Way Side. But who is link between Sevens and Way Side?

C2*a*. As a man was seen leaving the copse, none of the women mentioned is likely to have been the actual murderer. But she may have been an active accomplice.

D

PERSONALITIES CONCERNED

D1. Mr. Moffatt.

D2. Oliver Moffatt, son of above.

D3. Ena Moffatt, daughter and sister of above-mentioned.
D4. Leopold Leonard Larson, guest at Sevens.
D5. Edward George Pegley, visitor at Sevens.
D6. Henrietta Towers, Towers Poultry Farm.
D7. Edward Thoms, chauffeur at Way Side.
D8. John Hayes, tenant of Way Side.
D9. Reeves, butler at Sevens.

Points for and against above.

D1*a* (Mr. Moffatt, senior).

Against.

Blacklisted by steamship companies on suspicion of card-sharping. Known to have made secret visits to America and to have possessed an automatic now missing. No alibi.

For.

Country gentleman of old family and good standing it is difficult to imagine as card-sharper or confidence trickster. Said to be well off and to have a large sum invested in consols.

Deductions.

The secrecy about Mr. Moffatt's American visits suggests discreditable reason and possibility of connection with Bennett. The blacklisting provides obvious opportunity for blackmail. The disappearance of Moffatt's automatic suggests it may be the one used. His true financial position must be ascertained, if possible. As card-sharper and so on, a country gentleman seems incredible, but the impossible must not be deduced from the merely incredible, which sometimes turns out to be the actual.

D2*a* (Oliver Moffatt).

Against.

Amateur photographer, known to have been taking snaps at the time and in the vicinity of the murder. Liable to have dropped fragment of wrapper. Fellow member with Bennett of Cut and Come Again club. Sulky and refuses to answer questions or explain quarrel with Thoms. No alibi.

For.

General character inconsistent with murder, but, then, so is everyone's.

Deductions.

As he is the elder Moffatt's son, he may very well have known of the secret American visits and may have known of—resented—feared—connection between his father and Bennett. The common membership of the Cut and Come Again gives also the possibility of direct connection between him and Bennett. Another line to be followed up.

D3*a* (Ena Moffatt).

Against.

Only the lipstick incident and the fact that she is, like her brother, a member of the Cut and Come Again. Alibi supported by Mrs. Markham's evidence, but not conclusive, as distance might have been covered in time. Nervous manner suggesting she knows more than she has said.

For.

Some nervousness perfectly natural. Girls don't shoot.

Deductions.

The Cut and Come Again people must be questioned to see if there is any suggestion of a connection between her and Bennett. If there was any connection, and Bennett's visit was to meet her, her brother may have known, objected, and there may have been a quarrel between the two men on her account.

D4*a* (Leopold Leonard Larson).

Against.

Showed extreme dislike and enmity for share-pushers. Open hostility to Pegley, to whom he seems to have used insulting language. Frequent visits to America suggest possibility of previous knowledge (denied) of Bennett.

For.

No such connection known and no motive suggested. Alibi supported by Ena Moffatt and Mrs. Markham but not conclusive (see D3*a*), and further supported by loss and recovery of gold cigarette-case.

Deduction.

Larson's dislike of share-pushers and use of strong language to Pegley suggests that if he met Bennett, recognised him, used the same language, a quarrel might have resulted and ended fatally.

D5*a* (Edward George Pegley).

Against.

Suspected share-pusher. Has lived in America. No alibi.

For.

None, except vagueness of those against.

Deductions.

Suspected of share-pushing. May, therefore, have been associate or rival of Bennett and have had reason for wishing to get rid of him.

D5*a* (Henrietta Towers).

Against.

Told long story about bonds stated to have been stolen from her mother and of her suspicions that her stepfather had been murdered. She is of strong and decided character and would probably go far to protect her stepsister, Molly. Seems to have taken care to hide photographs of her stepfather and half-brother. Reeves used stepfather's name in his faked testimonials. Lipstick (see D2 and D8). Alibi confirmed by Mr. Hayes as his by her. Unsatisfactory.

For.

None, but none of this has direct bearing on the case.

Deductions.

Probably had some reason or motive for long story she told. Did she believe Bennett responsible for loss of her mother's bonds or the death of her stepfather? If so, she might have heard of him from Miss Molly, who had met him at the Cut and Come Again, made an appointment with him, shot him, either out of revenge or to recover the lost bonds or during a quarrel. If there was any previous connection between Bennett and the Oultons that, and not Mrs. O'Brien's name and address on their back, might account for Bennett's interest in Miss Molly's sketches. Or Miss Henrietta may have known Bennett was worrying her stepsister and have wanted to protect her. That might explain what she said about Hayes trying to seduce her. It was on her mind and had to come out somehow. She would certainly be capable of strong action to protect or help anyone for whom she felt responsible. Almost certainly there is some reason for the removal of the photos of her stepfather and brother. Obviously that can only be fear of recognition. Is it possible one or other of them, the supposedly dead stepfather or the missing brother, is identical with the murdered man?

Incidental moral.

Drawn from story about lost bearer bonds: Don't try to do the income-tax or the consequences may be unexpected.

D6 (Edward Thoms, Mr. Hayes's chauffeur).

Against.

Sulky and suspicious manner. Refuses to answer questions or explain quarrel with Noll Moffatt. Was engaged without references. No alibi.

For.

None.

Deduction.

Has something to conceal. Some point of connection between him and Noll Moffatt, fights between youngsters in their respective social conditions being unusual.

D7 (John Hayes, tenant of Way Side).

Against.

Denies knowledge of Bennett though Bennett had been asking the way to his house. Displays curious ability to clear up doubtful points before they are put to him. Has lived in America and was in possession of pistol of type used in murder. Claims to love the country but seems to be bored by it. Seems to wish to throw suspicion on Thoms. Said to have possessed second pistol (doubtful evidence of maid, Aggie).

For.

Alibi confirmed by Henrietta Towers as she confirms his. Not too satisfactory.

Deductions.

His coming to live in a secluded part of the country when the country evidently bores him, suggests that he wishes to conceal himself. Why? Can he, he has admittedly made money in America, be the confidence trickster the F.B.I. want to hear about, and, if so, was Bennett an associate, possibly a blackmailing associate, Hayes had to get rid of?

D8 (Mrs. (Laddy) O'Brien, Mr. Hayes's dismissed housekeeper).

Against.

Lipstick (see D2 and D5). Sudden departure after violent quarrel with her employer which might have been forced to explain this sudden leaving. No alibi, and admittedly in vicinity of scene of murder that afternoon.

For.

Hardly required, as satisfactory explanation of quarrel and sudden departure is provided by story of jealousy and the tale about the new hat and the quarrel with Hayes.

Deduction.

As she left on bad terms with Mr. Hayes, she may be willing to give information, if she knows anything—and can be found.

D9 (Reeves, butler to Mr. Moffatt).

Against.

Ex-convict. Cat burglar. Obtained present situation by aid of forged testimonials. No alibi.

For.

Lack of known motive.

Deduction.

Use of name " Oulton " suggests some connection with Oulton affair. All knowledge of Reeves, however, denied by Mrs. Oulton.

Note.—At present, Mrs. Oulton and Molly Oulton may be left out of consideration.

Final deduction.

Complete mix-up of a case.

He had just written these last words when a welcome summons to dinner floated up the stairs. He put down his pen, called a willing response, when suddenly a small, indeed a tiny, detail, on record indeed but that for the moment he had entirely forgotten, flashed into his mind.

" Couldn't mean anything, though," he told himself aloud.

" Dinner's ready, Mr. Owen "—his landlady's voice came up the stairs again.

Deciding to make a note later on of what he had just remembered, he descended to the kitchen, whence came a welcome smell of roast pork and apple sauce.

He found his host there, that moment returned from the

police headquarters where he was engaged on clerical work.

" Bit of news just come in," he told Bobby. " I was to pass it on to you. The bullets found in the Sevens grounds known to have been fired by young Mr. Moffatt out of the old gent's pistol are the same as what killed this Bennett bloke."

" The same type, fired from the same pistol ? " Bobby asked.

" That's right," agreed the other, who was no logical positivist and expected what he meant to be understood rather than what he said. " Means the bloke was done in with Mr. Moffatt's pistol."

" Have some more gravy, Mr. Owen ? " suggested his hostess, for, if men must work, women must cook.

Bobby accepted the gravy with gratitude.

" Not much good," he said, but certainly not meaning the gravy. " Mr. Moffatt kept the thing in an open drawer practically anyone could get at, and there's nothing to show when it was taken or when it was last seen."

" That's right," agreed the other again. " They was saying that at H.Q. Every one of the whole lot, even Thoms, Mr. Hayes's chauffeur. He's been at Sevens with messages from his boss and been kept waiting there. He could easily have pinched it."

Bobby wondered vaguely if the second pistol reported at Way Side by one of the maids, and deftly explained away by Hayes as an electric torch made to resemble an automatic, might by any possibility be the lost Moffatt pistol. Nothing to prove it was, of course, or that Hayes's explanation, so oddly offered before it was asked, was not perfectly correct.

Bobby sighed. All conjecture. All speculation. All

random guesswork. Hardly a proved fact of which you could say, Because that was, therefore this is. All of it together amounted to no more, he told himself gloomily, than confused noises in the head.

He applied himself to the roast pork; that at least was solid, firm, factual, admitting of no dual and contradictory explanation.

Later, as instructed, he took himself off to county headquarters and there presented his report to Colonel Warden, who read it, if not exactly with nods and becks and wreathed smiles, at any rate with a good many grunts.

"Very complete statement," he said finally. "The truth's there all right, only where? The murderer's there for certain, only which?"

Bobby was just about to mention that one little detail which had flashed so suddenly into his mind, whereof he had quite forgotten to jot down the note he had intended, when a constable appeared.

"A lady to see you, sir," he said. "She says her name is O'Brien and she can tell you all about the Bennett case."

CHAPTER XVIII

PASSED TO HAYES

THERE WAS A MOMENT'S PAUSE. The constable was excited. Bobby's face was blank. The colonel whistled softly.

" Glad to hear it," he said, and then: " Well, fetch her along."

Mrs. O'Brien appeared. She looked flushed, and spoke a little breathlessly. Plainly she was feeling the strain. The colonel very sensibly let her talk for a time, explaining herself and her errand. Both Bobby and he watched her intently. She was a big woman, loud in manner, in appearance, in dress, and Bobby remembered how Ena Moffatt had smiled at the idea of this huge woman with the spreading face and features adopting one of the new, flat, pancake-like hats that were at the moment fashion's latest vagary. He had a vision of her employer laughing at it and her, and of her snatching it off and throwing it down in her rage He wondered whether now it would pass into the possession at Way Side of the cook or of the maid. Though it was a chilly morning, Mrs. O'Brien's excitement was making her perspire a little, with disastrous results to the somewhat heavy make-up of powder and rouge she wore. The colonel took his opportunity when at last she paused for breath.

"We quite understand that, Mrs. O'Brien," he said. So far Mrs O'Brien had been explaining why she had not come forward before and how her sense of duty was now forcing her to tell all she knew, and never in all her life had she dreamed she would ever have anything to do with the police, but all must do what was right, and, after the way she had been treated, no one could expect her not to. "We fully appreciate your motives," the colonel continued, "and I am sure no blame will be attributed to you. I understand you knew the dead man?"

"Well, seeing we were married——"

"Married?" interrupted the colonel, surprised. "Your husband?"

"Divorced," explained Mrs. O'Brien.

"Oh," said the colonel.

"It was me was the wronged party," emphasised Mrs. O'Brien. "Mental cruelty—the little squirt!"

"Dear me," said the colonel, slightly at a loss.

"But wanted me back," Mrs. O'Brien continued. "Made all sorts of promises, if only we could come together again. Said he had never known a happy hour since we parted."

"Had you any intention of agreeing?" the colonel asked.

"Might have," she answered cautiously. "I didn't say 'yes' and I didn't say 'no.' Johnny—that's Mr. Hayes—was scared it was going to be 'yes.' Jealous, you know. That's why he did him in."

The colonel sat upright.

"You mean Mr. Hayes shot Bennett?"

"That's right," she answered calmly. "Plain enough, and not the first either, if all tales are true. Johnny's a thug, a killer; no heart; doesn't care for anything except his own precious skin. The things I've put up with from that man and then to treat me the way he did. Oh, it was him did Nick in all right."

"We shall have to ask you to make a formal statement," the colonel told her.

He gave her a brief lecture on the seriousness of what she said, and reminded her she would have to give evidence in court. She looked sulky and a little frightened, but stuck to her tale. A shorthand writer was called in. Her story was to the effect that she had first met Bennett in New York, where she had been proprietor of a large, flourishing, and important restaurant. On Broadway, she said somewhat hurriedly when asked for the address; but she had forgotten the exact number, even the exact position. It had closed down after she sold it, unable to survive the loss of her personality, and she had never got a penny of the purchase price. Mr. Bennett had been a customer. He was then a "drummer"—she used the old-fashioned word now generally replaced by "travelling representative"—in hardware. He made a lot of money speculating, but he hadn't treated her right—there was Another Woman, a hussy—and finally, though he had gone down on his bended knees to stop her, she had obtained a divorce. Afterwards she had obtained a position as housekeeper with Mr. Hayes and had returned to England with him. But she had held Mr. Hayes at arm's length in spite of his persistent advances, she having always kept herself respectable, as none could deny, and, when he heard that Mr. Bennett wanted her to come back, his frantic jealousy had overcome him, with the tragical result they knew.

Here her emotion overcame her and she shed a few tears. Then she produced documents which showed she had in fact been married in Denver, Colorado, to a Nicholas Bennett, and, less clearly, that she had been divorced from him on grounds of desertion and mental cruelty in Mexico a few years later. They might think it strange she had considered returning to Mr. Bennett after the way he had treated her, especially with Johnny Hayes going down on his bended knees like he was, but a woman, she explained, never quite forgot her feelings for her first love. There was something about a first love . . .

The colonel said somewhat hastily that he quite understood that, and what had actually happened? What had Mrs. O'Brien seen to make her sure Hayes shot Bennett?

Mrs. O'Brien said it was impossible for any man to appreciate her position. There she was, torn between the two men, each of them on bended knees, so to say. Colonel Warden and the other gentleman would understand. . . .

The colonel said they did indeed understand, and what actually happened. Jealousy was one thing, he reminded her. Murder was another.

"It was this way," said Mrs. O'Brien. "Nick put it straight. He couldn't bear the suspense any longer. He had got to see me and I must decide. Very masterful and determined. I didn't dare ask him to the house for fear of what might be if he and Johnny Hayes met. So I told him to wait for me in Battling Copse. I told him how to get there, and I met him, and he pleaded so hard I promised to come back. Transported with joy he was, poor fellow. Only I said I must tell Mr. Hayes first, me being straight with all as always, and pack up and leave, and when Nick had it all arranged for us to marry over again then he could come and see me, but not before, it not being proper."

"Not being——?" said the colonel, a trifle puzzled, and then: "Oh, yes, of course," he said, realising she meant him to understand how careful she was to observe all the proprieties.

"Somehow," she went on, "Johnny Hayes got to know. Cunning he is, a weasel if ever there was one, a stoat, a fox," said Mrs. O'Brien, and there apparently her zoological knowledge ran out, for she paused and continued inadequately: "Low minded, too, and when I was going back to the house I saw him and I knew something was up, for he glared something awful and never said a word. He was going towards the copse, and I hoped he wouldn't see Nick, as I wanted to tell him myself, and then I heard a bang. I didn't think much about it at the time, but now I know it was a pistol shot."

"A pistol shot?" Bobby asked, looking up. "Are you sure? Was it clear and distinct?"

"It was," she answered, "crack—just like a whip, only much louder. It did just cross my mind someone was shooting rabbits or something. I didn't think about it any more. I dare say I was a little upset, along of the momentous decision I had just made."

"What time was this?" the colonel asked.

"At four o'clock, because I looked at my watch," she answered, and Bobby, glancing at the wrist-watch she wore, saw that it was a small, expensive-looking thing—and saw also that at the moment it was not going. "And then I turned to look, and I saw as plain as I ever saw anything Johnny Hayes running out of the copse with his hat before his face and I thought Nick must have lammed him one and made his nose bleed. Never did it cross my mind that my poor Nick, who wanted me back so bad——"

She paused to wipe her eyes, but soon conquered her emotion and continued:

" When I told Johnny I was going to leave him you wouldn't believe how he carried on, the great bully. Couldn't bear to think of having done what he had all for nothing, and tried to scare me into stopping. I wasn't having any. I just packed and went, little dreaming my poor Nick——"

Again her emotion overcame her, but once again it was soon conquered. She was informed that her evidence would be required at the adjourned inquest, and Bobby asked casually:

" Have you lost a lipstick case recently ? "

She turned and stared at him, and it was a moment or two before she answered. Then she said slowly:

" I have not. You can look if you like. I've only two. They're both in my bag." She named the make. "It's what I always use," she said, " some preferring one and some another."

She signed the statement she had made, gave her address—she was staying with friends at Uxbridge, she explained—and then to Bobby was assigned the task of providing her with tea and of seeing her to the station to catch the next London train. By good luck there was one nearly due, a fact for which Bobby was profoundly thankful.

Returning from this duty, Bobby was told that the colonel wanted him again. He reported accordingly and found the colonel looking very worried.

" Whole thing in the melting-pot," he sighed. " I felt sure Thoms was our man after hearing what happened at the Cut and Come Again, and now there's this."

" There are points in Mrs. O'Brien's statement defending

counsel would jump on at once," Bobby remarked doubtfully.

"Anyhow, there is no doubt Bennett was really her divorced husband. Her story would explain what he was doing down here," the colonel pointed out.

"Yes, sir, but not why he was taking enough interest in Sevens to watch it through field-glasses."

"Her statement stands up where we can check it," the colonel went on. "There's corroboration that a man was seen leaving the copse with a hat held before his face."

"Yes, there's that," agreed Bobby, "but she may have picked up her knowledge afterwards. It's common gossip round here, told over and over again at the Red Lion, I expect. I think, too, gossip she had heard might explain the way she took it when she was asked about having lost a lipstick. She seemed a little startled but not surprised, I thought. Also she said she heard one report; sharp, clear, and distinct, like the crack of a whip. The other evidence is that there were two or three reports in quick succession. I noticed her watch wasn't going this afternoon, though of course that doesn't prove it wasn't then, and I don't think anyone returning to Way Side from the copse could see the spot the other witness says the man he saw left it from."

"If she's inventing the yarn, what for?" the colonel asked.

"It might be spite, to get even with Hayes after their quarrel. Or it's just possible she's heard that a wife can't be forced to give evidence against a husband and means to point that out to Hayes. Or it is even possible, if she's in with Hayes again, and Hayes is really the man we want, he may have put her up to telling this yarn in the hope you will act on unreliable evidence and he'll get an acquittal."

" Suppose her story's true, and she's reliable ? "

" Oh, yes, sir, there's that," agreed Bobby.

" Hadn't Hayes an alibi, though ? "

" Yes, sir. Miss Henrietta Towers's evidence."

" Oh, yes," the colonel said. " Yes, I remember. She'll have to be questioned again."

There was a knock at the door, and the constable appeared.

" Beg pardon, sir," he said as the colonel frowned, for he had said he did not wish to be interrupted. " Young lady here, sir. Says she has information to give about the Bennett case. Miss Henrietta Towers."

CHAPTER XIX

PASSED TO ENA

BOTH THE COLONEL AND BOBBY were a little startled. They exchanged surprised looks. The constable waited stolidly. The colonel snapped out with temper, for he was worried and uneasy:

"Well, fetch her in. What are you waiting for?"

The constable endured this injustice as subordinates must the unfairness of their superiors, and retired. The colonel glared at Bobby and said very angrily:

"What's this mean?"

Bobby, one of whose great merits was that he knew when to hold his tongue, said nothing, thus depriving the colonel of an opportunity for biting his head off. The shorthand writer, fearing the colonel's thunderbolts might descend next upon him, tried to pretend he wasn't there. The door opened and Henrietta came in—strode in, rather, with her usual swinging step. She was carrying a somewhat worn-looking suit-case in one hand, carrying it easily, too, though it was of a good size and weight. The colonel waved her to the chair Mrs. O'Brien had occupied and looked at her severely.

"I understand you think you have something to tell us?" he asked, as if he were warning her to think again.

"I thought you ought to know about this," she

answered, indicating the suit-case. " It was in a ditch on our land, near the road, close to a gate. It wasn't there before —before the murder. They say everything was taken out of the car before it was found, and I thought this might have come from it and you ought to see it."

This seemed interesting. The colonel's ill temper began to pass. Bobby got up and, taking the suit-case, put it on the table where the colonel was sitting.

" Locked," said the colonel, trying it. " How did you come to find it ? "

" It was Mr. Youngman," she explained. " He is our egg gatherer—for Weston Brothers. They take most of what we've got. It wasn't Mr. Youngman's regular day to-day. I think he just came to talk about the murder. Everyone is, you know. We've had a lot of reporters to tea to-day, and they've all been asking questions."

The colonel groaned. Well he knew it, this influx of newspaper men and their questions.

" You haven't said anything to them about this ? " he asked, indicating the suit-case.

" No," she answered. " I thought I had better not."

" Mr. Youngman told you about it ? "

" No. I think he was a little disappointed he didn't know anything at the time about what had happened. The other man—the one who heard the shots—has had the reporters talking to him, and he says he's going to have his picture in the London papers, and I think Mr. Youngman feels if he hadn't stopped to talk to Mr. Hayes the reporters would have wanted his photograph too."

" He says he was talking to Mr. Hayes at the time ? " the colonel asked sharply.

" Just for those few minutes," Henrietta explained. " He told me he looked at his watch and saw it was five minutes past four when he left Mr. Hayes. He had been talking to him for five or ten minutes, so if he hadn't stopped he would have been close to Battling Copse when it happened. He thinks he might even have seen the man who did it running away afterwards."

The colonel and Bobby looked at each other. This was unexpected confirmation of Hayes's alibi, and appeared to clear him and to show that Mrs. O'Brien's accusation had been purely malicious. Henrietta, unaware of the interest her story had roused, went on calmly:

" How I came to find the suit-case was because he said, too, he had noticed a lady's bicycle near the road, but on our land. He said he wondered at the time what it was doing there and if it was ours. I knew it couldn't be."

" Why ? "

" We keep ours in the shed, and I knew no one had had it out that day. No one uses it much except me. Mother never does; she can't ride and won't learn, and if Molly takes it she has to alter it. She isn't as tall as I am. I wondered a little what a bicycle could have been doing there. It wasn't there before the murder."

" How do you know ? "

" My sister or I would have seen it, and we hadn't. I asked Molly. One of the hens will insist on laying in that corner of the field where Mr. Youngman said he saw the bicycle. All the hens have their own little fads, and this one simply won't lay anywhere else. She has got it into her head that's the proper place, and she would rather die than use the nests. So every day Molly or I go and have a look, when she's laying. Sometimes she takes another hen with her. I suppose she tells them what a nice quiet place it is, and much better than the nests, and every self-respecting hen ought to use it. It's very trying, but hens are like that—terribly determined creatures. So we have to go and look or risk losing the eggs and stopping her laying, and Molly says there was no bicycle there that morning. She is quite certain, and Molly sees everything like that. If it had been there, most likely she would have made a sketch—pattern of bicycle spokes against the hedge or something. If she was dying she would want to draw the medicine-bottles. After Mr. Youngman had gone I thought I would go that far and see if it had come back and if there were any eggs. There were no eggs and no bicycle, but I found the suit-case. It was in the ditch, pushed under some brambles. It looked as if it had been hidden, only not very well."

"Can you show us the exact spot?"

"I broke off some branches so as to know it again."

"You didn't try to open it?"

"Well, it's locked. I did try, but I couldn't."

"Was this Mr. Youngman quite sure it was a lady's bicycle he saw?"

"I don't know. I suppose so. He said he thought it was mine, so he must have."

Bobby got out a large-scale ordnance map at the colonel's request, and Henrietta was able to indicate the exact spot where the egg gatherer said he had seen the bicycle. A path was shown near, crossing the field, and then a little further on entering a wood, through which evidently a cycle could be ridden in almost complete immunity from observation. On the map Bobby had already marked with a tiny pencil cross the spot where Ena Moffatt, Mrs. Markham, and Mr. Larson had all met. A brief calculation and a tracing out of the intersecting footpaths, which seemed numerous in the neighbourhood, showed it would be quite possible for anyone leaving the spot where the bicycle had been seen to reach in the given time the meeting-place of the three people mentioned.

Not till Henrietta had been thanked and dismissed did either man comment on this fact. But then, looking more worried than ever, the colonel said:

" Well, this means we have Hayes's alibi confirmed and Ena Moffatt's knocked out. Nothing in that, of course, but there it is."

" Yes, sir," agreed Bobby, and the colonel scowled, as if he exceedingly disliked this quite innocuous remark.

" No one can possibly suppose . . . " said the colonel, with one of his best glares. " Besides, girls don't shoot."

" No, sir," agreed Bobby, and let his eyes wander for a moment to an evening paper that happened to be lying near, one of its flaring headlines announcing in huge letters: " Girl shoots lover."

" Well, not girls like Ena Moffatt," declared the colonel crossly. " I've known her for years."

This did not in itself seem to Bobby to be entirely conclusive. But he held his tongue, and the colonel gave him another glare and said:

" Thank goodness, nothing about love in this affair."

" No, sir," agreed Bobby warmly. " Enough complication as it is without that "; and even the shorthand writer breathed a sigh of relief as he bent over his transcript.

The colonel turned his attention to the suit-case, examined it from various points, supposed it was no good expecting to find finger-prints on the blessed thing, and then pushed it over to Bobby and told him to get it open.

That did not prove a task of any great difficulty, and, when Bobby had accomplished it, he coughed gently as a signal to the colonel, standing staring frowningly out of the window as if for two pins he would arrest everyone in sight.

" A child like Ena," he was muttering indignantly to himself.

At the sound of Bobby's gentle cough he turned and marched resolutely upon the open suit-case, as upon the imminent deadly breach. The contents seemed to consist entirely of clothing, all of it either new or with the laundry and other marks carefully removed.

" All that can't have been done after the murder—or can it ? " the colonel said.

" Hardly likely, I think," Bobby answered. " I expect after my talk with Bennett about share-pushing he realised we were on him, got the wind up, and made up his mind to bolt. And he went through his things to remove everything that might identify him."

" I dare say that was it," agreed the colonel. " No papers of any kind, no letters—what's this ? "

He had found, pushed away between two shirts, a woman's handbag. It was small and looked fairly expensive. He opened it. Within, on the flap, was written Ena Moffatt's name and the Sevens address. Her personal cards were within, too, and in a small packet were a number of letters. The colonel looked at them distastefully and doubtfully at Bobby. Bobby said nothing, but his mouth was set and grim. The colonel swore softly in an undertone and then picked them up, his face crimson. He looked at Bobby imploringly but got no encouragement. Swearing with a vigour and a fluency of which he was quite unaware—he had no idea that he was uttering a word aloud—he began to turn the letters over.

" Love-letters," he said with a sort of muffled moan. " Very much so." His looks began to grow less embarrassed, became black and frowning instead. " Very much so," he growled again. " Bit thick—disgraceful. Filthy—obscene. A child like her—wouldn't have believed it. Dated from Brighton—an hotel. Addressed Mickey Mouse—my God—and signed, ' Quack, quack.' ' Quack, quack ' ! " repeated the colonel in a kind of wail that was far indeed from any suggestion of the comic. He stared at Bobby. " I've known her since she was a child," he said.

Bobby said nothing.

" Got to see it through," the colonel said heavily.

" Our job, sir," Bobby answered, " to see things through. And, if we don't, it's all the same, for it goes on by itself."

The colonel pressed the bell on his table. To the constable who answered he gave orders for his car to be brought round.

" Have to see it through," he repeated. " You had better come, too, Owen. What do you make of it ? "

" We ought to be quite sure of our facts," Bobby said cautiously, " before we come to any conclusions."

" Those letters are facts enough," the colonel answered. " And that bicycle—a lady's bicycle hidden near the scene of the murder. Well ? "

" It suggests very strongly," Bobby said as the colonel paused, obviously challenging him to give an opinion, " that someone knew what was going to happen and had arranged a way of escape. That's good logic, but there's no proof who that person was. There's an off-chance the bicycle is mere coincidence, though that's not likely. I think we must assume connection."

" A woman's bicycle," the colonel went on when Bobby paused, " and it can hardly have been Miss

Towers's, and Mrs. O'Brien was seen shortly afterwards, not on a bicycle, on foot. And Ena Moffatt's handbag with these letters in Bennett's suit-case. Well ? "

" It is easy to make a theory," Bobby said, putting into words the conclusions they were both conscious of. " Both Bennett and Miss Moffatt are members of the Cut and Come Again. Miss Moffatt denies all knowledge of Bennett. The fact remains they both went to the same club, though there is no proof they ever spoke there. Bennett may have got possession of the handbag without Miss Moffatt's knowledge—probably he did. But, having got hold of it and seen the letters he may have thought there was a chance of blackmail of one kind or another—money or something else, making use of her in some way. That might account for his spying on Sevens. He may have told Miss Moffatt she had to meet him, and she may have known about her father's pistol and taken it with her—for protection, perhaps; perhaps with some idea of frightening him into returning the letters. There was some sort of quarrel. The pistol went off."

" You suggest that's what happened ? " said the colonel aggressively.

" I think it is a plausible deduction from the facts," Bobby answered steadily. " I think it is one that would occur to anybody."

" I know," agreed the colonel. " Got to test it," he said firmly.

The constable appeared again, to say the car was waiting.

CHAPTER XX

PASSED TO MR. LARSON

THE DRIVE TO SEVENS was a silent one. Neither man spoke; both were busy with their own ideas, both going over and over again in thought the theory Bobby had advanced, looking for weak spots in it, liking it less and less as the distance to Sevens grew less. Only when they were quite near did the colonel exclaim suddenly:

"It was a man seen leaving the copse after the shots were heard."

"Yes, that is so," agreed Bobby, who had already reminded himself of the fact. "Prosecuting counsel would say it might have been her brother. No need, anyhow, for the prosecution to prove who it was or what he was doing."

"I expect," agreed the colonel bitterly, "that is just what a prosecution would say."

He said this very angrily, apparently considering Bobby was to blame for the suggestion. But Bobby had never been able to feel there was much sense in the ever popular game of pretending that facts aren't there, and it was entirely obvious that what he had suggested was what any prosecution would advance. Their business, prosecuting counsel would argue, was with what happened, not with guesses about unknown men whose very existence merely depended on the word of one easily mistaken witness. Not much help there, Bobby felt, if Ena Moffatt was to escape the danger threatening her.

The car stopped. They got out and knocked. Reeves appeared and regretted that Mr. Moffatt was out. Young Mr. Moffatt was in town. Miss Moffatt was in the drawing-room, and no doubt would be very pleased to see them.

"Tell her," said the colonel, "a handbag has come into our possession and we would like to know if she can identify it as hers."

Reeves departed with his message, and Ena appeared at once.

"Oh, have you got my bag?" she cried excitedly. "Oh, I am glad. Do come in. Wherever was it? Did someone find it? I am glad. Have you got it with you?"

They followed her into the drawing-room, where she had been engaged in her customary variety of occupations, by the testimony of the wireless she now turned off, a half knitted jumper with the needles still in it, an open novel, a letter apparently just begun, not to mention a plainly disgruntled Persian kitten stretching itself before the fire as if just disturbed from a comfortable and soothing lap.

The colonel produced the handbag.

"I may take it it is yours?" he asked.

"Oh, yes," she said, and looked a little surprised when, though she held out her hand for it, the colonel did not at once give it to her. "Where did you get it?" she asked. "I thought I had left it in town, at a club I belong to, but they said they hadn't seen it. You don't know how glad I am to get it back."

She was still holding out her hand for it, and the colonel was still holding it in his. He said:

" I ought to tell you we found it in a suit-case we have reason to believe belonged to the man killed in Battling Copse."

Ena stared, her eyes opened to their widest, and that was very wide indeed.

" Good gollywogs ! " she said slowly, and repeated the phrase, for it was one of her own invention and she was in secret a little proud of it. " Good gollywogs, however did he get hold of it ? "

Her air of extreme surprise seemed genuine enough. But the colonel knew that all women are born actresses. His manner was still severe and gloomy as he continued:

" I felt it was necessary to make sure you recognised the handbag as yours."

" Of course it's mine," Ena said, looking less surprised now, and instead puzzled and even annoyed, as the solemnity of the colonel's voice and manner began to impress her. " Can I have it, please ? " she said, holding out her hand again.

" I am afraid it will have to be produced at the inquest," the colonel told her. " It will be necessary, too, to call you as a witness. You will be asked to explain how it came to be where it was found."

" But I don't know. I haven't an idea. How can I ? " Ena protested. She was beginning to look frightened now. " I haven't an idea," she repeated.

" You will also be asked," the colonel continued, " whether you are quite sure you are correct in saying you have never seen Bennett before. You will, of course, be on oath."

" Oh," gasped Ena. " Oh."

There was no doubt now but that she was thoroughly frightened. The colonel got to his feet.

" I am not going to ask you any questions," he said. " I think it advisable for you to consult Mr. Moffatt. I should suggest legal assistance, too. Of course, that is for you and Mr. Moffatt to decide. All I wish to do to-night is to be sure that you recognise the handbag as yours, and to inform you that your presence at the inquest will be necessary. You will probably be questioned about it, and also about certain letters in it that may be thought to have some bearing on the case. It is very largely on account of those letters that I think you would be wise to secure legal assistance."

Ena looked not only thoroughly frightened, but also even more bewildered.

" I . . . I . . ." she stammered. " I don't know what you mean," she burst out. " Please, can't I have my handbag now ? It's mine, isn't it ? Why can't I have it ? It's the letters. I must have them before anyone sees them."

" You will be questioned about them," the colonel repeated.

" Oh, but I can't be," said Ena, with much decision.

" It will depend on the coroner," the colonel told her. " As in my opinion the handbag and its contents provide important and relevant evidence, it will be my duty to place them in his hands."

" Oh, you mustn't," Ena cried. " I mean, not the letters, not for anything. You see," she explained, " they are just simply, most awfully horrid."

The colonel made no comment. He knew that already. He was edging towards the door. Ena made a run and got between him and it. She wasn't so much frightened now as angry—though anger is a poor word to use. No fury like Ena in a paddy, her brother had once said, and she was at the moment fully living up to that fraternal judgment. She and the colonel faced each other. A slightly awe-struck Bobby looked on and thanked all the gods that be that he wasn't in the colonel's shoes. The absolute silence in the room was broken only by the purring of the kitten, now reconciled by the warmth of the fire to the loss of even so comforting a lap as Ena's. Ena herself was dead white with rage. The colonel was nearly as pale, though with him it showed more, he having no make-up to disguise his pallor. Ena said in a penetrating whisper:

"You haven't—read them?"

The colonel said nothing.

Ena understood his silence. She said very loudly and distinctly:

"You cad!"

"Miss Moffatt," said the colonel, "no purpose is served by continuing this extremely distressing and painful scene."

"Painful yourself!" said Ena.

Then she boxed his ears. Good and hard. Bobby gave a little gasp. Never, never in his wildest dreams had he ever thought to witness such a thing. Chief constable of a county, too, and how clearly Bobby perceived what advantage sometimes appertains to the mere sergeant's humbler rank. The colonel was superb. He could not prevent himself from staggering slightly under the impetus of what may be fairly described as a good in-swinger from the right, beautifully timed, most accurately aimed. Nor was it his fault that a kind of crimson splash, so to say, appeared promptly where ear and Ena had made such resounding contact. But that was all. The incident passed without further comment, as the newspapers would have said. He made her a little bow.

" We must be going now," he said. " Ready, sergeant ? "

Ena collapsed into a chair and wept aloud.

The colonel passed through the door into the hall. His gait was stately and unmoved. Bobby followed. As he went he cast one awe-struck glance at Ena. She wailed:

" They aren't mine, and I promised no one should see them—oh, oh, oh."

" Eh ? " said Bobby. " What's that ? "

Ena sprang to her feet, the tears streaming down her face till, in comparison, Niobe would have seemed a mere spot of Sahara.

" Jane's father's a dean, and awfully, awfully strict," she lamented. " Oh, whatever shall I do ? "

Bobby dashed after the colonel, who, absorbed in his own thoughts and quite unaware that Bobby was not with him, had entered the waiting car and had just signalled to the driver to start.

" Beg pardon, sir," Bobby panted, for he had come at a run. " I think there's a mistake, sir. It's someone called Jane. Her father's a dean."

" Mr. Moffatt," said the colonel, coldly and decisively, " is not a dean."

" No, sir, that's Jane, sir—I mean, Jane's father," Bobby explained. " They aren't Miss Moffatt's at all; they are Jane's."

He explained further. They returned to the drawing-room, where Ena still wept, huddled in a chair.

" Go away," said Ena, seeing them appear again. " The dean will kill Jane, and Jane will kill me, and it's all you. Beasts ! "

" Yes, yes, quite so," said the colonel soothingly. " Do you mean those letters were not written to you ? "

" Of course they weren't," said Ena, sitting up. " I

wouldn't let any boy write to me like that. I think it's simply disgusting of you if you think I would."

"They were in your handbag," the colonel pointed out as meekly as ever yet did colonel speak since colonels were.

"Jane gave them me to read," Ena explained. "Her dad's dean of St. Ermines. Most likely he'll be a bishop some day, unless Jane can stop it. He's most frightfully strict, so, of course, Jane's a bit the other way. It's reaction or something, she says; and then she likes it—she really enjoys cocktails," said Ena, slightly bewildered at the idea, "and she said those letters were awful fun. It's some man she met at Brighton. She stays with an aunt there, and so she always goes for a long walk on the Downs in the afternoon when there's *thé dansants* at the hotels. That's where she met this boy, and she gave me his letters because they would make me laugh my head off, she said, but they don't a bit; they're just silly and rather beastly. I was just writing when you came in to tell Jane I had lost them somehow and they weren't funny a bit, only silly. You can read it if you like."

She indicated the half-written letter she had been busy with when they entered. The colonel gave it a glance where it lay open on Ena's blotting-pad. The colonel beamed. His ear was still sore, but what did he care?

"My dear child—my dear young lady—my dear Miss Moffatt," he babbled, "relieved . enormously great relief . . . very much . . comfort . ."

"It won't be a comfort to Jane, if you go and tell on her," Ena said.

"I don't think it will be in the least necessary for anything to be said now," the colonel declared. "So long as the letters have no connection with the murder, there will be no need to."

Ena was beginning to see light now.

" My sacred gollywogs ! " she exclaimed, using the strongest expression she knew. " Did you think it was me ? "

The colonel said nothing, but the red patch in the neighbourhood of his ear became merged in one universal spreading crimson that bathed his countenance from cheek to chin.

Ena said:

" Well ! "

But how she said it !

It made the colonel feel about a foot high. Bobby felt a little less than that. Ena surveyed them both.

" Well ! ! " she said again.

Once again the only sound in that silent room was the purring of the contented kitten by the fire.

" I think," said the colonel, trying to sound brisk and cheerful, " now everything is satisfactorily cleared up, we had better be going. Ready, sergeant ? "

" Yes, sir," said Bobby with alacrity, and never were two of the masculine sex more ready, and indeed anxious, to depart from the company of a pretty girl.

" Good night," said Ena coldly. " I'm not a bit sorry I slapped you."

" I am," said the colonel simply.

Ena was looking at herself in the glass.

" Me—murder," she murmured. " Murder—me." Unconsciously she put on a slight swagger. It was as if she felt she was quite as capable as anyone else of an odd assassination or two. " Oh, well," she said tolerantly, " I suppose you didn't really mean anything, and if you really want to know who killed that poor man, I can tell you. It was Mr. Larson."

CHAPTER XXI

PASSED TO MR. MOFFATT

"WHAT'S THAT?" said the colonel sharply.

Ena had turned to the mirror, endeavouring to repair the ravages recent events had caused to her complexion. She paused in the complicated and careful technique she was employing and repeated over her shoulder:

"It was Mr. Larson. Didn't you know?"

The colonel sat down heavily on the nearest chair and stared blankly at her. Bobby was reduced to the expedient of rubbing his nose and looking almost as helpless as he felt. Ena bestowed on them each a bright smile and resumed her task, giving it all the grave care and attention it required. The colonel looked at Bobby, and Bobby looked nowhere in particular. The colonel said:

"Miss Moffatt, do you realise what you are saying?"

Ena turned and stared at him.

"Of course," she said. She finished with her nose—and whether one prefers the feminine nose a violent red, or more white than nature ever meant a nose to be, must remain a matter of personal taste. She sat down, picked up the kitten, and said reflectively, "I look awful, don't I? It's the way you bullied me."

"Eh? What?" exclaimed the colonel. "We? You?"

"I suppose," said Ena complacently, "you always

treat suspects like that. It's the third degree, isn't it? I expect you thought you would get me to confess, didn't you?"

It was a view of recent events the colonel found slightly bewildering. Reflectively he put up a hand to his still tingling ear. Third degree indeed! But he felt argument and remonstrance would be alike ineffective. He said:

"Miss Moffatt, you have made a very serious accusation."

"Oh, I haven't," she interrupted indignantly. "I only told you who did it."

"I should like to know your reasons, if I may," suggested the colonel.

"It isn't reasons," Ena retorted with a certain contempt; "it's because I know. Anyone would if they had seen the way he looked at Gwendolene."

"Gwendolene?" repeated the colonel, and Bobby produced his notebook, ready to take down full particulars of this fresh personality now appearing on the scene.

"Yes. Mr. Larson had been with dad talking about investments and things, and he came out of the room, and Gwendolene was there, and the way he looked at her, it was awful!" Ena sat upright. She squeezed the kitten so hard it emitted a protesting mew. "If it hadn't been for me, he would have killed her—that's how he looked; just too murderous. It saved her life, I'm sure, me being there."

But the colonel was growing suspicious, and Bobby had already sighed gently and put away his notebook again.

"Who is Gwendolene?" asked the colonel.

Surprised, Ena held up the kitten.

"This is Gwendolene," she said. "Isn't oo, precious?" she asked the kitten. "She got under his feet—Mr.

Larson's, I mean—and it was just as much his fault as hers, because he wasn't looking, and if anyone ever looked like murder, he did. If I hadn't screamed he would have kicked her ever so hard—he had his foot up, and when I screamed he looked as if he wanted to kill me instead, and I expect he did, too, only he didn't dare. I picked Gwendolene up and we ran, didn't we, sweet 'ums? I locked my door to feel safe, and I didn't come out till after I had seen him drive away."

"Miss Moffatt," said the colonel sternly, "are you accusing Mr. Larson of murder because he was annoyed with your kitten?"

"Oh, no," she answered, "it was the horrible way he looked. Besides, you remember dad's pistol he's lost and no one knows where it is? Well, that's because Mr. Larson pinched it."

At this the colonel and Bobby exchanged glances. Here at last seemed evidence that might be of real importance.

"How do you know?" the colonel asked. "Miss Moffatt, please be very careful what you say. A man's life——"

"I suppose he'll be hanged, won't he?" observed Ena meditatively. "They always do murderers, don't they?"

"Why do you say Mr. Larson took your father's pistol?" the colonel repeated.

"I saw him," said Ena simply. "It was a month ago—the 10th. I know, because I was writing to Uncle Alexander for his birthday and I told him.

"You told him you had seen Mr. Larson taking Mr. Moffatt's pistol?"

"Well, I didn't know what it was at the time," Ena said. "I went into the library to get some stamps—only don't tell dad, because he's always so stuffy about his stamps if there aren't any when he wants them—and Mr. Larson was there, and he was taking something out of one of the drawers and he saw me and he glared. I didn't see plainly what he had, but it was something bright and hard-looking. I thought it was a flashlight, and I thought it was funny, and I told uncle when I was finishing my letter."

"Didn't you tell Mr. Moffatt?"

"No-o. Dad was fussing about his old stamps and I knew he suspected me. Besides, I saw the flashlight on the hall table afterwards, so I thought Mr. Larson had put it there and it was all right. But now I just know it was the pistol, and that's why he looked at me the way he did. At the time I thought he was only being horrid because I had caught him at dad's desk, but now I know he was afraid."

The colonel listened gloomily. If all this meant that the weapon with which the murder had undoubtedly been committed was now identified with Mr. Larson, the fact was certainly of the utmost significance. But could Ena's story be relied on? How would such a tale stand up under cross-examination?

"Why should Mr. Larson want to kill Bennett?" he asked.

"Oh, he hates share-pushers," Ena explained. "Didn't you know? Mr. Bennett was one, wasn't he? And Mr. Larson's something to do with shares and things, too. Mr. Larson was always saying share-pushers ought to be shot, and so he did, I suppose. I expect they've skinned him some time and he wanted revenge."

The colonel looked more and more worried. The pistol traced to Larson. Larson uttering threats. The possibility that Larson had suffered financial losses through Bennett!

" Would your uncle be likely to have your letter still ? " he asked.

" Oh, rather," Ena assured him. " Uncle Alexander has every letter anyone has ever written him from the year one. He has them all filed and indexed and all that —stacks of them."

" I should like to see it," the colonel remarked. " Could you give me his address ? "

Ena provided the address, and, in answer to a casual question Bobby dropped, explained that the kitten incident had only happened two days ago. It was the awful look in Mr. Larson's eyes, Ena explained, that made her understand quite suddenly. She shivered and was a little pale as she described the look he had sent after them as she and the kitten made their escape. After a few more questions the colonel and Bobby took their departure, and in the car the colonel said :

" Well, what do you make of all that ? "

" Well, sir," Bobby answered slowly, " it needs thinking over. Mr. Larson is, of course, one of the possibilities in the case. If we accept Miss Moffatt's story——"

" Yes, but can we ? " asked the colonel. " Can we put her in the witness-box to tell a story of that sort ? She admits herself she thought at the time it was a flashlight. I dare say Larson did look as if he wanted to kick the kitten across the hall—cats do make some people feel like that. But a look's not evidence. We couldn't even mention it. There's the letter she says she wrote. We'll have to see what she actually said in it. That is, if it's not been destroyed. Larson has an alibi, too, but how strong is it ? What's there to prove that cigarette-case hadn't been lying there for days ? "

"Reeves says he saw it in Mr. Larson's possession earlier that afternoon."

"Can we trust Reeves's evidence? As a witness he would be discredited the moment he was asked about his record. Very difficult case. Better sleep on it. Come and see me to-morrow. Ten o'clock. No. I've an appointment; no time to attend to anything just now. Eleven; make it eleven. We shall have to follow it up somehow, but blessed if I know how. Have to talk to Larson again, I suppose."

Neither did Bobby see his way very clearly. Little good questioning Larson, he thought. Even if Ena's story were true, Larson would simply deny it. Nor was there any proof that Ena's suggestion of previous transactions between Larson and the dead man had any foundation in fact. He was still as undecided as ever when next morning, on his way to keep the appointment the colonel had given him, he saw a tall man waving to him from across the street and recognised Larson himself. A light rain was falling at the time. Bobby was wearing a raincoat and a hat with a brim pulled down to protect his face, but Larson, he noticed, was bare-headed as usual, and had not even an umbrella. When Larson came across to him, Bobby said something about the risk of catching cold, and Larson laughed and said that he had never had a cold since he gave up wearing a hat.

"Try it, sergeant," he urged.

"Well, I did at one time," Bobby answered, "and then a fellow tried to palm his own hat off on me one day. In a way that's how I came to join the police, and in uniform, of course, you have to have a helmet, so I got out of the way of going without."

"Start it again," urged Mr. Larson. "Still busy with

the case of that poor devil who was shot here? Making any progress?"

"Oh, we think so," Bobby answered. "We may be able to make an arrest soon. I believe the chief constable was thinking of asking if you could come to see him again. There are one or two small points he thinks you might be able to clear up."

"Delighted, of course," Larson answered readily, "if there's anything I can say to help. Nasty business. Could I see him now, do you think? Save a special journey from town, perhaps."

Bobby said he thought that would be a good idea. They proceeded together, accordingly, to the police headquarters, chatting amiably on the way. Bobby asked if Larson had had a good trip from town, and Larson said he had come by train and had had a most disagreeable journey, a woman with half a dozen brats, all sucking peppermints, and with a basketful of vegetables and kippers, having invaded his compartment. He was half humorous, half really indignant, at having been forced to put up with such travelling-companions, and then they reached their destination, where, in response to the message Bobby sent up, they were ushered immediately into the colonel's room. The colonel said how good it was of Mr. Larson to come along, and how lucky it was he happened to be in the town again, and Larson explained he had come to see Mr. Gregson, a leading solicitor in the district.

"Bit of bad luck," Mr. Larson told them ruefully. "I happened to see a motor accident the other day, and now they've laid violent hands on me for a witness—awful bore. At Winders Green it was. I was passing and saw it all—motor-car and cyclist mix up. Cyclists," said Mr.

Larson feelingly, " are God's own pests on the roads, but this time I'm bound to say the motorist was to blame."

" Oh, yes," said the colonel, " there was a report came in. Something about a cat, wasn't there ? "

Larson nodded.

" The whole thing turns on the cat, apparently," he said, smiling. " The cyclist says there was one. The motorist says there wasn't. Unluckily for him I saw it as plainly as ever I saw anything in my life—big animal; a Tom, I should say; black, with white feet. At least, I saw it unless I was suffering from incipient delirium tremens, and then it would be rats, not cats, wouldn't it ? Anyhow, it seems I shall have to appear in court and solemnly swear there was a cat, a whole cat, and a lot else as well."

The colonel was listening with great interest. He glanced at Bobby and saw he was listening, too. For the accident at Winders Green had happened on the same day, and almost at the same hour, as that at which the murder had taken place in Battling Copse, and certainly a witness of the accident could not possibly have been anywhere near Battling Copse at the time of the murder. The colonel was fiddling with the report now.

" I don't think your name was mentioned, was it ? " he asked.

" In your man's report ? No, it wouldn't be," Larson answered. " I didn't much want to be mixed up in the thing if I could help it—takes time and worry and all that. To tell the truth, I don't think I've quite got over the shock of my own experience. I still dream of it, and this brought the whole thing back so vividly."

" An accident ? " the colonel asked.

" Fellow in a sports car banged right into mine," Mr.

Larson answered. " It was near Winders Green too—some very nasty turnings about there. I had been at Sevens to see Mr. Moffatt and I was driving home. Next thing I knew I was in bed in hospital, with a strange female giving the nurse blue fits."

" How was that ? "

" Police muddle," explained Larson, chuckling. " Happens sometimes, I suppose. By some extraordinary chance, there was nothing in my pockets to identify me—no cards, letters, anything. Then a policeman had a look at the car and found an envelope addressed to a business pal of mine. They must have gone over that car with a toothbrush. They found it at the bottom of one of the pockets where it must have been lying for months, and jumped to the conclusion it meant me. Then there was some further muddle over the phoning, and finally a poor lady turned up in the full belief she was a widow. When she found a stranger she had never seen before—well, she expressed herself freely."

" Mistakes will occur," said the colonel. " When did this happen, do you remember ? "

" I remember well enough," answered Larson grimly. " Made me miss an important appointment for that day—the tenth it was, last month. I believe the man I failed still thinks I fixed it all on purpose to disappoint him."

The colonel looked at Bobby. This seemed important, for if as a result of this accident—and the truth of Larson's story could easily be tested—his car had been examined so closely by the police soon after he left Sevens, then if he had had any pistol in his possession it would certainly have been found. Ena's story seemed disproved, then, just as by his earlier statement his alibi seemed to receive further confirmation.

"But you don't want to hear about my troubles," Larson went on smilingly. "I believe you wanted to see me about something?"

"Yes," the colonel answered. "We are very worried about Mr. Moffatt's pistol. It's missing, you know. We should very much like to get some idea of when it disappeared. Did you ever see it?"

"No, not that I remember, and certainly I should," answered Larson. He smiled again. "I think I've said as much before. The little Moffatt girl been saying things?"

The colonel started.

"Why do you ask?" he inquired cautiously.

"Oh, I'm definitely in her bad books," the other answered smilingly. "She called me a horrid man and a murderer the other day. That wretched kitten of hers nearly tripped me up. I felt like scragging the little beast, and I dare say I looked it. The little Moffatt lady was very indignant. I asked if she minded if I broke its neck—not quite all in fun either; I felt like it. She called me a murderer, or words to that effect, and rushed off in a temper. She's got a little temper of her own, that girl."

"Yes, I've noticed that," agreed the colonel, thoughtfully feeling his ear.

"I'm not sure," Larson continued, "that she doesn't suspect me of picking and stealing as well. Moffatt was raising Cain about his stamps having vanished from his desk, and Miss Ena saw me just before alone in the room. I had left my cigarette-case there and I went back for it, and she came in just as I was picking it up. I am sure she thought it was the stamps I was after."

The colonel glanced again at Bobby. Apparently both matters mentioned by Ena could now be regarded as satisfactorily answered, and he drew a breath of deep relief. He thanked Mr. Larson warmly for the assistance he had given, and the frankness with which he had spoken, and Larson said with a certain hesitation:

"There is another thing I've had on my mind. Did you know——" He hesitated again. He made a deprecatory gesture with his large, well-manicured hands, from which, Bobby noticed, that fine diamond ring of his had vanished—only for evening wear, it was, perhaps, Bobby thought; too valuable for every day. Larson said: "It's just this: did you know Moffatt was being blackmailed?"

"Blackmailed?" the colonel repeated, sitting up abruptly. "Are you sure? Who by?"

"By Bennett," Larson answered. "Very likely you knew, but I felt I had to mention it because—well, it's a possible motive, I suppose."

CHAPTER XXII

PASSED TO MR. PEGLEY

IT WAS A MOMENT OR TWO before the colonel spoke. He was endeavouring to readjust his ideas. He looked round quickly at Bobby, whose face was impassive, giving no hint of the tumult of confused and contradictory ideas seething in his mind. Larson told himself that Colonel Warden looked hopelessly bewildered, and his attendant sergeant too stolid to be bewildered by anything. He waited gravely; a little amused, too. He had said what he felt it necessary to say, and now he waited the outcome, if any. The colonel drew a deep breath and said:

"That is a very serious statement, Mr. Larson. It may mean——"

Larson held up his hand.

"No, no," he said quickly. "What it means or doesn't mean is your affair. Nothing to do with me. I should very much prefer not to be mixed up in the thing at all. Does a business man no good. Takes up a lot of valuable time as well. Bad enough that I may have to give evidence in this motor accident case at Winders Green. But I felt I had to ask if you knew. I gather you didn't."

"I take it you are certain of your facts?" the colonel asked.

"What I do know is that Bennett was boasting about

being able to squeeze Mr. Moffatt. And I have seen a bundle of notes to some considerable value said to have been paid over by Moffatt—naturally I was not a witness to the transaction. Also I know Bennett was threatening what he could do if Moffatt didn't 'pay up and look pleasant.' I know Moffatt seemed to be having considerable difficulty in meeting ordinary calls on his pocket. Which explains, I suppose, why he was trying so hard to pump me for Stock Exchange tips. In passing, I never give them. I don't operate on the Stock Exchange, don't believe in speculation. Moffatt told me in so many words it was a matter of life and death to him to raise money."

"But he is a rich man?"

"He was quite frank about that," Larson explained. "He has a good income—but every penny mortgaged—and no capital at all. A curious, difficult position, I admit. There's a trust fund of £100,000 in old consols. It was established many years ago, apparently by his grandfather, or great-grandfather perhaps. The trustees have absolute power. They can withhold the income or any part of it at their discretion. When the trust was established some time in the last century, stringent precautions were thought necessary. Apparently the then heir was an irresponsible sort of person—poet and that sort of thing. The consequence is, no loan can be raised on the security of the trust fund. Moffatt might be told any moment that only his board and lodging would be paid, and the rest of the income allowed to accumulate for his heir. And what he gets from his estate is fully mortgaged, too. He was finding it more and more difficult to satisfy Bennett's demands—or so Bennett said—and Bennett was using a good many threats."

"You are sure of all this?" the colonel asked.

" An old schoolfellow of mine turns up to see me every now and then with a hard-luck tale. Not a very satisfactory person, I'm afraid, but well—old school memories, you know. I generally give him a fiver to get rid of him. A month ago I was rather surprised to see him doing himself well in a West End restaurant. He saw me, and came across and insisted on repaying the last fiver I had lent him. He showed a thick wad of notes. I wondered what had happened, and he told me he was in partnership with a man who could get all the cash he wanted from a rich friend. I didn't say anything more. I thought it sounded fishy, but no business of mine. Two days ago he turned up to get the fiver back. I was curious, and after a bit of pressing it all came out. His friend had been drawing large sums from a Mr. Moffatt, and now his friend was dead and there wouldn't be any more money coming in. I asked if his friend's name was Bennett. He said yes, and went on directly to accuse Moffatt. So far as I know he had no actual grounds to go on. But I felt you ought to know."

" Undoubtedly," said the colonel. He drew a writing pad nearer. " This man's name and address ? " he asked.

" Carter. Robert Carter. But I'm not sure he uses it now. He's passed under others, I fancy, though I don't know. Dodging creditors, I expect. I don't know his address—and I've often wished he didn't know mine."

" It may be difficult to find him ? "

" You might try the Rowton Houses or a Salvation Army shelter, places like that," Mr. Larson suggested. " I'm afraid if he hears the police are asking for him he will probably vanish. I have my suspicions about some of his recent proceedings. Probably he'll turn up to see me again when he thinks another fiver is due, but that won't be just yet. I'll let you know when he does, of course."

"What you are telling us is entirely what Carter told you?" the colonel asked. "Can it be trusted, do you think?"

Mr. Larson shrugged his shoulders.

"That's for you to say," he answered. "I wouldn't trust Carter too far myself, but his story seemed to fit. And I don't quite see what object he could have in inventing a set of elaborate lies to tell me."

"No," agreed the colonel. "But a man in Mr. Moffatt's position—have you any idea what Bennett knew, or thought he knew, about him?"

"Not the faintest. I was very surprised myself. Possibly he had been trapped in some way. I've known it happen. I expect you've had cases. You know the sort of thing—woman, compromising position, indignant husband round the corner, and a scandal the victim daren't face. But I don't know. All I can tell you is that it was something that happened on one of the American liners."

The colonel could not prevent himself from whistling softly. He turned and looked at Bobby, who, too, looked a little startled.

"Mr. Moffatt was asking your advice about investments?" the colonel asked after a pause.

Mr. Larson shrugged again those broad shoulders of his whereto his unusually small head for his height made so odd a contrast.

"One of the penalties of the, I suppose, rather unusual position I occupy in City affairs," he explained. "It happens that often I am in possession of highly confidential information—if, for example, I am trying to arrange a merger of some kind. Obviously, if only for my own sake, I keep that information to myself or else the merger would soon be off—and my usefulness at an end, incidentally. But many people can't understand that. They seem to think I can use my knowledge in speculation, when, if I did, it would be cutting my own throat. I'm a company promotor and agent, not a speculator in stocks and shares."

"You didn't give Mr. Moffatt any advice, then?"

"Well, I gave him the only possible advice in present circumstances. With the new Government rearmament programme, a child can see base metals must rise. Common sense, not speculation. Buy fifty or a hundred tons of tin to-day, hold a while, bound to sell at a profit. I don't mind passing that tip on," he added, smiling, "and I don't mind adding that my own profit in base metals is—well, not five figures yet."

The colonel looked dazed, admiring, envious. He nearly rushed to the phone to order someone—he didn't quite know who—to buy a hundred tons of tin. Then it occurred to him that possibly that would require more money than his available cash balance at the bank amounted to. But didn't one buy things on the Stock Exchange without having to pay for them? Only perhaps that didn't apply to base metals. Bobby, knowing well that his balance at the post office came to less than, not five, but three, figures, was spared this temptation. Dismissing his momentary dreams, and with a new note of respect in his voice, the colonel went on:

"I think I remember it being mentioned that you crossed to New York once in the same boat with Mr. Moffatt?"

"That is so. I didn't see much of him, but that is when our acquaintance began."

"Do you remember a game of poker on that voyage?"

" I don't think so. Why? Anything special about it? I have played with Moffatt once or twice, but I'm not much of a card-player. Moffatt plays a remarkable hand—holds good cards, too, as a rule; but, then, he knows how to play them."

The colonel pressed him further, but apparently any poker played on that voyage had passed entirely from Mr. Larson's memory. He offered, however, to look at his diary. He explained he had kept a diary for many years. It was a practice he had often found useful. Probably if he had played poker on that voyage there would be a note: " Poker," and a further note—so much won or lost.

" Probably lost," said Mr. Larson ruefully. " It generally is."

With that the interview ended. The colonel conducted Mr. Larson to the door with all the respect due to a man who acknowledged that his dealings in base metals had not yet brought him a profit amounting to five figures. Bobby contented himself with looking out of the window. The colonel came back, sat down, and began to think. He leaned his head on his hands and sighed, for by now it was not only his ear that was aching. He said moodily:

" Every time we get anything, it turns out to be something else."

" Yes, sir," agreed Bobby, almost as dejectedly, " every time the rabbit comes out of the hat, it turns into a pigeon and flies out of the window."

" Funny thing about Moffatt's money being tied up like that," the colonel went on. " Explains why he's always grumbling about the rate of interest you get from old consols and yet never tries to change."

" I'm beginning to think," Bobby said slowly, and

more to himself than to the colonel, " that the trust fund may prove to be the explanation of the whole affair."

" Well, anyhow," declared the colonel, " Larson seems to be cleared. Miss Moffatt is clearly wrong in thinking he had taken her father's pistol. If his car was searched in the way he says it was—and we can easily test that—his possession of a pistol couldn't possibly have been overlooked, and he had hardly had time to get rid of it. And he can't very well have been committing a murder in Battling Copse and witnessing a motor accident at Winders Green at the same moment."

" No, sir; that much is plain," agreed Bobby.

" One fact we are certain of," the colonel went on, " is that Moffatt's pistol was used—and he's the one person in whose possession it would be in the ordinary way."

" In a case like this," said Bobby, " it's a comfort to have even one fact to be sure of."

" He was in the library alone all afternoon by his own account," the colonel continued. " Perfectly easy to slip out and back unseen. And this blackmail story. We know there was something, though apparently Larson didn't. Fatal for a man in his position if it got about he had been blacklisted by the steamship companies as a card-sharper."

" I suppose so," Bobby agreed.

" Might do a good deal to prevent that coming out," declared the colonel. " I don't like it one bit, not one little bit. It's got to be followed up. Better get some lunch, and then we'll drive over and see what he has to say."

Later, then, that afternoon, once more the chief constable's car drew up at Sevens. This time Mr. Moffatt was in, and Reeves accordingly ushered them into the library, where Mr. Moffatt was busy writing letters and looking,

Bobby noticed, very much less calm and composed than usual.

"How do, colonel?" he said. "Come about that murder again? Ena was telling me you were here yesterday. Seemed to think you had been suspecting her. I told her not to be a little fool. Can you bring an action for criminal libel against a company?"

The colonel looked a little scared by this abrupt demand. True, he wasn't a company, but he was a colonel, and a chief constable as well, and had he laid himself open to an action for criminal libel?

"Because," said Mr. Moffatt fiercely, as he got up and planted himself before the fire, like Horatius before the bridge, "I'm going to bring one against the Atlantic steamship companies. I am writing to Meadows to start at once—my lawyer, you know; Meadows & Scott, Old Jewry." He stood there swelling with an indignation that very nearly choked him. He spluttered a little before he could get out what he wanted to say. Not difficult, Bobby thought, to see where Ena derived her temper from. "If it costs me the last penny I have in the world," he said when at last he could control his voice, "I'll teach 'em to blacklist me."

"Blacklist—you?" repeated the colonel.

"Just found out," said Mr. Moffatt. He swallowed hard. He gave the impression that at any moment he would start smashing furniture and throwing things out of the window. "I was thinking of going across to America last year. They wrote me all cabins were booked up. I thought their letter rather curt, but just then I went down with influenza, and, of course, that put any trip to America out of the question. Then I heard the boat I had inquired about had been half empty that trip. I thought it a bit queer, but I thought there had just been some muddle or stupidity of some sort. But when I wrote the other day asking about sailings and so on, I got a letter back regretting that the information asked for couldn't be supplied. Well, I thought that was going a bit too far. I sent the letter on to Meadows and asked him to take it up. Well, Meadows had some difficulty in getting anything out of them, but he rang me up last week—the day of the murder, as it happens; the same afternoon, four o'clock it was, too; almost the same time—and told me there was some misunderstanding. I had apparently been confused with someone thought to be undesirable, and did I want him to go on with it? I didn't take it very seriously, though I did think Meadows sounded a bit worried. We were talking nearly ten minutes on the phone before finally I made him understand he was to take every possible step to find out what was at the bottom of it all, and to insist, too, on a written apology. I won't accept any apology now. I'll have damages."

The colonel's head was beginning to ache worse than ever. Mr. Larson's story had seemed to shed a gleam of light on the affair, and here was darkness and confusion back, worse than ever. Whatever the truth might be, Mr. Moffatt's attitude was certainly not that of one who had submitted to blackmail, or committed murder, to keep secret a story he was now showing every anxiety to proclaim to all the world so that his grievance, and the wrong done him, might be as widely known as possible. Besides, if he had really been talking to his solicitor for nearly ten minutes on the afternoon, and at the hour, of the murder —and the truth of that could easily be checked—he had certainly an absolutely complete alibi.

" I inquired if you had been indoors all that afternoon,"

the colonel remarked resentfully, for he felt this complete alibi ought to have been offered him before.

" Well, so I had, hadn't I ? " snapped Mr. Moffatt. " What did you expect me to say ? " Then he returned to his grievance. " Blacklisting me—me—a Moffatt of Sevens. I'll—I'll—I'll——" He swallowed again and tried to control himself. " Sorry," he said. " Bit upsetting, you know—the insolence of the thing. I'll deal with 'em. Was it about your talk with Ena last night you wanted to see me ? "

" No, no," answered the colonel hurriedly, for, indeed, that was the very last subject on earth he ever wanted to hear mentioned again. " You told us you didn't know Bennett ? That he was quite a stranger to you ? "

" Yes. Well ? "

" Do you think it possible he had got wind of this business with the steamship companies ? "

Mr. Moffatt stared.

" Good Lord, no, I shouldn't think so. How could he ? Not that I know of, anyhow. I wish he had. The more people I can prove did know of it, the bigger damages I can claim. I'll claim enough to build the new cottage hospital they're always talking about."

" There is one other point," the colonel continued. " I understand you consulted Mr. Larson about your investments ? "

" Well, hardly that. I had a chat with him about doing something with a few hundreds I have in consols. Why ? "

" A few hundreds ? I understood I thought I had heard you say—mention a much larger sum ? "

" There's a trust fund," Mr. Moffatt answered. " Can't touch that; tied up. Life interest, that's all. Too bad, all that money at two and a half, but there it is. No getting round the trust deed. I asked Meadows long ago. I don't save much, I know—impossible these days, with all the claims there are on one. Hard enough to meet them all. Income-tax, too. But I have scraped up a little—between two and three thousand. In consols, too. I asked Larson what he advised. He didn't seem to have much idea—didn't want to give anything away, I suppose. Close lot, these City men. Advised buying tin. Good Lord," said Mr. Moffatt, exploding again. "I'm not a metal merchant. Sound advice, I dare say, but no good to me. Anyhow, he didn't recommend Highland Developments, like Pegley."

"Mr. Pegley recommended that?"

"Yes. Larson gave me a hint to be careful. Larson said: 'Never mind what I think. Ask your solicitors.' So I did, and Meadows said he couldn't even trace the thing. Bogus concern, he thought. Meadows said Pegley was after my cash. Don't trust the man myself. Larson called him a share-pusher. Look here, it's none of my business, but have you thought of Pegley in connection with this other affair?"

"The Bennett murder? Mr. Pegley? No. Why?"

"Well, if you inquire at the Oakley Road House, you'll find Bennett and Pegley lunched there together that day and had a row, and Bennett called for help and accused Pegley of having tried to murder him."

CHAPTER XXIII

PASSED TO NOLL

IT WAS TOO MUCH ALTOGETHER for the chief constable. With a sort of muffled moan he got to his feet and stood facing Mr. Moffatt. For a moment or two they remained thus, Mr. Moffatt frankly bewildered, the colonel unable to speak. He turned and looked helplessly at Bobby.

" Yes, sir," said Bobby, and all the sympathy he felt was expressed in those two simple words.

The colonel took out his handkerchief and began to mop his forehead. He was grateful for Bobby's sympathy, though it was not sympathy but light and leading for which he yearned. Mr. Moffatt began to bristle—he was in a mood to bristle.

" If you don't believe me," he snapped, " go and ask for yourselves."

The colonel put his handkerchief away. He said sadly to Bobby:

" The moment we seem to be getting anywhere, it always turns out to be somewhere else."

" Yes, sir," agreed Bobby again. " It is pretty awful, sir."

He had the impression that the colonel was about to burst into tears. Instead, he walked out of the room. Mr.

Moffatt stared after him. "Cracked," he said. "The fellow's cracked. Plumb crazy."

"The case is crazy all right," said Bobby grimly.

He hurried after the colonel and said something to him. They came back into the room together. Mr. Moffatt continued to stare. The colonel said:

"Sorry. I think I felt I wanted air—air."

"Oh," said Mr. Moffatt.

"You see, Mr. Moffatt," interposed Bobby, "you have been so extraordinarily helpful."

"Oh," said Mr. Moffatt again, but this time an "Oh" in a different key.

"There's another point," the colonel said, "that Sergeant Owen has reminded me of. It has possibly some connection with this muddle about the blacklisting. Our information is that you have been in the habit of visiting America nearly every year, but apparently did not wish your visits known."

Mr. Moffatt glared and scowled and hesitated. It was plainly to be touch and go whether he exploded or explained. Finally explanation won over explosion.

"Private affairs," he said. "I don't mind telling you, provided you keep it to yourself. I don't want—well, no good raking up old tales. There's Ena, too; shock for her. The fact is, I go to see a daughter of mine."

"Daughter?" repeated the colonel, surprised.

"Illegitimate," explained Mr. Moffatt, coughing in an embarrassed sort of way, for at heart he was an old-fashioned kind of person. "When I was a boy. All boys are fools. Got mixed up with a girl—barmaid, as a matter of fact. Unpleasant story. Ashamed of it still. Needn't go into details. My father hushed it up. Girl and baby packed off to the States. Mother dead now, but I've slipped over sometimes to see the child—woman now, of course, married and all that. It's why I've been trying to scrape a bit of money together. I thought Larson might help; told him how badly I wanted a bit of spare cash. All he could talk about was tin—thought I wanted to set up as an ironmonger, I suppose. I'm trusting you to keep all this to yourselves. Wouldn't care for Ena to know. She's no idea things like that happen; wouldn't understand; young girls don't, you know."

Neither the colonel nor Bobby was quite sure of that. But they both murmured promises that the information would be regarded as entirely confidential. The colonel expressed his gratitude for Mr. Moffatt's frankness.

"Clears the atmosphere, and that's always a help," he said. "You are inclined to think Pegley may be Bennett's murderer?"

"Looks like it to me," declared Mr. Moffatt, grateful for this change of subject. "Couple of share-pushers. Knew I had scraped together a bit of money and thought they would like to get hold of it. I've only a life interest in the trust fund and the land, but any savings I can do what I like with. I wanted to be able to settle something on Hetty—my girl in America. That's what Pegley and Bennett were after, if you ask me. But Bennett didn't trust Pegley. That's why he was watching through field-glasses that afternoon—to see what Pegley was up to. Later on they met in Battling Copse. Appointment, probably. Pegley expected trouble, and borrowed my automatic to take along. He had plenty of opportunities of knowing where it was kept. They had a row. Pegley whipped out the pistol and Bennett got shot. Pegley tried to conceal Bennett's identity, hoped it would pass for an accident. That's my idea."

"Upon my soul," exclaimed the colonel, impressed. "I shouldn't wonder if you haven't hit on the truth."

Mr. Moffatt chuckled, well pleased.

"When you resign, I'll apply for the job," he said, his good-humour quite restored. "Glad you called—given me something else to think of. That blacklisting impudence got me annoyed. Upon my soul, when you got here, I believe I was on the point of throwing things out of the window. Well, young man," he continued, turning to Bobby, silent and watchful, "you're Scotland Yard, aren't you? What does Scotland Yard think?"

"I think it's very important indeed."

"My idea about Pegley?"

"Oh, no, sir, not that. I meant very important that you were on the point of throwing things out of the window."

"Eh?"

"But not so important as that it was raining this morning."

"What do you mean?" demanded Mr. Moffatt, beginning to bristle again. "What's raining this morning got to do with it?"

"I am not clear yet," Bobby said, though as much to himself as to his companions, "but it may turn out conclusive."

"Rubbish," announced Mr. Moffatt with simple brevity.

"But, anyhow, one thing is clear," Bobby added. "Neither Bennett nor Pegley knew anything about your private savings. Very likely neither of them would have minded lifting it, but we can be quite certain that neither together nor separately had they ever given it a thought—or even knew you had any savings."

"Oh, they hadn't, hadn't they?" exploded Mr. Moffatt. "Then what was their game, eh?"

Bobby made no answer. Colonel Warden came to himself with a start. He had been absorbed in his own thoughts, and had only heard vaguely what the other two had been saying. He said now:

"We had better be going—plenty to do. Bewildering business, all this. Switched off on a new line at every point."

Therewith he and Bobby departed, and in the car the colonel said presently, after a long period of silent thought:

"What was that you were saying to Moffatt? Something about rain this morning?"

"Just an idea of mine," Bobby answered. "It fits in with a vague sort of notion that I can't quite get into shape. I can't even get down to think it out," he added complainingly, "when we get new ideas and facts sprung on us every hour or two. I only said what I did to Mr. Moffatt to puzzle him a bit and prevent him from talking too much—no good his letting himself in for a libel action. Besides," added Bobby, fearing to seem too altruistic, "if he were, we might get roped in as witnesses. They hate that at the Yard when it's not their own case."

But the colonel was not listening.

"Looks to me," he said, "as if Moffatt has hit on the truth. No actual proof, but plausible. Pretty nearly good enough for an arrest. If there's real evidence of a quarrel at this road house, that'll be something. Prove Pegley lied when he said he didn't know Bennett. Why? Threats, and a pistol produced, apparently. That pistol's the crucial point of the whole thing—if only we could find the pistol and identify it with someone."

" Yes, sir," agreed Bobby, " only if Pegley had a pistol at the road house at lunch-time, he wouldn't have needed to take Mr. Moffatt's when he went to meet Bennett—if he did."

" No, that's so," agreed the colonel, " but he might have taken it some time before. What's worrying me is why did Larson tell us all the things he did ? "

" I think," Bobby said, " he must have heard something about the blacklisting—of course, that sort of thing does get about."

" So it does," agreed the colonel. " It's possible this Carter person he talks about was just putting him off. Carter didn't want to explain where he had actually got that wad of notes from Larson saw in his possession. When Larson began asking questions about Bennett, Carter just followed. Saved him the trouble of inventing lies for himself. Quite likely Carter had never heard of Bennett before Larson asked about him. Of course, he would know something from what he had read in the papers. Anyhow, both Larson and Moffatt seem cleared now."

After that he was silent, and Bobby was not sorry for the opportunity to try to readjust and rearrange his own thoughts that were buzzing and humming in his mind like a colony of bees at swarming time. He hoped, but not too confidently, that presently, like the swarming bees, they would arrange themselves into that coherent and ordered whole which at present he felt himself quite unable either to grasp or to express.

" If it hadn't been raining this morning," he reflected, " I might never have given it another thought—after all, very likely it means nothing."

The drive to the road house did not take long. When

they arrived the tea-hour was over and dinner not yet, so that the place was almost deserted. The manager received them in his private office. He was a round, smiling, nervous little man, named George, and very anxious to do all in his power to please and propitiate anyone so important as the chief constable of the county. He remembered that some sort of quarrel or dispute had occurred on the day named between two customers—an event, he hastened to assure them, extremely rare in an establishment so well conducted as his. He did not know much about it himself, and he had not seen either of the disputants. The affair was over, and the two parties to it had driven away, before he could reach the scene—a prudent man, this Mr. George, Bobby thought to himself, and one with no itch to meet trouble half-way. It had all been quite a trifling business, Mr. George insisted; he had not paid it much attention; there had been no reason to report it; certainly neither he nor any of his staff had thought—why should they?—of connecting it with the Battling Copse murder of which naturally they had all read in the papers. Bobby received a clear impression that Mr. George had been by no means anxious that there should be any such connection. Road houses have their reputations, and like to keep them unsmirched by any hint of murder, theft, or other such unlawful happenings. Pressed, Mr. George admitted having heard that something had been said about a pistol one of the disputants had produced, and that threats had been used. Yes, he remembered being told that the word "murder" had been uttered, but he had only taken that to mean that the pair of them had been doing themselves too well at lunch. Certainly there could be no objection to the chief constable asking any question he wished to put to any of the staff. But Mr. George doubted very much if any description of the two disputants could be obtained. Lunch-time was busy; that day had been specially busy, and they a bit short-handed. Moreover, two of their waiters had left—probably, Mr. George thought pessimistically, the very two who might perhaps have been able to give some further information. Just possibly the garage attendant might be able to tell them something.

The garage attendant was accordingly summoned but had little to say. He did not seem a very intelligent or observant person, and was plainly on the defensive and afraid of saying too much for fear of getting into some difficulty or trouble or another. Apparently he half expected to be arrested on the spot. He admitted reluctantly that there had been a quarrel; he believed a pistol had been produced; certainly threats had been uttered. But that was all. After lunch, gentlemen were sometimes inclined to be excitable and to lose their tempers over nothing. He had hardly seen anything of it himself. Someone had told him there was trouble and so he had gone along to see what it was all about, and there were the two gentlemen rowing at each other. Someone had shouted a warning about a pistol, and one of the gentlemen had laughed and said something about the other wanting to murder him, only probably he would wait for a better opportunity, with fewer people about. Then they had both driven off, and he, the garage attendant, had returned to his work, having plenty to do and no help—this last with a reproachful glance at Mr. George.

Bobby pressed him about the registration numbers of the cars. The garage attendant scratched his head and finally recollected that one number—that of the car belonging to the disputant who had expressed a fear that murder was to be his fate—had ended in three sevens. Bobby and the colonel exchanged quick glances, for the number of the car found at the bottom of the Battling Copse chalk-pit had also ended in three sevens. That seemed to prove one of the two disputants had been the unlucky Bennett, and his fear of murder but too well founded. The garage attendant had no recollection of the number of the other car, but, stimulated by the interest now shown in his statements, remembered that when they were all talking about the affair afterwards, a waiter had remarked that one of the gentlemen concerned had left his card on the table.

The garage attendant had in fact seen the card in this man's hand. But he hadn't looked at it. Didn't matter to him. Waiters liked to know names, if possible, so they could address their customers by name. If they could do so, customers were often pleased, and that might mean a bigger tip. But names were nothing to him in the garage.

The colonel, his hopes now roused to the highest, asked for the waiter to be sent for. But his hopes were promptly dashed, for it seemed that the pessimism of the manager was justified and this man one of the two who had left. But Mr. George thought it just possible the card might have been put away in the man's locker—possible, but unlikely; and might still be there—also possible, but still more unlikely. However, search should be made, and—unexpectedly—it was successful. There was the card, very dirty and thumb-marked, and, what was more, there was noted on it the wine that had been supplied: a Liebfraumilch hock.

"Wanted to show he remembered if he ever served the same customer again," Mr. George remarked. "Sound idea enough."

But the colonel was hardly listening, for it was Mr. Pegley's name and address he was looking at.

" Have to see what Mr. Pegley can tell us," he remarked, but, much to Bobby's satisfaction, thought also that as all this had taken up time, and it was getting near the dinner-hour, they might dine first.

" Begins to look," said the colonel, enjoying an excellent dinner—for there is little a road house will not do to win a chief constable's favour—" begins to look to me as if we were on the right track at last—thanks to Mr. Moffatt."

After dinner, they drove on to London, and found Mr. Pegley's address was on the top floor of a new and very smart block of service flats. By good fortune, Mr. Pegley was at home, and he received them amiably enough, though with a certain visible nervousness, in his luxury flatlet, as the management described it—meaning thereby, apparently, that a room not much larger than a cupboard was provided with telephone, built-in cocktail cabinet, refrigerator, radio, in fact with every modern device that could be thought of, though not with those old-fashioned commodities known as light, air, and space.

Mr. Pegley agreed readily that he had lunched that day at the road house in question, reminded them they had already been informed of that fact, but denied firmly and emphatically that he had ever been concerned there at any time whatever in any sort or kind of dispute or unpleasantness. Incidentally, he had had beer with his lunch, not hock. As a matter of fact, he must, he said, have left about half past one, since he had that day an appointment at two-fifteen, so certainly had been nowhere near the road house at two o'clock or any time thereafter.

" Besides," he added, " I've told you before I never set eyes on the poor devil you're inquiring about. I know I can't prove an alibi for four that afternoon, if that's when he was done in. I haven't the least idea where I was exactly at four and I don't see why you should expect me to know. Could you say where you were at four any day last week ? You can't reasonably suppose I murdered a man who was a total stranger to me. Anyhow, I can prove I kept my appointment." It was, he explained, as he had told them before, a call made on a lady living in the neighbourhood for a chat about investments. " Nothing decided," he went on, " but she can tell you all about it." He gave details that could evidently easily be checked. " And I hope," said Pegley, " that will satisfy you I had nothing to do with any row at the road house. What makes you think I had ? "

The colonel produced the visiting-card he had brought away from the road house.

" Our information," he said, " is that this was left on his table in the restaurant by one of those concerned in the quarrel."

" It's mine all right," Pegley agreed, examining the card with interest. " All over finger-prints, too, if that's any good to you. Trace anyone by finger-prints, can't you ? I suppose that's why you've got it wrapped up so carefully "—Bobby had placed it in one of his cellophane envelopes before they left the road house. " Very interesting. Got this address on it, you notice, and I've only been here three weeks. Temporarily, you know. I am looking out for a little place in the country—not too big, not too small. Takes some finding. Now, who have I given a card to recently ? " He paused, trying to remember, and then suddenly burst out : " Why, yes, of course, young what's-his-name was there—at the road house, I mean. Lunching. He didn't know me, but I did him. I had seen him with the old man. I remember now. I spoke to him as I was leaving; told him who I was; said we should meet at dinner. I remember quite well I put my card down on the table by his side. He must have forgotten and left it there."

"Who is young what's-his-name?" the colonel asked, though he felt he knew already.

"Young Noll Moffatt," answered Pegley. He looked very astonished, even disturbed. He whistled softly. "It must have been young Moffatt had the row with Bennett you've been talking about." He whistled again. "Now, what does that mean?" he muttered.

CHAPTER XXIV

CAT AND DOG STORY

IT WAS ALTOGETHER TOO MUCH for Colonel Warden. He flung out his hands in a gesture of despair, and he was not a man of many gestures. He said loudly:

" Young Moffatt now. Much more of this and I shall go off my head."

" Well, it looks like that young man, doesn't it ? " Pegley said cheerfully.

" Talk about a will-o'-the-wisp, talk about a wild-goose chase," muttered the colonel, who was beginning to look a little wild.

But Pegley had an air of enormous relief. His previous apparent uneasiness had dropped away. His eyes were bright, his look alert and smiling; he had the manner of a man who sees suddenly vanish a danger he had deeply feared. Bobby watched him with puzzled interest, asking himself why a suggestion that the Moffatt boy might be guilty should bring him such relief. Pegley turned to the built-in cocktail cabinet and produced bottles and glasses.

" We'll celebrate," he declared. " Ought to have known it all the time. Jealousy. Just jealousy. Nothing else after all." He began to be busy preparing cocktails. " What shall it be ? " he asked, beaming on them. " White Lady ? Gin Fizz ? Or one of my own private particular poisons ? "

" Why are you so—relieved, Mr. Pegley ? " Bobby asked.

Pegley turned sharply, shaker in hand, and stared at him.

" What's that ? " he demanded.

" Why are you so relieved, Mr. Pegley ? " Bobby asked again.

Something of his previous nervousness came back to Pegley's manner. His eyes lost their smile and grew watchful and suspicious. He looked at Bobby distrustfully. He said:

" Well, now then, pretty plain who did it, isn't it ? Well, then—well, it lets the rest of us out, doesn't it ? Jealousy. That's all. Over that Molly Oulton girl. Noll Moffatt smitten with her. So was Bennett. Been some sort of kick-up with Bennett before—at the Cut and Come Again, I think."

" Oliver Moffatt had nothing to do with that," Bobby remarked.

" Hadn't he ? " said Pegley. " Another victim, was it ? Explosive young lady. Girls are like that sometimes, and, when they are, best to have nothing to do with 'em. Don't care for that sort myself anyhow—like 'em best when you know where you can get off with 'em."

" Why is it a relief to you to know that Oliver Moffatt has come under suspicion ? " Bobby asked once again.

" More than suspicion, isn't it ? " Pegley retorted. " I told you, didn't I ? If it's young Moffatt, it isn't—well, anyone else. When you blew in to-night I half thought you might be trying to push me in, and now—well, there it is. Not that I've anything against the boy. How could I ? Hardly know him. I don't deny I had the old man in my eye as a possible client. Hurt me to think of

£100,000 tied up in old consols. I could double, treble the return; more. Nothing doing, though. Trust fund. Did you know? The old boy can't touch a penny. Don't know why the devil he couldn't have said so at first. Dead loss; waste of time; rotten luck all round. Trust funds ought to be illegal. Oh, well, I've seen worse. Tough on the old man. Not that I care, but there it is—a row, a threat to murder at lunch, and a corpse by dusk. Pretty plain, if you ask me."

He returned to his cocktails. The colonel roused himself from his gloomy and bewildered thoughts.

"I am much obliged to you for the help you have given us, Mr. Pegley," he said. "I need not remind you, I'm sure, that all this must be regarded as strictly confidential. Naturally what you have said to us is privileged. Anything said to others would not be so—and might help to defeat the ends of justice."

"Right-oh," said Mr. Pegley. "I don't want to get in your bad books and I don't want to run any risk of libel actions either. Nothing to do with me, anyhow, except——" He paused and looked again at Bobby, once more with a certain manner of unease, as if he began to think that possibly he had said too much. "Well, how about it?" he asked, indicating his cocktails. "Just a spot to celebrate?"

"I am not aware of any cause for celebration," said the colonel stiffly. "Good night, Mr. Pegley. I regret it was necessary to disturb you, and I thank you again for the information you have given us. Sergeant."

He stalked out of the room. Mr. Pegley winked at Bobby.

"Goes for you, too?" he asked. "That'll make three for little me. I never could abide waste."

"Good night, Mr. Pegley," said Bobby in his most amiable voice. "You've given me quite a lot to think about."

Pegley looked at him quickly, as though somehow he did not much like the turn of this last phrase. Bobby was already at the door, hurrying after the colonel. He had it nearly closed, then opened it again.

"Mrs. O'Brien been to see you to-day?" he asked.

Pegley's mouth opened.

"How did you know?" he asked.

Bobby made no reply. He closed the door and hurried to join the colonel, who was standing by the automatic lift shaft, angrily pressing the button.

"Celebrate, indeed," he said indignantly. "What was that about Mrs. O'Brien?"

"I asked if she had been to see him to-day. Just a guess."

"Well, why shouldn't she?" grumbled the colonel. "What about it? Young Moffatt!" He turned. He said slowly: "Young Moffatt—and his own father sent us here."

The lift appeared. They entered it. The colonel growled again:

"Celebrate, indeed. I felt like rubbing his nose in his own gin." He added, for he was a fair-minded man: "Natural enough in a way, I suppose. He feels there isn't any risk of his being suspected now. Relief, no doubt."

"I doubt myself," Bobby said slowly, "if he was ever uneasy about his own position. There's nothing much to suggest he had anything to do with what happened. If he had been guilty, he would have had a nice little alibi all ready. And I don't think he is the murderer type, either."

" You can never be sure of that," the colonel said.

The lift stopped at the ground floor. They made their way to their car and found a stern policeman, watch in hand, standing by it. However, when he understood who they were, he decided thoughtfully that the obstruction caused had not been serious and he might exercise his discretion.

" Respecters of persons, I'm afraid, the police," said Bobby disapprovingly, but not till the constable had saluted and gone on his way. He repeated: " Pegley was uneasy, I agree, but not about himself. If he is innocent—well, an innocent man is so sure of his innocence, he generally thinks it must be plain to everyone else as well. If he is guilty, he must know there's no real evidence against him. I take it that means he was worried about someone he thought might be guilty, and now he's tremendously relieved to find he was wrong."

" Why should he be ? " the colonel demanded. " He's nothing to do with any of the rest of them, has he ? You don't mean you think there's some connection with Mrs. O'Brien, and he suspected her ? "

" Oh, no, I don't see how it could be Mrs. O'Brien. Or, if it was, why that should worry him. They seem to have been complete strangers."

" Well, then, who ? "

" I'm trying to worry that out," Bobby said with a very worried air.

" Mr. Moffatt himself ? " asked the colonel. " Moffatt's the only one of the lot Pegley seems to have been in touch with—purely as a client, though. Not much in that, either, especially as Moffatt's money is all tied up and Pegley can't get the job of reinvesting it. There's Larson, but apparently Larson tried to put a spoke in Pegley's wheel, so he might be rather pleased than not to see him brought in. Thoms ? But why should Pegley care about Thoms ? Or the Henrietta Towers girl ? He talked about her sister, too, but he can hardly have been thinking of them. I expect," decided the colonel, "all it means is, when he realised one of the party was suspected, it suddenly struck him he might have been in the same boat and he felt jolly glad he wasn't."

"It might be that," agreed Bobby.

"If we've got to the end at last," the colonel said abruptly, "and it really is young Moffatt, I'll resign. I couldn't stand it. Not a boy like that—known him since he was a kid; his father and sister, too. I'll have to see it through. Got to. Can't shirk the job. Then I'll go."

Bobby felt it would be disrespectful, and might be misunderstood as well, to clap his companion on the back and say "Good man," as he felt inclined to do. Decent sort of chap, the chief constable, though. Wonderful how many of the decent sort you did run across, even in his kind of job. It took him into the valleys often enough, but sometimes to the heights as well. After all, the surgeon, whose job it is to cut off the gangrenous limb, must often have cause to admire the healthiness of the rest of the body. Not his place to sympathise or approve, however, though he did say:

"Oh, well, sir, I hope it won't come to that. Nothing like a clear case yet."

The colonel only grunted. He was an excellent driver, but now he was so worried he as nearly as possible ran down a pedestrian on a Belisha crossing he had not noticed. The pedestrian, an elderly and peppery gentleman who knew his rights and meant to stand on them, no matter what the risk to life or limb, expressed himself fluently and loudly. The colonel offered an undesired and unvalued apology and drove on. He was now not only worried but also extremely annoyed with himself, and Bobby felt the time was appropriate for complete silence. A lightning conductor's existence is no doubt useful, but must be uncomfortable as well. But presently, when they had driven a good way further and were nearly home again, he ventured to say:

" I wonder, sir, if you would mind putting me down at Winders Green ? "

" What for ? " growled the colonel.

" I just thought," Bobby explained meekly, " I would like to get some more details of the car accident Mr. Larson saw there."

" All in the report," the colonel said testily.

" There wasn't anything about the cat, sir," Bobby reminded him. " I feel interested somehow in the cat."

The colonel looked at him coldly. But Bobby made no effort to explain. He knew better than to attempt to put before his superiors an only half-baked theory. He preferred his cooking to be thorough and complete before he sent his dishes to table, or he might be met, not only with incredulity, but even with a direct order forbidding further investigation on such unconvincing lines. And Bobby hated to disobey direct orders, unless it was really necessary, and even then only with his heart sometimes in his boots and sometimes in his mouth, but never in its right place. Nor did he ask how the chief constable meant to follow up the information received about young Oliver Moffatt. That, of course, was Colonel Warden's own responsibility, since in his hands lay the direction of the inquiry. Bobby knew what line he would take himself, but knew also he must wait till his advice was asked. The colonel stopped the car.

"Winders Green," he said briefly.

Bobby thanked him, asked for instructions, got none of any interest except to report next day as usual, and so alighted.

The colonel put his head out of the car window.

"Owen," he said, "I'm worried about young Moffatt—very worried."

Bobby thought to himself he had noticed that already. The colonel drove on without waiting for a reply. Bobby made his way to the local public-house. It was not yet closing time, though very nearly so. The bar was fairly full, and Bobby having been served took his glass over to watch a game of darts that was in progress at one end of the room. He made some remarks about it, and the rather complicated system of scoring in force, and presently found an opportunity to ask about the car accident he heard had taken place recently in the neighbourhood.

There was a kind of general giggle. One or two of the dart-players assumed panic. Another opined that old Sammy Hooper's heart would break when he knew. Bobby, puzzled, asked what the joke was. There were more grins, and finally it came out that the Mr. Hooper referred to had been an eye-witness of the accident, that he had visions of a trip to London, all expenses paid, to give his testimony, and that he had told the full story so often, and at such length, that finally a resolution had been put to the vote and carried unanimously that if he mentioned the subject again he would have to stand treat all round.

"So he went off home in a huff," said one man. "Gave his old woman the shock of her life to see him back before closing time. Break his heart to think there was someone asking about it and him not there to tell the whole story all over again from start to finish."

" All details complete, eh ? " smiled Bobby.

" That's right," said the other.

" Something about a cat, wasn't there ? " Bobby asked.

There was more grinning and chuckling. Presently it came out that Mr. Hooper had put the whole blame for the accident on a cat, specifying the cat, describing it down to the last hair on the tip of its tail, and identifying it with a big Tom belonging to a Mrs. Adkins, a neighbour of Mr. Hooper's, with whom apparently he was at deadly feud.

" Along of that same Tom," it was explained to Bobby. " He says it was her Tom did in his brood of prize Wyandottes this spring and she says it wasn't. Anyhow, it wasn't her Tom had anything to do with the accident, because she had it along to the vet that afternoon; ingrowing toenails it had, seemingly."

" Ingrowing claw," corrected the landlord, a literal soul.

" But Mr. Hooper said he saw it ? " Bobby asked.

" Swore to it up and down, told us all over and over again about its white paws and how he knew it at once. All made up, because it couldn't be there and at the vet's, too, as Mrs. Adkins proved when she heard what he was saying. But he told about that cat so clear-like everyone who heard him fairly saw it there, running across the road."

" Oh, well," said Bobby, " I expect Mrs. Adkins was quite pleased to be able to show he was wrong."

To that they all agreed, except that pleased was no word for it. No word, indeed, existed adequate to describe her satisfaction and delight. Poor, unfortunate Mr. Hooper would never hear the last of it. She had been cunning enough, too, to lie low for a while and let him commit himself fully and with increasing vividness of detail to his story till presently—only, in fact, a day or two ago—she had produced the veterinary surgeon's evidence and blown Mr. Hooper and his story equally sky high. Now it was fairly certain that it was a neighbour's mongrel dog Mr. Hooper had actually seen.

Bobby said it was the most amusing story he had heard for a long time, and everyone laughed a great deal at unlucky Mr. Hooper's discomfiture, and then Bobby, having finished his drink, departed, well pleased.

For, indeed, it seemed to him that this story of the cat, the mongrel, and Mr. Hooper fitted well into the theory he was building up; the theory that, when it was completed, he meant to produce for the inspection of his superiors, impregnable to all official doubts and hesitations.

CHAPTER XXV

PASSED TO REEVES

IN THE MORNING, however, Bobby came to the conclusion that, though his case was certainly not yet complete, though it might well be that he was attaching too great importance to what might perhaps turn out to be merely unimportant trifles, yet it had become his duty to explain in detail to Colonel Warden the exact lines on which his mind was moving. Obviously, however, this new hint of suspicion pointing to young Noll Moffatt must be dealt with promptly, and obviously, too, if that developed in any way, then, Bobby told himself, his own tentative theory would have to be abandoned as inconsistent with any such new information.

At any rate, it seemed to him clear he had now reached a stage in his own theoretical reconstruction of what had happened when his superior officer must be informed. With that intention, therefore, clear in his mind, he proceeded to the local police headquarters, where he was informed that the chief constable had developed a touch of influenza, and had been ordered by his doctor complete rest for a day or two.

" Means his missus when it says doctor," opined the worried chief superintendent and deputy chief constable to whose presence Bobby had been shown. " This blessed

Battling Copse case has got the old man down proper—sort of nervous breakdown, as you might say."

Bobby agreed. He knew better than most how deeply Colonel Warden had felt his responsibilities, how troubled he had been by the swift twists and turns of suspicion that had characterised the investigation, how deeply he had been affected by this latest suggestion that the guilt might rest upon the son of an old friend and neighbour.

"Some of those involved may turn out to be friends of his," Bobby remarked. "He's let it get on his mind."

"Young Moffatt," said the chief superintendent. "I know. I had my own ideas about that from the start. Known to have used the pistol and not one of the steady sort. Drink and all that, and at odds with his father because he wants to go one way and old Mr. Moffatt wants him to go another. Well, what's next? You're better up in the case than I am. What do you suggest?"

The chief superintendent had, in fact, of late been almost entirely occupied with ordinary routine duties, from the burden of which he had relieved his superior while the investigation of the Battling Copse crime was occupying so much of Colonel Warden's time. And routine has to be attended to, no matter what more sensational incidents may intrude upon it. The chief superintendent knew, of course, the broad outline of the investigation, but only a little of that background which alone makes bare facts significant, which is, indeed, to the bare fact much what the breath of life is to the body. His mind and time were therefore chiefly occupied by the mass of daily documents of one kind or another wherewith the complicated machinery of modern life floods every day every police office in the land. So he was only too glad to cut Bobby's explanations as short as possible, and agree that Bobby was to carry on as best he could for the present, till it was known when the chief constable would be able to return to duty.

"Very awkward, of course," said the chief superintendent. "You'll have to do the best you can, as you can. Oh, there's a report from your people in London that Mrs. O'Brien has been seen visiting Larson, if that's of any interest. If the colonel stops sick, I shall ask the Yard to send someone down to help you. I can't spare the time, with all I've got on hand. I suppose they'll curse me, but you're better staffed there than we are."

"We don't think so," Bobby protested hotly.

The chief superintendent smiled in a superior way.

"You don't know up there what being short-handed means," he said. "You haven't a Watch Committee to pare you to the bone." He paused for a moment to brood darkly on a Watch Committee, amiable as individuals, but as a body possessed by seven times seven devils of cheeseparing. "Oh, well," he said, "carry on, but there's one thing I've noticed. I sat up all hours last night going through the papers in the case. Well, what strikes me is this: there's something against everyone mentioned except one person. They're all of good character and good standing except one person. And that one person's the same."

"Reeves?" asked Bobby.

"Yes. Mr. Moffatt's butler. Ex-convict and all that. And yet, so far as I can make out, he is the one person concerned left entirely to one side."

"There seems nothing to implicate him at present," Bobby said, looking thoughtful.

"Well, carry on," repeated the chief superintendent, "only don't forget Reeves; that's my tip. Don't forget

Reeves. Better see first what young Moffatt has to say for himself, but don't press him. Report to me when—er—when you have to," he concluded, plainly meaning that, unless Bobby had to, he wasn't to, and that " had to " meant—well, just that.

Thus dismissed, Bobby left the chief superintendent to his forms, his reports, his schedules, and on a police motor-cycle he managed to borrow—when the sergeant in charge was out and the constable taking his place a little overborne by the prestige of the London man—made his way to Sevens, where he found Noll Moffatt busily occupied in packing up some " stills " he was sending to a friend who knew someone who had a cousin who had been at school with the secretary of the chairman of the Hyper Film Consolidated Association. Noll's hope was that the " stills " would be carelessly left lying by the secretary on the great man's desk, and that he, on seeing them, would be so struck and interested by their excellence, and so impressed that he would instantly ring up Noll and engage him then and there as camera-man.

" Though," said Noll, a little gloomily, " they do say just at present he never speaks to anyone except to give them a week's notice. Gave his wife a week's notice the other day from sheer force of habit, I heard."

All the same, Noll was not much inclined to worry about his " stills." As easy to resist them, he thought, as to resist Mr. Jack Dempsey's straight left. Alas ! how little did he foresee that day when, on finding those " stills " upon his desk, where, after incredible adventures, they duly arrived, the chairman was to sweep them impatiently into the waste-paper basket without so much as giving them a single glance. But that was of the future, and to-day, still radiant in hope, Noll Moffatt greeted Bobby cheerily enough.

"Look here, though," he said, "what's all this about Ena? The kid's so cocky these days there's no holding her. What's up?"

Bobby said untruthfully that he didn't know.

"Haven't found the dad's automatic yet, have you?" inquired Noll.

"No. I wish we could," Bobby answered. "You remember, when you saw the body, you told us it was a perfect stranger—someone you had never seen before?"

Noll looked less cheerful. He left his beloved "stills," and his expression grew, Bobby thought, both sulky and uneasy.

"I said I didn't recognise him, and I didn't," he answered. He shuddered slightly. It had been the first time he had seen death, and, to the young, death still seems a stranger and an enemy, as indeed to the young death is, since to them death bears the threat of unfulfilment. "I didn't look too close," he mumbled.

"I have a photograph of the body here, if you would like to look at it again," Bobby said.

But the boy didn't wish to. He gave it a glance and looked away.

"What for? Why should I?" he grumbled.

"In case you wish to correct your previous statement."

"Look here," demanded Noll violently, "what are you driving at?"

"From information received," Bobby said gently, "we have reason to believe you were concerned in a quarrel that took place on the day of the murder at lunch-time at the Oakley Road House. It is also suggested that the other party to the quarrel was the murdered man, and that threats were uttered."

"Oh, hell, you've dug that up," young Moffatt muttered.

"Do you wish to say anything?" Bobby asked. "If you do, I should like it in writing. Probably you may want to see a lawyer first—or your father."

"Oh, Lord, not dad," Noll said. "He would go in off the deep end for keeps if he knew. Look here, I suppose you think I'm a blasted liar. I'm not. I didn't know him again at first. I hardly looked; made me feel queer somehow. Besides, he was all different. It was only afterwards I began to think who it was." He paused. "It's gospel truth," he said. "In bed that night, I saw his face much more plainly than I did in that beastly barn place."

Bobby was quite prepared to believe this. It is the fact that death often brings great changes. Even close relatives called to identify a body may fail to do so. It is as if, when life is left, life's troubles and complications are left, too, and what remains is a peace life has not often known.

"Do you mind telling me what your quarrel with Bennett was about?" Bobby asked.

"Yes, I do," Noll answered defiantly. "Private. I did tell him he wanted his brains blown out, but of course I didn't mean it—at least, I mean I meant it all right, but not like that."

The remark was hardly a model of clarity, but Bobby felt he understood well enough what the other wished to convey.

"Perhaps," he observed, "the trouble was about the same thing that you and Mr. Hayes's chauffeur quarrelled over?"

Noll went very red, spluttered, hesitated, and finally burst out:

"Well, anyhow, look here, if you think it was me, I

can jolly well prove I was nowhere near Battling Copse at four that afternoon."

" You told us you saw no one all the time you were out, and you agreed you were in the neighbourhood? You said you meant to take photos, but didn't, and you wouldn't say what you were doing."

" Yes, I know, but I did take one or two. Look at that," Noll said, and, snatching up an unmounted photograph from a number lying about, he slammed it down before Bobby. " There," he said triumphantly; " that's one."

It showed a bull standing under a fine beech—a good photo and a clever composition. Bobby looked at it with interest.

" Jolly good," he said doubtfully, " but I don't see where it comes in. It doesn't show you and it doesn't show when it was taken."

" Yes, it does," retorted Noll. " I didn't know myself, but it does. Lucky for me, too. You ask old Dawson—it's his bull and his field. And the brute was only there that particular day and hour. You see, it's always the lower field they let it run in when it's not in its stall. But that afternoon they found a gap in the lower field hedge and the bull trying to get through. Well, you can't risk having a pedigree bull running loose, especially one that's a bit queer tempered, so they turned it into the beech-tree field while the gap was mended. And it hadn't been there ten minutes, and I had just happened to get that " still," when some chap turned up with a cow he wanted served immediately. So old Dawson had the bull brought up to the home paddock. You'll find time and names and everything entered in his service book. Means a photo of that bull under that tree in that field could only have been taken on that one day, somewhere within a few minutes, one way or the other, of four o'clock in the afternoon."

"Seems good enough," Bobby agreed.

There was, of course, the detail that the photograph provided no proof in itself that it had actually been taken by Oliver Moffatt in person. But it should be easy to show that he had left home carrying his camera, that the photo came from a camera of the same type, and that no one else possessing either a similar camera or the ability to take such a picture was in the vicinity at the time. Bobby said:

"Do you mind if I take the photo? What you say will have to be checked up on, of course, but it sounds all right. I'm very glad," he added with a friendly smile, "both for your sake and for our own. The more people we can rule out, the better. In these cases our motto has to be: 'Every man's a suspect till he's proved innocent.' What we have to do is to rule out name after name till only one is left—if we can."

"Yes, I see that," Noll said, and hesitated, and looked uncomfortable. "Look here," he said, as Bobby gravely waited. "I know it's rather a beastly thing to say, but have you ever thought of Reeves?"

"Your butler?" Bobby asked, surprised and startled. "Why do you ask?"

"Well, the fact is," Noll said, "I hate sneaking, but I happened to find out. I didn't mean to say anything to anyone so long as the chap seemed running straight, but if it's murder—well, there you are. It makes things a bit different."

"You mean," Bobby asked, "you know that Reeves is an ex-convict?"

"Oh, Lord," exclaimed Noll. "You knew all the time?"

" He gave himself away almost the first time I saw him," Bobby answered. " Have you known long ? Does Mr. Moffatt ? "

" Oh, he doesn't know," Noll answered. " Rather not. He'd have a fit. I've known about six months. I didn't mean to split unless I had to. After all, we're insured. I thought—well, you know, turning over a new leaf and all that. Of course, if you knew all the time, then I haven't split on him now, have I ? "

" Certainly not," agreed Bobby. " You know something else ? Remember," he added, as Noll still hesitated, " it is—murder."

" Yes, it is, isn't it ? " agreed Noll. " Well, look here. I do a bit of prowling round at night. I've an idea of my own for taking night snaps. If I can work it out, it may be a big thing. Well, last night I was experimenting a bit. And I saw Reeves. He was at Way Side by their side gate. He was talking to Hayes—I mean, not just talking. Pretty excited they both were. You could see that."

" Did you hear what they were saying ? "

" No. Didn't try. None of my business. But I thought it jolly queer. And I saw Reeves hand something over. Something bright and hard-looking. Well, we've all had that missing automatic pretty well rubbed in. Dad keeps thinking of new places every day where it might be. Well, I thought at once what Reeves passed over looked jolly like it. Mind you, I can't swear to it, but that's what I thought."

" I see," said Bobby, wondering if now at last they had been given a pointer to the truth. Odd that hitherto the ex-convict had seemed outside suspicion and now was brought abruptly into the centre of doubt. " Are you sure it was Reeves ? " Bobby asked.

" Oh, rather."

" And that it was Hayes ? "

" Well, who else could it be ? I couldn't see him plainly —at least, not his face. Most of him was in the shadow. But when they had finished he walked off back to the house, and it was someone in plus fours so it can't have been the chauffeur bloke. The light went on in Hayes's study, too, as soon as he got in."

" I see," said Bobby slowly. " I'm very glad you've told me. It may turn out important."

Encouraged by this, Noll went on:

" Well, the moment I saw them I felt sure they were up to something together. Look here, you know Hayes takes photos ? "

" Many people do," Bobby observed.

" Yes, but Hayes is keen on it. Well, look here, there was a bit of film or wrapper or something found, wasn't there ? You can't identify a thing like that, I suppose. But that means it was either Hayes or me was there. Because no one else would be likely to be taking snaps in Battling Copse at that time of day. Well, look here, I know it wasn't me, so it must have been him, mustn't it ? "

" At any rate," Bobby agreed, " it seems a sound piece of deductive reasoning."

CHAPTER XXVI

ABSTRACT REASONING

BOBBY LEFT SEVENS feeling that Noll Moffatt's story of the nocturnal interview at Way Side raised new difficulties, new questions not easy to understand.

That the young man was telling the truth both when he said he had in fact failed to recognise Bennett's body, and when he protested that the quarrel at the Oakley Road House had no connection with the subsequent tragedy, Bobby was inclined to believe. But the story of an apparently secret and agitated nocturnal interview between Reeves and Hayes he did not see how to fit in with the provisional theory he had formed from the facts as he at present knew them. He still believed his theory was correct, but he knew well, of course, that the discovery of new facts at present unknown might prove it entirely mistaken.

His motor-cycle soon covered the distance to the Towers Poultry Farm he had decided was to be his next destination. As he dismounted by the entrance-gate he saw Henrietta come to the door of the cottage and stand there, tall and firm-footed, on the threshold, as though she would guard it against all comers.

" There is something she knows," he told himself with one of those flashes of insight that occasionally visited him, " and what it is she will never tell."

She stood there, motionless and gravely watching, as he leaned his cycle against the gate-post, and removed his gloves and goggles. He thought to himself:

" She was expecting someone—but not me."

He walked up the garden path and greeted her. She acknowledged his presence and salute with a slight movement of her head, but she did not speak and made no movement to invite him within. Her eyes were watchful and alert, her attitude tense; she gave the impression of being prepared to do battle to the last, and Bobby's rare smile touched the corners of his mouth as he said:

" I wish you weren't so ready to regard me as an enemy, Miss Towers."

A little disconcerted, she said:

" Why do you say that? I have only seen you once or twice. I suppose you have to do your duty."

" Yes," he agreed, more gravely, " and I think you feel that anything that threatens yours threatens you."

" I don't know what you mean," she said, but now she was plainly troubled.

" I suppose it's a woman's attitude," Bobby mused. "Your hens will fight for their chickens, won't they ? "

" Have you come to tell me that ? " she asked.

" No, no," he said ; " musings by the way, so to speak. Trying to get on terms. There's one thing I wanted to ask, though. What have you done with the photographs that used to be in the frame next to the one of Mrs. Oulton ? "

Calmly, steadily, she met his questioning gaze. For a full moment their eyes challenged each other. She said slowly:

" I don't know why you ask what seems an impertinent question. I do not propose to answer it."

"Will you answer this, then?" he said, a little crossly now, for he was tired of this fencing. "Is the real name of Mr. Hayes's chauffeur, not Thoms, but Oulton, and is he your half-brother? And are the two photographs I asked about of him and of your stepfather?"

Henrietta was a little pale now—as pale, at least, as the tan of wind and weather on her cheeks permitted. But her voice was steady still, her eyes still calm, as she replied:

"I don't see why you should think so, and I have told you I do not propose to answer your questions."

"Well, of course, that's for you to decide," Bobby agreed. "But it won't stop us going on putting two and two together. Our job, you know. We add two and two together and see what it makes—generally comes out three or five and then we know there's a mistake somewhere. But now and again we get four for an answer, and then it looks correct. I think it does this time. The important thing is, does that four spell—murder?"

She made no answer, but stood, erect, unmoved, and still, so that he wondered a little at the force of her self-control. Yet he knew well how that last word had struck home. Upright she stood and waited, magnificently quiet. Bobby went on:

"I thought you might help me, but I can see you won't. Perhaps I can help you, though I can see you won't believe that. I don't think myself that two and two in this case makes—what I said. But I have to make sure. I would make sure though it meant my own life and that of everyone I know."

He had said these last words with a force that matched her own. More quietly he went on:

"But I think my two and two does make a four that

means Thoms is Oulton and your half-brother. You might as well say so, too; it will be easy enough to check that. You know you told me a good deal about what happened in the past—your stepfather's death, and those bearer bonds that were stolen from your mother and so on. I didn't see you as likely to confide stories like that to strangers, or even to police officers, without some good reason, and I wondered a good deal what that reason was. I lay awake at night wondering—at least," Bobby added candidly, " I did till I dropped off. I knew there had been a row between Thoms—to use his official name—and young Moffatt. In the course of duty "—Bobby's voice grew wistful and sad—" I had to stop a jolly little set-to between them. They wouldn't say what it was all about, but, when two boys start scrapping, a girl is as likely a bet as any. I remembered young Moffatt and Miss Molly were both the artistic sort, and it was quite on the cards they met pretty often while she was out sketching and he was out looking for likely shots, and I remembered, too, that old Mr. Moffatt put on a bit of a scowl—the heavy father sort of air—when he heard this place mentioned. Then what you said about Mr. Hayes—you put it quite plainly—made me think it was hardly likely you personally were concerned, so that again made it likely it was Miss Molly was the attraction in Noll Moffatt's eyes. So I started wondering where Thoms came in. He wasn't the artistic type, and Miss Molly was hardly the sort of girl to take any interest in the ordinary chauffeur. Did that mean Thoms wasn't quite an ordinary chauffeur? I argued that if he and Moffatt had quarrelled about Miss Molly, Thoms hadn't interfered as an ordinary jealous rival, but because he was interested in Miss Molly for some other reason. An obvious deduction was that

that other reason must be a blood relationship. Suppose Thoms was some kind of relative—say a brother—and had heard gossip about young Moffatt and Miss Molly? Evidently old Mr. Moffatt had heard something, so there was talk going on, and if Thoms had heard it, too, and had tried to interfere or say anything—well, the little scrap I saw was nicely explained. And the suggestion that Thoms might be a relative of yours seemed again to link up with your saying you had no photograph of your half-brother when I asked you. I noticed that the frame with Mrs. Oulton's photograph in it was meant to hold three photos, and now only held one, and obviously it would have been only natural if the other two had been of her husband and her son. A natural deduction was that the photos had been put away to avoid any risk of recognition, and a further deduction was that a risk of recognition from a photo seen in this house meant the risk referred to someone in the neighbourhood. Another point was that Mr. Hayes mentioned once that it was his chauffeur told him the Way Side property was to let, and a possible deduction from that was that Thoms might have some reason for wishing Mr. Hayes to settle in this neighbourhood. So then I had to try to reason out what was behind all this, and there the story you told me about your stepfather's death and the lost bonds began to come in. I expect if you could manage to lay hold of those bonds again, once they were in your possession, whoever has them now would find it very difficult to claim them back or to establish proof of legal ownership. There would be no record, I suppose, of when or where he bought them. Perhaps you have?"

"We have no details," she answered slowly. "We have my stepfather's accounts, with a note that simply says what their value was and that they were bought for mother with her money. But we believe if they are our bonds they have my stepfather's signature on some of them, and a note in his writing that they belonged to mother. And we think they would bear his finger-prints in the ink mother upset. At the time our lawyers advised us to keep specimens of his finger-prints on record for comparison, if necessary."

"I take it, then," Bobby said thoughtfully, "that if you could somehow get possession of the bonds again, you would be able to prove your right to them as your legal property, if you were challenged. The question is, where are they, and in what way and by what means could you get hold of them again?"

To that Henrietta made no reply. She had listened intently, breathlessly indeed, but her fine self-control remained unshaken. Bobby waited for a moment or two to see if she would say anything further. When she did not, he resumed:

"I rather got the idea that when you heard of Bennett's murder you—well, I don't like to say panicked. I don't see you in a panic somehow. But I think you did wonder if Thoms—may as well go on calling him Thoms; no other name admitted as yet—if anything had gone wrong; if he had gone too far; if somehow he might be involved. You thought it would be well to tell me part of the story so that the facts could be on record, so to speak, beforehand. You didn't think what you said could implicate your half-brother in any way, or give any kind of pointer to him, and you did think it might be useful afterwards if you could say you had told your story at once. Well, that was all right; you didn't say anything that pointed to Thoms, but you hadn't calculated on the scrap between him and young Moffatt or on the chance of my happening to see it and starting to wonder what it was about. Of course," said Bobby apologetically, " I know all this is a lot of abstract reasoning from probably insufficient data, and abstract reasoning and concrete fact don't always agree. But there it is, for what it is, and unless I'm shown a flaw in my logic, or any new facts inconsistent with it, I shall have to go on thinking it all seems to fit pretty well."

" What has all this got to do with who committed the murder ? " she asked abruptly.

" Yes, there's that, isn't there ? " Bobby said.

" Have you anything more to say ? " she asked.

" I was rather hoping," he answered, " that it might be you who would have something to say. Wouldn't it be wiser ? "

She shook her head—a faint, almost imperceptible gesture, but one strangely decisive all the same.

" I think you're wrong, if I may say so," Bobby told her. " Perhaps you'll think it over and let us know if you change your mind. After all, you know, the police are there to help all law-abiding people. Our job. It's only when people go outside the law that there's apt to be trouble."

" Is that a warning ? " she asked, with a touch of scorn in her voice.

" I suppose it is what it is," he answered.

" The law," she said, and there was a deeper scorn in her voice. " The law——"

" Oh, yes, I know," Bobby interrupted, " an ass and old Father Antic and all the rest. I know. I'm a servant of the law, and they say none are heroes to their servants. All the same, the worst law is better than no law. Anyhow, where there's law you do know where you are, and that's something in a world like this. If you change your mind about having another talk, you'll let us know, won't you ? "

With that he bowed formally and turned away, and he was conscious that, as he walked down the path to where his motor-cycle stood, she was still standing as he had left her, looking after him.

CHAPTER XXVII

MR. HAYES IS WORRIED

WAY SIDE, Bobby had decided, was to be his next place of call, for he felt it was important to secure, if possible, confirmation of Noll Moffatt's story. And, if it were true, then Bobby felt he would very much like to know what was the subject of this interview between Mr. Hayes and the Moffatts' butler.

His interview with Henrietta had been more than a little disappointing. She had remained so much on her guard, so plainly hostile and distrustful, that he had achieved little by his talk with her. Nor was he at all certain that the warning he had felt it his duty to convey had had the least effect.

" Might as well have held my tongue," he thought. He smiled wryly. " Wouldn't even let me into the house. Possible she hasn't much say in it all, though."

He told himself moodily that things were taking their own course, and one that he at least had not foreseen or understood. The question of the murder seemed to be slipping into the background, a crisis was approaching, he felt, and how to deal with it he did not know.

" All depends," he thought again, " on what all these people are really up to, and how far Bennett's death is connected with whatever it is that's going on now. And if I am right about the actual murderer, why is he hanging about? Why doesn't he bolt while he's got the chance?"

He gave these questions up as beyond his comprehension till at least he had new facts to add to those already in his knowledge. He had reached Way Side now, and, almost as he dismounted, the door opened and Hayes appeared on the threshold, smiling a welcome.

"Well, well," he called, "am I glad to see you? I should say. Jumping Moses, why, I was just on the point of giving you people a ring."

"Oh," said Bobby, mildly surprised, for seldom on his official visits did he find himself so warmly greeted. "Anything up?"

"I'm worried," Mr. Hayes said. "Come along in. What'll you have? A spot of the best?"

"Nothing, thanks," Bobby answered, following his host into the study, as it was called. "Too early for me for one thing, and on duty for another."

"Well, you don't mind if I do, do you?" Hayes asked. "I need it and that's a fact."

He poured himself out a stiff drink. Bobby took a chair his host indicated and regarded with interest a fine diamond ring lying on a sheet of paper on the table by the side of a magnifying-glass.

"That ring looks as if it were worth something," he remarked.

Hayes took a drink. He put down his glass, ignoring Bobby's remark, and said slowly:

"I want protection."

"Eh?" said Bobby.

"Protection," repeated Mr. Hayes. "I've been rung up twice and told I was getting mine. I don't like it. Nervous, I suppose. And I'm all alone."

" Alone ? But there are the servants ? "

" All gone," Hayes answered. " The housemaid left yesterday. Heard of a place that suited her—had to go at once if she wanted it. Then this morning the cook got a wire her aunt or someone was dying and off she went, too, or there wouldn't be much of the furniture left for her, she said. Says it's valuable, and unless she's on the spot she won't get her share. Wouldn't wait another minute. I wanted her to wire for confirmation, but she wouldn't. She said if her aunt wasn't ill she would be vexed. Said she must see for herself."

" But your chauffeur ? Isn't Thoms with you ? "

" Sacked him," said Hayes. " He had something to do with that Battling Copse affair. I've felt that all the time. Got on my nerves, thinking he was a murderer and perhaps I should be the next. I asked him straight out if he knew anything about it—the murder, I mean. He as good as admitted he did it."

" Did he, though ? " exclaimed Bobby, startled.

" Yes ; not in so many words, of course, but that's what he meant and what he knew I knew he meant. Laughed and said the police would never prove anything ; they were a lot of dummies anyhow. I told him to clear out. Gave him a month's wages and saw him off the place then and there. I don't," said Mr. Hayes, with a slight shudder, " I don't like murder ; never did. Makes more fuss than anything."

" So it does," agreed Bobby. " Was this yesterday ? "

" Yes. That's not all, either. He was back hanging round here after dark last night. And he wasn't alone. Someone with him. I couldn't see who. I heard someone prowling about, and I slipped out to see. I was jumpy. I told you I had been rung up and threatened. It was

Thoms all right. I saw him plainly. He was by the garden gate with another man. They were talking. Excited, they were. Arguing. I think Thoms was urging something the other man didn't quite like. Murdering me, perhaps," said Mr. Hayes with a nervous laugh.

"Could you hear what they were saying?"

"No. I tried, but I couldn't get near enough, and then they separated and I bolted back to the house and turned all the lights on."

"You didn't recognise Thoms's companion?"

"No. He kept in the shadows. I couldn't see him plainly."

"You are sure it was Thoms?"

"Oh, yes; saw him plainly enough. I know that plus fours suit of his, too. He always wore it on his days off."

Bobby was silent for a moment or two. Unless Hayes was telling elaborate lies for no apparent purpose, it was Reeves and Thoms who had been seen by young Moffatt, not Reeves and Hayes. But that made it all seem more puzzling still. Apparently, too, as Thoms had been discharged earlier in the day, this meeting by the Way Side garden gate was a result of a previous appointment.

But for what purpose, and, if Hayes's story was true, what was it Thoms had been urging and to which Reeves had been reluctant to agree? What the bright object Noll had seen handed over?

It occurred to Bobby that if Thoms—Oulton—had been sent off in the way Hayes described, it was quite likely he had taken refuge at the Towers Poultry Farm.

"Perhaps," Bobby said to himself, "he was there, listening, all the time I was talking, and that's why Miss Henrietta was so keen on not letting me indoors. Well, if he did hear what I had to say, all the better."

Aloud he said again:

"That's a valuable-looking ring you have there."

"That? Oh, yes," agreed Hayes, looking slightly surprised at this sudden change of subject. "I was just giving it a look over when I heard you coming." He picked the ring up and examined it lovingly. "Worth a hundred pounds, if you ask me," he said, "and I got it for twenty."

"Good bargain," Bobby suggested.

"Fellow hard up; wanted the cash," Mr. Hayes explained. "I promised to let him have it back any time he wanted at the same price—if I still had it. I won't," said Hayes with a faint chuckle, "not me. I shall have the cash instead."

"It looks," said Bobby cautiously, "like one Mr. Larson was wearing."

Hayes, plainly surprised by this observation, gave Bobby a quick and searching glance, and then determined apparently to admit the fact.

"That's right," he said. "Larson didn't want it known, but, as you spotted it for yourself, no use saying it isn't. Big deal he has been planning for years gone west—a complete wash-out. Knock-out for him. Sore about it, too. Came to see me because he knew I made my money in the States and he thought I might like to make some more. So I would, but not on the proposition he wanted to interest me in. Said he was going across in a day or two and could handle things on the spot. I told him I was going across, too, right away, and could do all the handling on the spot myself. So when he saw it was no good he said he was a bit pressed for the ready and what would I give him for his ring. I offered him twenty, cash down, and he jumped at it. Wanted it to pay his fare back to town, perhaps."

Bobby reflected again that Larson, the first time he saw him, had arrived at Sevens in a magnificent Rolls-Royce. Then, when Bobby had met him later on, he had spoken of a train journey in what from his description of his fellow-passengers had sounded like an overcrowded third-class compartment. And now he was apparently disposing of a valuable ring for considerably less than its real value. All significant, Bobby thought, of an increasing financial pressure, and perhaps significant of more besides.

" You told Mr. Larson you were leaving for America ? " Bobby asked. " Isn't that rather sudden ? "

" I'm fed up," Hayes explained. " I thought I should like the country—quiet, a change, new life, all that. Didn't expect—well, murder and that sort of thing. I'm getting out."

Bobby looked at him thoughtfully. A little like flight, he told himself.

" I think," he said cautiously, " Colonel Warden was hoping you would be available till our investigation was complete."

" What for ? " demanded Hayes. " I don't know a thing about it; nothing to do with me."

" If it is your chauffeur . . ? " Bobby suggested.

" Well, I can't help that. Not my fault."

" No, but it's such a very complicated case; cross-currents, one thing and another," Bobby explained. " It's almost beginning to look as if Bennett's murder was incidental to something else that may be going on. You were saying you have had threatening messages over the phone ? "

" Yes; that O'Brien woman. She tried to disguise her voice, but it was her all right. Trying to get even because

I wouldn't put up with her tantrums and her airs any longer."

" What was it she said actually ? "

" Oh, I was going to get my own, and all that sort of talk. I didn't take much notice. Told her to shut up and hung up. Tried it again later on. I hung up at once. But I began to think I was alone here except for two women servants—that was after I had sacked Thoms—and then the housemaid said she wanted to leave at once. I had told them I was giving this place up and leaving for the States and they must look out for new jobs. The girl had heard of this one and was all set on going off at once—suited her specially well for some reason. So she went, and then this morning the wire I told you about came for the cook. No holding her; she wasn't going to miss her share of her aunt's goods. Somewhere in Ireland it is. So off she went, too, and that means I'm all alone in the house. I don't like it. You've taken my gun, too. Can you get it me back ? I should feel safer. I suppose you can send a policeman along as well ? I'll pay for his time, of course—anything you like. And stand him a drink as well."

" I think I can promise that," Bobby said. " I'll report what you say, and I think you can depend on an officer being here before dark. He will stay the night if you wish it. But don't stand him any drinks, please. Regulations are very strict, and he will be on duty."

" Oh, that's all right," Hayes said, and seemed a good deal relieved. " It'll only be for the one night, you know. I'm going to an hotel in town to-morrow. But there are a lot of papers and stuff here I've got to clear up first."

Bobby took his departure then, a good deal more

puzzled even than on his arrival. This story of Larson's visit to Way Side on pretext of discussing some financial enterprise in America seemed a curious development, especially when taken in conjunction with the Scotland Yard report of Mrs. O'Brien's visit to Larson in town and with her threatening messages over the phone.

It struck him that possibly these threats of Mrs. O'Brien's had really been intended as a reminder of what Hayes had lost in losing her and as an offer to resume relations. It might have been wise, he thought, from Hayes's point of view, if he had been more willing to listen to what she had to say. His cutting her off so quickly would not tend to improve her temper.

And it seemed to Bobby, too, that possibly it might be the news of Hayes's intention to leave for America that was the chief agent in this apparent coming to a culmination of all the tangled affair.

But, even if it were so, he could not get clear in his mind the various parts the different players were likely to take in the final act of the drama whereon, as it seemed to him, the curtain was about to rise.

Back at police headquarters, he spent some time on the phone, talking to Scotland Yard. A message came through presently in reply to his inquiry. It said that Mr. Larson was not at his address, which was in a block of service flats in Bloomsbury. He had not said where he was going. He had been carrying a small suit-case when he left, and the hour at which he had departed was one that would get him to Paddington in time to catch a train due in at the local station almost immediately. It seemed worth trying, and Bobby, hurrying to the station, was just in time to see the London train arrive and Mr. Larson alighting from a third-class smoker.

Bobby waited, and greeted him pleasantly as he came off the platform.

" Paying us another visit, Mr. Larson ? " he asked.

" Came along to see if you want to run me in," explained Mr. Larson, smiling a little. " It's getting on my nerves a bit. I've been followed these last few days. The porters at the flats where I live have been asked questions. They're beginning to look at me. I can't stand that sort of thing. Not in my position. Stories soon get about. My position in business depends on my reputation. I can't afford gossip. It's got to stop. I made up my mind to come and ask you if you have anything against me or have I got to see my solicitors ? I don't want to, but if I'm forced——"

He left the sentence unfinished, and Bobby said protestingly :

" My dear sir, when we have anything against a man he doesn't have to ask. He knows. And are you sure you're correct in saying you have been followed, or that porters have been questioned about you ? Was it perhaps Mrs. O'Brien——? "

He left his sentence unfinished in his turn, and Mr. Larson looked relieved.

" Oh, it's her, is it ? You can't suspect her, surely ? "

" That's a question with only one possible answer," Bobby replied. " Every man may be innocent before the courts till he's proved guilty; but, for police work, every man is suspect till he's proved innocent. And that generally means till someone else is proved guilty."

" You can have proof of who's guilty, if you like," Larson said quickly. " Search Hayes's house and you'll find your proof all right."

" What makes you say that ? " Bobby asked.

" Intuition, if you like. What Mrs. O'Brien has told me, if you prefer that. But search and you'll find all right enough."

"Just what we can't—without proof," Bobby explained. " Vicious circle sort of business. We can't go into a house to look for proof till we've proof the proof is there. We might know there was a signed, sealed confession of guilt in Mr. Hayes's writing-table drawer——"

" There may be, or something just as good," Larson interrupted.

" No good to us," Bobby said. " We can't touch it till we have proof to satisfy a magistrate he can give us authority to act on. Police have no right of search."

" If someone gave you that proof? "

" Why, then," said Bobby formally, " he would be serving the ends of justice and would be entitled to the thanks of all law-abiding citizens."

" I don't know," retorted Mr. Larson, " that all that interests me, but I'm a bit keen on ending this state of things. I tell you candidly, I'm not willing to let it go on as it is. There are stories going about the City. No one believes them yet, but that'll come if they're not cleared up soon. The merest whisper about a man in my position and no more confidential business comes his way. My reputation is my stock-in-trade."

" If there is any information you can give us——" Bobby suggested.

Larson shook his head.

" I have my own ideas," he said, " but I'll keep them to myself for the present. Mrs. O'Brien has been telling me things, I admit, but—can one trust her? I don't intend to allow myself to be dragged into any libel action to gratify her spite against Hayes. And I don't mean to appear as a witness in a sensational murder case. Not the line for a City man handling big mergers and other confidential business. No. If I knew anything, I tell you candidly, I should pass it on to you confidentially. I shouldn't mind what you guessed yourselves, but I should see that there was nothing I could be brought in on. Can you imagine—well, say, the Governor of the Bank of England appearing in a sensational murder case and being cross-examined by defending counsel? It wouldn't do for him, and, though I'm not the Governor of the Bank of England, it wouldn't do for me, either. But I will give you one hint. Hayes is fond of photography."

"Yes?" said Bobby, non-committally.

"Would a photograph showing Hayes was present in Battling Copse at the time of the murder—would that interest you?"

"Immensely," Bobby said.

CHAPTER XXVIII

THE EMPTY GLASS

IT WAS DUSK, the dusky hour that lingers in 'the English countryside before the closing in of night, when Bobby came again to Way Side. He knocked, and when he heard sounds within, but the door remained closed, he called out his name, and went and stood in the light of the lamp of his cycle, so that he might be seen. The door opened then, though still cautiously, and the nervous voice of Hayes called:

"No one's come. Why hasn't someone come? They rang me up to say a policeman would be here before dark, but no one's come and the phone's gone dead."

"Gone dead?" repeated Bobby. "You know, I half expected that. The wire goes across fields nearly a mile, doesn't it? Easy to cut it somewhere. Looks as if we might really expect visitors."

"I'm all alone," Hayes said. "Mrs. White hasn't come, and there's no message from her."

"Probably she's been stopped," Bobby suggested. "Had a note or a message to say you had changed your mind and didn't want her, but her money was enclosed. She wouldn't ask any questions after that. Looks like careful preparations being made. Any idea what's up?"

" Robbery, burglary, theft, housebreaking," Hayes answered in a breath.

They were standing in the hall now, into which, too, Bobby had wheeled his cycle, fearing that, if it were left outside, it might take it into its head to disappear.

" Yes, but I meant who ? " Bobby said. " That's what I want to know."

" Robbery, burglary," Hayes repeated. " That's what." He had become very pale; he was plainly badly frightened. " Murder," he muttered. " Why hasn't a policeman come ? They promised."

" Well, one has come, hasn't he ? " Bobby asked.

" No. No one. Not a sign."

" Oh, come, I say," Bobby protested. " I am someone after all. I do exist."

" But—why—oh," Hayes said, and stared, as if only just understanding.

" I'm a policeman," Bobby pointed out, " and I've come, haven't I ? I'll stay the night, if you like. For you to say. The local people are very short-handed. All police are. Parliament doubles police duties every week almost and never thinks any more staff is needed. What makes it worse here is that Colonel Warden has gone sick. His deputy, the chief super, is carrying on, but it means an upset. He jumped at it when I offered to take on your job. He's coming round himself later on to see how we are getting on, but my impression is he thinks you're exaggerating. Can't believe in open threats, assault, deliberate violence, anything of that sort. Outside his experience. Outside most people's, for that matter."

As he chatted on he had been watching Hayes closely, and he felt very sure that his appearance was not altogether welcome; that Hayes would very much have preferred an ordinary local constable, knowing little of the case and quite willing to show himself and his uniform as a general warning, to ask no questions, and to see no more than what was under his nose.

"I didn't think it would be you," Hayes muttered, still with that slightly disconcerted air.

"Oh, well, if you don't want me you can always chuck me out," explained Bobby cheerfully, and, when Hayes shook his head with a manner of suggesting that he would have preferred anyone to Bobby, but Bobby to no one, Bobby continued: "Why didn't you go down to the village for someone else when Mrs. White didn't turn up and you found the phone had gone dead? It's not far."

"Far enough. Getting dark as well, and not another house or cottage the whole way," Hayes answered. "I should have had to leave this place empty, too."

"Why not? If you have something valuable here in the house you were afraid to leave, you could have taken it with you."

"And got done in on the way?" Hayes retorted.

"Mr. Hayes," Bobby said, "I put this to you. We don't understand your attitude. Who are you afraid of, and why? A householder, a law-abiding citizen, has no reason to be so alarmed. He knows he has the law behind him. If he suffers injury, he can appeal to the law for redress. Is that the case with you?"

"What do you mean?" Hayes retorted with violence. "I've been threatened. I told you so. My phone's been cut. I'm alone. My servants have been enticed away or prevented from coming. I may be beaten up—or anything. I don't know what's up, as you call it, but I ask for police protection. I'm entitled to it, aren't I? I'm ready to pay."

" It is because you are entitled to it that I am here," Bobby answered. " But my feeling is that you are not being frank with us. It almost seems as if you felt that if you were attacked and robbed, you would not dare to call in police assistance afterwards."

" Well, I've called you in before, haven't I ? " Hayes asked. " I don't know what you're getting at."

" At this," Bobby answered, " that you may have something in your possession that, if you lost it, you would have difficulty in proving a rightful claim to."

" Mighty clever, aren't you ? " Hayes snarled. " All nonsense, of course. Pity, as you're so clever, you haven't found out yet who shot that poor devil in Battling Copse."

" The odd thing about that," Bobby remarked, " is that it seems to be broadening out so. Most remarkable."

" If I'm murdered," said Hayes gloomily, " a fat lot of good you'll be."

" We never are," agreed Bobby. " Not after murder. No real good hanging whoever did it. We generally do all the same. Professional pride, I suppose. Will you tell me who you are afraid might murder you to-night ? "

" Don't know; can't say. I'm just nervous, that's all."

" Thoms, for instance ? "

" I wouldn't put it past him."

" Why should he ? "

" Sacked without a character."

" Doesn't seem much of a reason. Anything else ? "

" Ask him."

" He's not communicative. What about Mr. Moffatt's London financier friend, Mr. Larson ? "

Hayes gave a little jump.

" You're on him ? " he said.

" Well, you said he called to see you. Sold you his

ring. Sounded as if he were hard up. Might have been a kind of preliminary look round—if he's heard or knows of anything valuable you have in your possession, that is ? "

" If it's that," Hayes muttered, " Mrs. O'Brien's behind it."

" Or Noll Moffatt ? "

Hayes looked genuinely surprised.

" Young Moffatt ? Why ? "

" ' Why ' is what I'm always asking and you never answer."

" I'm not going to, either," retorted Hayes. " I asked for protection, not for a cross-examination. Get that ? I've been threatened—personal violence. Perhaps there'll be a burglary attempted. Your job to see there isn't one. That's all. Understand ? "

" There's hardly anything about this business that I do understand," Bobby sighed. " My head's nearly bursting with guesses, too—some of them about you, Mr. Hayes, and none very complimentary."

Hayes greeted this with a scowl.

" Keep them to yourself," he snapped. " Do your job you're here for and that I'm paying for. See ? "

" That job being, I suppose," Bobby remarked, " to make sure that nothing happens to-night, so that you may get away in the morning with anything valuable safe in your pocket, and anything here you don't want to be seen safely destroyed. Safety first, in fact, all the time and all the way. You know, Mr. Hayes, there are times when I think you're a very clever man."

" Thank you for nothing," growled Hayes. " Anyhow, perhaps I could teach you a thing or two. Have you brought my automatic back ? I asked for it when I rang up."

Bobby produced two formidable-looking weapons.

" One for you, one for me," he said.

Hayes snatched the weapon from Bobby's hand.

" It's not loaded," he said, looking to see. " I think I've got a clip somewhere, though."

" I wouldn't bother," Bobby told him. " They've a tame expert at headquarters here, and I believe he's fixed it so it can't be fired—not until it's unfixed again. Fear of accidents, you know."

Mr. Hayes stared, gaped, verified Bobby's statement, indulged in an outburst of profanity. Bobby looked pained. He said:

" Mine's not loaded, either. Safer that way, don't you think ? The great British public doesn't expect police to shoot. Awful fuss if we do. Not playing the game. Cheating almost. Bad as body line, or kicking a goal at Rugby when you haven't said you meant to. Worse if a policeman lets someone he's with do the shooting. The High-Ups simply won't stand for it. A funeral if you're shot, and the sack if you shoot—that's their idea, and no wonder a policeman's lot is not a happy one."

" What's the good of the bally things if they aren't loaded ? " demanded Hayes—only he didn't say " bally."

" Well, the other fellow doesn't know that, does he ? " asked Bobby.

" It's playing the fool," cried Hayes angrily. " I've a good mind to tell you to get out."

" The merest hint will be accepted," Bobby told him. " Even a gesture towards the door and I'm off."

Hayes nearly choked. Bobby watched him unsympathetically. Hayes gasped, gurgled, swore. He said finally:

" What's your game, anyhow ? "

" The truth," Bobby answered, and he said again: " The truth."

Hayes hesitated, and seemed to come to a decision. " Now you're here, you had better stay," he said.

" Better the policeman that you know than others that you know not of," Bobby suggested.

" I thought they would send one of their own lot along," Hayes muttered.

" And I've come instead," Bobby answered. " You builded better than you knew."

All this had passed in a kind of outer hall or lobby that was just within the front door, separated by another door from the main hall that had also been intended for a small lounge. Through this Hayes now led the way, past the stairs, to the side passage that ran past the room he called his study to the garden door. He said over his shoulder:

" I'm going to bed. You can do what you like. If anything happens, you'll be on the spot. I don't suppose it will, now you're here. I'll have a drink first."

He opened the study door and went in.

" What's up ? " Bobby asked, for Hayes was standing on the threshold staring, gasping, making strange noises in his throat.

Bobby, whose own nerves were taut, looked over his shoulder, expecting to see he hardly knew what. Something strange, daunting, formidable, perhaps. Armed enemies, it might be, or some imminent threat of danger or of death.

But to his eyes all seemed perfectly normal. A fire burned in the grate. The lights were switched on. On the table stood a bottle of whisky, soda, glasses. Pushed out of the way on a side table was a tray with plates and the remnants of a meal of cold meat and tinned fruit. A pile of torn-up letters and bills and other papers was on the floor near the fireplace, and more papers had evidently been burned. Bobby said:

" What is it? Anything wrong? "

Hayes pointed a shaking hand at an empty glass on the table.

" Look there," he stammered. " Look."

" That glass? " Bobby asked. " What about it? "

Hayes looked at him wildly.

" It was full," he said in a strangled voice. " It was full when I went out, when you knocked."

" Are you sure? " Bobby asked.

" I had just filled it," Hayes said. " I was putting in a splash of soda when I heard you." He looked at Bobby again. " It's empty now," he said.

Empty it certainly was. Bobby looked at it thoughtfully. He did not touch it, but stooped and smelled it, and then, taking out his handkerchief and holding it very carefully, he put it aside on the top of the wireless cabinet.

" There may be finger-prints on it," he said. " Seems as if there must be someone else in the house."

Hayes had collapsed on one of the chairs.

" Who . . . why . . . ? " he muttered. " There can't be. Every door and window's locked."

" If someone drank your whisky while we were talking," Bobby said, " there must be someone—well, someone who did drink it. That," he explained meditatively, " is what is called deductive reasoning. Anyhow, we had better have a look round. Coming? " he added, as his companion showed no sign of moving.

" I . . I think we had better stop here," muttered Hayes. " What's the good . . . if anyone . . . well, we are all right here . . . let it alone."

Bobby shook his head.

" Wouldn't look well," he explained, " if I had to report to-morrow the house had been broken into while I was sitting still, doing nothing."

" It wouldn't matter," Hayes said. " There's nothing anywhere else—nothing that matters."

" Dear me," observed Bobby, " that's interesting. Means that anything your expected visitors are likely to be after is in here ? More deductive reasoning."

Hayes still muttered protests. He was evidently very unwilling to be left alone, but Bobby insisted that the rest of the house must be searched. Necessary, he repeated, to root out anyone who might be there in hiding. Hayes could lock the door, and at any suspicious sound he could ring the bell and Bobby would return at once, even if he himself had heard nothing. Bobby made sure the window was fastened securely, and a glance round the room told him there was in it no possible place of concealment.

" I shan't be long," he told the still protesting Hayes. " Why not come along, if you don't feel like being left alone ? "

Hayes, however, preferred solitude to the proposed expedition. He adopted the suggested precaution of locking the door as soon as Bobby left the room, and Bobby listened thoughtfully to the sound of the key turning in the lock.

" Scared all right, and pretty badly, too," he told himself. " That part's genuine enough, whatever else he's up to."

Carefully and methodically Bobby proceeded to go through the house, paying special attention to outside doors and windows, and, when he could find the key, locking the door of each room he had entered as he left it again. The back door was secured by two strong-looking bolts he withdrew to make sure they had not been tampered with. He looked in all the kitchen cupboards and store-places. He went into the dining-room, and there even looked under the table over which was a damask cover that hung nearly to the ground. The drawing-room, he found, had never been furnished, but he saw the bolt of the French windows was pushed home. Neither of these rooms had keys in their doors. Upstairs, he went into all the bedrooms, looked everywhere, took the opportunity in Hayes's own room of giving a glance inside the drawers of the different pieces of furniture. There was plenty of clothing in them still, so that Hayes had apparently not as yet done much packing. In one of the drawers, thrust among some shirts in what seemed but a half-hearted effort at concealment, he found an automatic pistol.

Lifting it with every precaution, he examined it carefully. He had no note with him of the registered number of Mr. Moffatt's lost automatic, but in make, calibre, in the dent on the barrel and slightly damaged foresight Noll had spoken of, it seemed to correspond with that weapon. Bobby placed it in one of his cellophane envelopes and then put it in his pocket.

By now he was convinced there was no other living being in the house, and he returned downstairs, wondering whether Hayes had been allowing his imagination to run away with him, or whether, as seemed more likely, the whole thing had been a trick to obtain a few moments' solitude wherein to carry out some operation or another for which he desired no witness.

" No one in the house," Bobby assured Hayes when he had been readmitted to the study, " but I found this in one of the drawers in your room. Looks to me like Mr. Moffatt's missing automatic the murder was committed with."

Hayes stared and gaped for a moment, then jumped to his feet in a passion of fear and anger.

"That's a lie!" he shouted. "You never did! If you did, you put it there yourself."

Bobby shook his head.

"I found it where I said," he answered, "and I certainly did not put it there."

"Well, someone did," Hayes repeated. "If you think you've got something on me, you haven't. I didn't shoot Bennett, and, what's more, I can prove I didn't, and I can prove who did. I've the evidence right here in the house; it's the same man who planted that thing where you found it."

"Who's that?" Bobby asked.

A slight noise at the window made them both turn. Someone was looking in at them from outside, through a gap where the curtains did not fully meet. The face, pressed closely against the glass, was clearly visible.

"Noll Moffatt," Hayes cried.

CHAPTER XXIX

CHASE AND PURSUIT

INSTANTLY THE FACE VANISHED, withdrawn into the night. Bobby jumped to the window, jerked aside the curtains, threw up the sash. He heard Hayes shouting to him to stop, not to go out; that it was dangerous out there. Without heeding him, or his final wailing appeal not to be left alone, Bobby flung a leg over the sill, jumped out. It was only a drop of some four or five feet. He ran forward, sideways, paused, ran back, and then on again. He found himself blundering across flower-beds, colliding with shrubs and bushes. In the darkness he could see nothing. The moon had not yet risen. No stars showed. The light from the open window poured out into the night, cutting into it, as it were, leaving on each side the darkness more intense.

Noll had vanished as though he had never been. Bobby half wondered if their glimpse of that pale, pressed face against the window-glass had been a kind of joint illusion. He stood still and listened. The air was very quiet, full of all those small innumerable sounds that together make up the strange stillness of the night. Far away a dog barked and was silent. A bat, or a beetle perhaps, went blundering by. From somewhere near, quite near, came the sound of running footsteps as of one in desperate haste. Bobby began to run in the direction whence he thought the sounds came. They ceased. Bobby paused to listen again. From behind, whence he had come, he heard a faint and cautious tread, as of one who went in deadly fear of being overheard.

The light from the open window suddenly vanished. Someone had closed the window, drawn the curtains.

Uncertain what to do, whether to follow where the desperate runner had seemed to pass, to return to seek that other who went so silently, so cautiously, Bobby stood still. It was all quiet again, quiet and very still. Now the silence seemed complete. It was as though those running footsteps, that stealthy tread, had hushed all other sounds; as though the house, the garden, the surrounding night, all alike waited in a breathless pause for what might happen next.

Someone not very far away cried aloud, as if in fear or pain. A more distant voice called out twice over:

"Take care, take care."

"Who is it? Who is there?" Bobby shouted, and then was inclined to be sorry he had so announced his presence.

There came no answer, nor was the warning cry repeated, or that cry he had taken to be of fear or of pain. As he had spoken once, he thought he would try again. He shouted at the full force of his lungs:

"There is a police officer here—police."

He thought he heard someone laugh and that was all.

He moved in the direction whence he thought this last sound had seemed to come. He ran into a growth of rhododendrons and then blundered into a holly hedge, with no resultant improvement to his temper, which was becoming sadly ruffled. Backing away from that prickly hedge, his foot caught in some obstruction and he fell. He got to his feet again and stood listening. He had the absurd idea that all the garden was shaking with secret laughter at his expense. He found his cheek was cut and was bleeding slightly. He thought to himself:

" I'm getting scared. Nerves. Never knew I had any. I'm doing no good here. I'll get back to the house."

Then he thought:

" I was a silly fool to leave it. Most likely I shall get told so when I report."

He began to make his way back towards the house. It stood up black and heavy in the night, a huge overpowering shadow with no glimmer showing anywhere, a dead thing uninhabited in the night, it seemed, and yet Bobby was aware of an impression that it was the scene of fierce and swift activities, of uncontrolled passions that had broken at last through the veneer of civilised life. The garden seemed to have fallen quiet now; it was as if all that was happening had become concentrated on the dark and silent house. He began to run. He nearly fell again. The treachery of the darkness made him slacken his pace. The thought came to him that most likely he would find the house closed, barred and shuttered against him, so that he would have to remain without, shut out and helpless.

It had been foolish, he told himself again, to yield to his first impulse that had sent him running in pursuit of Noll Moffatt, a pursuit he might have realised the darkness would render futile. A nice fool he would look if, for instance, the deputy chief constable arrived before his time and had to be told that he, Bobby, had been locked out.

He reached the wall of the house. The study window

he had jumped from was a little further on—to the right, he thought. He groped his way along by the wall, got tangled up in a border planted with rose-bushes, and a beam of light shot out suddenly a little way ahead. The curtains over the study window had been drawn a trifle aside. Someone was peeping out into the night. Hayes, presumably, anxious for Bobby's return, but no more anxious, Bobby thought, for that return than Bobby was himself.

He hurried on. He reached the window. The curtain, drawn aside, gave him a clear view of the lighted interior. Someone was standing there between the half-open door and the table. It was Noll Moffatt. He looked very pale, and in one hand he held a pistol. By the table, near the chair Hayes had been sitting in, lay a still and crumpled human form. By it was the bottle of whisky, overturned, its contents spreading out in a slowly increasing pool.

Bobby leaped to a standing position on the window-sill. With his elbow he smashed one of the upper panes. The glass fell in a tinkling shower; the crash sounded like an exploding bomb. The thought crossed Bobby's mind that perhaps Noll would shoot. If he did, he could not want an easier target. Bobby put his hand through the opening he had made, unlatched the window Hayes had evidently fastened after Bobby's precipitate exit, and flung it up. He tore the curtain down and jumped through into the room.

All this had taken not much more than thirty or forty seconds, but that had been long enough for Noll Moffatt to vanish. The door was still quivering, though, with the vibration from the bang wherewith it had been closed.

Bobby turned to the crumpled form lying there, supine, by the chair. He turned it over. He saw that it was not

Hayes, but Pegley, unconscious, bleeding from a contused wound in the forehead.

Bobby merely gaped for a moment or two. In the first paralysis of his astonishment he did not even ask himself how Pegley had got there. It came into his mind that he must be suffering from some strange illusion. He looked all round, almost expecting to find that the room, too, had endured some strange transformation. But it at least was still the same as it had been before, though the man prostrate there was Pegley and not Hayes.

Bobby put a hand upon the table, as if to keep hold upon some solid fact that would not change and alter. This person, this Pegley-not-Hayes, was not dead, anyhow. He had been knocked out by that blow on the head, but, possibly, if he could be revived, he could give some explanation of his appearance and what had happened. But then there was Noll Moffatt, too—seen twice, so he could be no dream—and what was he doing here? Bobby was still standing there in this kind of frenzy of bewilderment when he heard the door open.

He swung round instantly. In the doorway Reeves was standing, calm and imperturbable as a well-trained servant should be, neat, unruffled, as if he had just come in with the letters or to announce the arrival of a guest. Bobby blinked at him. For a moment or two they remained looking at each other. Then, without a word, without a change in his expression of the butler carrying out his ordinary duties, Reeves stepped back, closed the door gently. Bobby heard quite plainly the key turn in the lock.

That galvanised him into life. With a kind of muffled roar he leaped across the room, seized the door-knob, turned it, shook the door with all his force and in vain, for it was securely locked.

He stood back a little way and hurled himself against it. With no effect. It was a strong, well-made door—a pre-war door, in fact, of the time when solid work and wood were still put into construction. Most post-war doors would have gone down before the fury of his assault, but this held fast. It had not even panels to offer a point of attack, but was all one solid piece.

He gave up the effort to smash it down by his own strength and looked about the room for some implement to aid him. He found none. Even the fire-irons in the grate were small, finicking modernities with no weight to them. In a fury he pounded on the door with his fists and shouted, and then was ashamed of so futile a display of temper and of helplessness.

He found himself beginning to wonder if he had really seen Reeves or if he had dreamed him. He turned to make sure it was in fact Pegley lying there, unconscious and bleeding, by the chair that Hayes had been sitting in just before.

It was all, he thought, exactly what one would expect to happen in a madhouse suddenly deprived of doctors, nurses, and keepers.

What had happened to Hayes? Who had attacked Pegley, and why? What was Reeves of all living people doing here, and why did he continue to look so exactly like the butler that he was? And what was Noll Moffatt up to?

Standing looking bewilderedly from fastened door to prostrate Pegley, Bobby reminded himself ruefully that he had come here to-night precisely and exactly because he had thought developments were possible.

But not developments like these.

What was happening now was outside, he felt, the

boundary of sane explanation. It was because of that belief of his that events were drawing of themselves to some unknown crisis that he had asked Colonel Warden's deputy, the chief superintendent, for permission to come alone, and why he had been careful to arrive at dusk and as unobtrusively as possible. It had seemed to him a good idea to allow full scope for their development to whatever plans might be in progress; and so again he had not wished to be accompanied by anyone in uniform. For he knew well how much virtue there is in a uniform, how intimidating, how authoritative in quality a uniform can be, containing, indeed, in itself so strange a magic it can even make a dictator and throw whole nations into thraldom.

But now Bobby felt that the presence of a constable or two in uniform would be a help, and, though the chief superintendent had promised either to come himself, or at least to send help, before midnight, that hour was still far distant.

He made another attack on the door, again without result. No doubt he could break it down in time, but time the task would take, and time was precisely what he could not spare, he who had no knowledge of what might or might not be happening on the door's further side. He turned to the window. Exit there would be easy enough, but would he be any better off outside? He might find all the rest of the house secure against him, and even this window barred and barricaded if he tried to return by it. Again the vision came into his mind of the chief superintendent on his arrival finding him standing helplessly outside, on the doorstep.

As he hesitated there broke out a wild tumult of noise, a rush of feet, shouting, a confused and general clamour, wood breaking and splintering, glass smashing, blows given and returned, then someone screaming wildly, incoherently. Bobby turned towards the open window. Anything was better than standing helplessly there, listening and wondering.

He heard someone at the door and stopped abruptly, half way to the window. The door flew open and a man rushed in. It was Thoms. Bobby jumped forward to stop him. The impact and impetus of Thoms's rush flung him aside. Thoms seemed hardly even aware of Bobby's presence. He made a dive through the open window and Bobby heard him running fast as the darkness hid him.

" Oh, well, now then," Bobby said aloud.

He ran out and along the study passage into the hall. It was quiet and deserted now. Clear enough though were the signs of the struggle or pursuit Bobby had heard. Furniture was upset and broken, crockery and vases were lying about in fragments; a gaping breach in the banisters showed where three or four had been broken off, the door into the small room used as a cloak-room hung drunkenly on one hinge, the front door was wide open, and through it from the night without came a sound of more shouting, more running to and fro.

" Mr. Hayes ! Hayes ! " Bobby shouted.

There was no answer, and Bobby ran out through the open door to take part in the lunatic pursuit and chasing to and fro that seemed in progress without. He ran down the drive, keeping to the gravelled path. From his left there rang out pistol shots in swift succession, and he saw how little darting flames stabbed through the darkness.

Someone screamed.

Bobby ran wildly in the direction whence the shots had come.

Another shot rang out, and then silence dropped, dropped as the curtain drops when the play is over and it is time to go home.

The holly hedge again checked Bobby's progress. He turned back towards the drive, listening intently, walking slowly and carefully. In the silence that had followed on that earlier tumult he thought he heard small steps creeping slowly, not far off. He turned in that direction and caught his foot and fell full length. It was a body he had tripped upon. He could not tell whose it was. He felt for a match. By its light he was able to recognise the blood-stained face of Hayes. Those creeping steps were nearer now, and Bobby thought he saw near by a shadow move. He leaped and seized it in a grip that was not gentle, for indeed he was in no gentle mood. A muffled scream and he relaxed at once his hold.

" The devil ! " he exclaimed.

" No, it's me," a low voice answered—the voice of Molly Oulton.

CHAPTER XXX

ARREST AT LAST

FOR THIS NIGHT AT LEAST Bobby's capacity for surprise was entirely exhausted. In a matter-of-fact tone, as one greeting a casual acquaintance in the street, he said:

" Oh, it's you. What are you doing here ? "

" I'm looking for Noll," she explained, equally matter of fact. " Have you seen him ? "

" He's up there somewhere," Bobby answered, nodding towards the house. " What's he doing here ? "

" Henrietta sent him," Molly answered. " She hadn't any right to. She wanted him to stop Teddy. You can't stop Teddy, he's so stupid and pig-headed. Reeves told me, and I told Henrietta, and she got Noll to go after them, and so I came for him."

" Oh, yes," said Bobby, trying to get this clear. " Yes. Have you seen your brother ? He's Teddy, isn't he ? "

" Well, of course," she said, and before she could continue, at a little distance, the headlamps of a car blazed suddenly, making in the vast ocean of night a little island of bright light.

Its radiance hardly reached them where they stood, but in its full glare there showed the figure of a man, quite still, as if astonished and held fast by that sudden beam of light flung at him from the darkness.

"There he is," said Molly calmly. "Teddy, Teddy," she called.

Teddy—Thoms—Oulton—turned at the summons. At the same instant another pistol-shot rang out, and Bobby heard plainly the wicked, evil scream of the bullet as it flew by, between him and Molly, snarling, as it were, its disappointment that its message of death had failed. Simultaneously Bobby tripped Molly up, and pushed her, as she fell, under the shelter of a near-by bush.

He heard her cry out in surprise and anger at this rough handling; he snapped an order to her to lie still; he ran towards that bright illumined oblong patch the motor headlights made and that he saw was now empty.

He heard a hoarse, passionate voice shout:

"Give them back, quick, now, or you're getting yours. Hand over or——"

There was a note of finality, of triumph almost and achieved certainty, in that hoarse voice that made it seem the speaker knew success was his at last, that the end had come, and had come as he had wished. But the answer—the instant answer—was a snarl of defiance, and Bobby felt and knew that the reply to that would be the report of a pistol fired at close quarters, fired from so near that to miss would be impossible, death given and received—even in that moment of suspense he wondered, given by whom, by whom received? For that hoarse voice he had heard, distorted by rage and threat and triumph, he had failed to recognise.

But what he actually heard was unexpected. For there sounded no loud summons to death to come, obedient and swift, at the pressing of a trigger, but merely a sharp, snapping sound, as of an ineffective hammer driving home a useless tack.

Then followed an oath, screamed aloud in frantic surprise and disappointment, and hard upon it a sound half-laugh, half-sob, full of a wild relief. Bobby realised that the pistol had been empty, its cartridges fired away, its magazine exhausted. The thought came to him that the automatic of our advanced civilisation has, however, its disadvantages when compared with the club or knife of our merely barbarian ancestors. Club and knife do not exhaust their deadliness in their wielder's hands or turn abruptly useless. He heard a voice, apparently that of the man who had just laughed:

"Well, now then, come and get them if you can."

A curse, a shout, a sound of stamping and of struggling told that the challenge had been accepted. Into the island of light that lay between impenetrable walls of darkness came now two stumbling, interlaced, and struggling bodies, locked in such an ecstasy of hate and combat they had no heed of Bobby, though he, too, was now within that same radius of light. They rolled over each other on the ground, they tore at each other, they clawed, they fought as the beasts fight, with all nature had given them to fight with and with nothing else. Bobby stood for a moment as they rolled and fought at his feet. They knew no more that he was there than they knew aught else in the frenzy of hate and fear that held them in their primeval lust of combat. No sound came from them but their heavy breathing; their limbs were intertwined, their hands clawed at each other's throats. So closely interwoven were their bodies by their hate, it seemed as if nothing but death would part them. One rolled somehow uppermost and with a gasp of triumph got his hands about the other's throat. The next instant they had rolled over again, and now the other was on top and striking wildly down with his clenched fist on his adversary's head.

" Oh, stop them, why don't you ? " Molly's voice said at Bobby's side. " You've torn my frock," she added reproachfully. " Oh, stop them, please."

Bobby jumped forward, only just in time. The one of the two wrestlers who was now the uppermost had somehow caught up a heavy stone and with it was about to batter out his opponent's brains. Bobby only just managed to grab wrist and stone, wrench the stone away, fling it aside.

" That's enough," he said.

The man whose blow he had arrested screamed a curse at Bobby and struck out at him viciously. Bobby drew back. The other who had been undermost, whose life Bobby's intervention had probably saved, wrenched himself free, got somehow to his feet. He stood for a moment quite still, breathing heavily, a little bewildered. Bobby recognised him as Thoms. He saw now that the other was Larson. Larson did not seem to recognise Bobby. He was standing close to the car, and abruptly he put back his hand and snatched up a big spanner that had been lying within. His face was distorted with his fury; his eyes were frantic; there was froth and blood dripping from his mouth some chance blow had cut. He seemed to see Bobby all at once, and, lifting the spanner, ran at him, yelling as he ran. Bobby stepped sideways and with one clear, straight, well-delivered blow sent him crashing to the ground.

An instinct made him turn. Thoms was running at him now. Somehow he had picked up the empty automatic. He held it like a club. He, too, blinded with fury and the strange rage of conflict, did not appear to have recognised Bobby, perhaps even did not distinguish him from Larson with whom he had been at such deadly grips. Bobby gathered himself together, meaning to meet that charge with a flying tackle, when Molly stepped between them.

"I'll tell Henrietta," she said severely. "You wait till Henrietta knows."

Thoms stopped short in his rush. He looked at her bewilderedly and passed one hand across his face, as if wiping something away.

"Oh, well," he said, "she can jaw till doomsday, but I've got 'em all right." He looked at Bobby as if seeing him clearly for the first time. "Oh, Lord, it's the cop," he said, and turned and ran.

"Here, come, I say," protested Bobby.

From the darkness a voice floated back:

"I say, Molly, don't be a sneak."

"Yes, I shall," said Molly determinedly.

Bobby turned to help Larson, who was slowly getting to his feet, still more than a little dazed from that tremendous blow with which Bobby had sent him flying.

"Hold up. All right now?" Bobby said to him, and then added to Molly: "Does that mean your brother's got the bonds?"

Molly did not answer. Instead, Larson said:

"My bonds . . . bearer bonds . . . he's got them, robbed me . . fifteen thousand pounds' worth. He robbed me, got me down and robbed me."

"You've been robbed?" Bobby asked.

"That's right," Larson said. "It's my head. A tree fell, or something . . . I can't remember." He felt gingerly the spot where Bobby's fist and his skull had made contact. "No, it was him, I suppose. He must have had a club or something."

"Think so?" said Bobby, flattered to the very depths of his being. One could almost hear him purr. Ambitious schemes flashed through his mind of entering for the next police boxing championships at the Albert Hall. " It was a bit of a whack," he admitted modestly. " The timing does it," he explained.

Mr. Larson was in no mood to appreciate technicalities of the ring. He was in fact still finding some difficulty with an earth that seemed much less firm than usual; inclined, indeed, to tie itself up in knots under his feet. He sat down on the footboard of the car, though even that seemed less steady than are well-conducted footboards as a general rule. All the same, he felt safer there. He said:

" Why aren't you doing something? What are police for? Get after him. Why don't you? "

" You mean you intend to charge him with theft? " Bobby asked.

" Yes; robbery, assault. Couldn't you see for yourself? " retorted Mr. Larson indignantly. He felt his aching head again. " Violent, brutal attack," he complained. " Theft and robbery; highway robbery."

" Oh, it isn't," interposed Molly indignantly. " I don't know how you can say such things! If he means the bond things and Teddy's got them," she explained to Bobby, " then they're ours—mother's, I mean. Teddy's got them back, that's all. He said he would."

" Sounds more like a civil action," Bobby remarked. " Ownership disputed, apparently. Of course," he added to Larson, " if you can prove ownership and forcible removal from your custody, no doubt you could proceed criminally."

" So I will, so I will," declared Larson. " I'll see he gets penal servitude for this."

" They're mother's. You can't. They aren't yours;

they never were," protested Molly. " You tell the most awful stories," she added gravely.

" In the meantime," Bobby said, " you might explain what you are doing here and what all this is about."

" Doing your job; helping you out," Mr. Larson told him sternly. " This is what I get for it. Robbed and assaulted." He paused for sympathy. None came. In an even angrier tone he went on: " I could see you were just blundering along, doing nothing, getting nowhere, just as you are now. I tell you I've been robbed of £15,000 and all you do is to stand there with your hands in your pockets and talk. Police, indeed. Same with the murder. Doing nothing; getting nowhere; hopelessly incompetent. I felt I had to do something."

" Yes ? " said Bobby as he paused.

" I felt I had to do something," Larson repeated. " I don't choose to remain under even the faintest touch of possible suspicion of being connected with such an affair in any way whatever. There are some people in the City only too ready to whisper stories. Get some gossip started about me and they might have a chance to get some of the business I handle. I couldn't afford it. I knew perfectly well where there was hidden conclusive proof of the guilt of the real murderer. I knew your out-of-date, incompetent, muddled official methods would never get it, and I knew it might be destroyed any moment. I decided to act. I entered the house where I knew it was hidden." He put his hand in one of the pockets of the car and brought out an envelope. " If you look at what's inside there," he said, " you'll find something to interest even your slow official mind."

" Photographs ? " asked Bobby meekly.

" Yes. I've only had time to give them the merest

glance, but you'll find snaps taken by Hayes of Mrs. O'Brien and Bennett in Battling Copse that afternoon. You remember a lipstick was found there? Hers. You remember a bit of film wrapper—wasn't it?—was found there, too? Hayes dropped it. I dare say he hadn't intended murder then. He wanted the snap for proof Mrs. O'Brien's husband was still alive and that she was meeting him on the quiet. That divorce of hers wasn't even near valid; wouldn't have held water even in American courts, or Mexican either. Hayes thought that snap would let him out of any promise of marriage she might have wheedled out of him. Most likely there was some sort of row afterwards. Perhaps Bennett tried to get the snap away. I don't know."

"How can you prove the photo was taken that day?" Bobby asked, studying it intently.

"Because of the hat Mrs. O'Brien is wearing, quite plainly shown," Larson answered. "You can easily get proof it was only delivered that morning and only worn by her that afternoon. She never wore it on any other occasion, and her movements can easily be checked. And you can soon satisfy yourself that that snap comes from a type of camera Hayes has and no one else owns about here. Proof absolutely convincing that Hayes was there that afternoon watching Mrs. O'Brien and Bennett just before the murder was committed, and with no one else near. Good enough?"

"Seems good enough," agreed Bobby, putting away the photograph with great care.

They heard someone else coming. It was Hayes, pale and excited, uncertain on his feet, wiping the blood from his face. He shouted to Bobby:

"I've been robbed—knocked down and robbed."

" You too ? " Bobby said. " Bearer bonds to the value of £15,000 ? "

" You knew ? You've got them back ? " Hayes cried.

Bobby shook his head.

" Oh, no," he said.

" Then I'll lodge a complaint," Hayes told him angrily. " I'll see what your superiors think of this. I'll sue them. You were there for protection and this is what happens. Disgraceful. I'll take it into the courts. I'll see my solicitors. Gross negligence. Or worse."

" Worse, if you ask me," Bobby agreed. " Who do you think robbed you ? "

Hayes pointed to Larson.

" Him," he said. " He did it; planned it and all. He's got them."

" I don't think he has," Bobby said, " and, if you accuse him of theft, he has just accused you of murder."

As he spoke he took from his pocket a pair of handcuffs.

" That's right," said Larson approvingly.

Hayes gave a kind of strangled gasp.

Bobby fitted the handcuffs neatly to Larson's wrists.

" It's you I'm going to charge," he said.

CHAPTER XXXI

CONCLUSION

ATTENDANCE AT HIS OFFICE was still forbidden Colonel Warden, who, indeed, had not yet been allowed to leave his room. But, doctor or no doctor, wifely anxieties or none, he had insisted on receiving in person Bobby's report. Now he was sitting up in bed, looking more than a little worried, when Bobby was shown in. He said to him:

"Are you sure we can hold Larson? It's proof we want—proof, evidence, something a jury can see for itself, not just logic or reasoning or anything like that. Something they can touch and handle."

"That's what we've got, sir," Bobby answered. "I think myself the case would have been good enough without, but there it is, proof anyone can touch and handle as much as they want, and the odd thing is, Larson himself gave it us."

"Larson?" exclaimed the colonel, startled. "You mean—Larson?"

"Yes, sir. But for him we might never have got it. This photo, sir."

He produced the photograph Larson had given to him and handed it to the colonel.

"And then, too," Bobby said, "we've traced the

lady's cycle he bought and had in readiness for his escape from Battling Copse after the murder. Pegley and Hayes have both been talking as well. I've had chats with them both, and I've paid another visit to the Towers Poultry Farm. Pegley is badly scared and pretty sick, too, at the way Larson knocked him out when they found the bonds where they were hidden in Hayes's study. He's told as much as he thinks won't incriminate him in the conspiracy he and Larson were engaged in to get hold of Mr. Moffatt's money. Hayes has talked a bit, too, but he's more cautious, more dangerous altogether. Pegley's only the jackal type. He knew nothing of the murder at the time, but he suspected Larson and was afraid of being implicated with him. That's why he was so relieved when he thought after our visit that it was Noll Moffatt who was guilty."

But the colonel was hardly listening. He was intent on the photograph Bobby had given him.

"Bennett and the O'Brien woman talking together, isn't it?" the colonel asked, studying it. "In Battling Copse? Is that someone else behind those bushes?"

"Yes, sir," answered Bobby. "Larson himself. It will be plainer in the enlargement, though through a magnifying-glass his face is plain enough. What's more, he's holding a pistol in his hand—the light just catches it under that branch. When it's enlarged, the bent foresight and dented barrel will be quite plain and will identify it as Mr. Moffatt's missing automatic we know was used. Larson had plenty of opportunities for getting hold of it. Miss Moffatt saw him once, looking in the drawer where it was kept, though probably he didn't take it then. Most likely he only saw it that time and afterwards remembered where it was."

"You say Larson himself gave you the photo? What on earth . . . ?"

"He didn't realise he himself was shown on it; he was trying to implicate Hayes, and at the same time provide an excuse for his presence at Way Side. He knew—Mrs. O'Brien told him—Hayes had taken a photo of her and Bennett together. He did not know, as we did, that Hayes had a perfectly good alibi for the actual moment of the shooting—thanks to the egg gatherer's testimony. All Hayes had wanted was actual evidence that Mrs. O'Brien still had a husband living and was meeting him in secret. The moment he got that by snapping them together he slipped away, and, luckily for him, met the egg gatherer. Larson had no idea he had been caught in the same snap; he didn't realise how plainly his face showed behind the bush he thought covered him. Hayes knew it, of course; knew it as soon as he developed the snap. He was holding the evidence up, partly to keep a hold on Larson and partly because gentlemen like Mr. Hayes like to keep as far away from police inquiries as they can. But chiefly, I think, because he wanted us to arrest Thoms. He was getting nervous about Thoms."

"Where does Thoms come in?" the colonel asked. "I don't understand that. You say his name is really Oulton?"

"It's a long story," Bobby answered. "Begins years ago, when money was easy in the United States, and if a man was swindled out of a few thousand dollars he didn't bother much. He merely bought some shares and waited for the rise they all took for granted in those days was quite certain, to sell them at a profit and get back all he had lost. Larson, Pegley, Bennett, and Hayes were all in the game. Denver seems to have been their headquarters, at least for Larson and Pegley, who generally worked together. Bennett and Hayes were often in Denver, but generally operated outside, in the smaller towns. Larson was always a bit too much of the gunman, and, from what the F.B.I. people say, he made Denver finally too hot for him. Protection broke down, and he had to clear out, though he still kept in touch with Pegley. They worked the same game. Pegley made the opening moves. Larson came on the scene later, won the victim's confidence in some way. Sometimes he did that by giving a warning against Pegley; once or twice apparently he pretended to catch out Pegley playing a crooked game at poker. Pegley faded away after that and Larson was established as the honest friend. Afterwards, of course, Pegley got his share of the loot. Larson seems to have worked both tricks with Mr. Moffatt, by the way—warning him against Pegley and making a pretence of exposing crooked play at cards. After Larson had to leave Denver, he spent a good deal of time on the Atlantic boats, looking out for likely victims. He was always very careful to make a good impression on board. He got to be known as a wealthy business man with influential connections on both sides of the Atlantic. It was on these voyages that he got in touch with Mr. Oulton, and, later on, with Mr. Moffatt.

" That was some time ago. Men like Larson are often prepared to wait years. Difficult to believe that a man you have known for long enough as a wealthy business man, extremely correct and discreet, is really a long-range swindler waiting his chance to trap you. It seems Oulton was the easier prospect. Moffatt was put in cold storage, so to say. Oulton was cleaned out successfully. Larson and Pegley got nearly every penny he possessed. Then he was found dead, with a revolver in his hand. It passed for suicide. Almost certainly Larson shot him to prevent him from prosecuting. There is no doubt Oulton had realised by then that he had been swindled, and meant to take steps against Larson. I've been at the Towers Farm again, too, and his widow, Mrs. Oulton, has shown me letters that make that plain. They were some written from New York when he first began to suspect he had been swindled. They are almost incoherent—I suppose the poor devil was pretty well out of his mind with excitement and worry. The Oultons were in a pretty helpless position after his death. They knew hardly any details. Mr. Oulton had been persuaded to consent to a high degree of secrecy. They knew the name, Bennett, but nothing about him. They knew, too, that a Mr Moffatt had been mentioned. They knew, again, that the man who called himself Bennett, really Larson—he went by many names; in this case the assumed name, Bennett, seems to have been part of the secrecy Oulton was persuaded to agree to on the usual plea that, if Larson's own name was used, envious rivals and competitors would be put on the track of the operations on the market supposed to be in train—they knew that once or twice he had motored to this neighbourhood. Most likely Larson had given Mr. Moffatt's name as a partner or friend of his. He had found out that Mr. Moffatt was a man of some position, and any claim of friendship with him would help to impress Oulton.

" By this time both Hayes and Bennett had also found America a bit too hot, and, after the slump, a little less like a Tom Tiddler's ground for picking up gold and silver. They came back to England. Bennett heard Larson had been using his name, and, guessing some game was on, tried to join in. Larson didn't want him, and from what he says now—he has talked a little since he knew how the Hayes photo was evidence against him—he even threatened Bennett with giving information to us about him. He knew the Denver police wanted Bennett. Bennett told him two could play that card, but, all the same, thought it prudent to stand out. But he told Hayes Larson was playing a rich sucker. Bennett was in funds at the time, and didn't want to run risks while he had money in his pocket to enjoy himself with. Hayes did a bit of spying, found out there were funds in a Paris bank Oulton had refused to touch and Larson and Pegley thought it best to leave alone considering the much bigger prize they were working for. When Hayes heard of Oulton's death—both he and Bennett suspected it was murder, and Larson's work—he saw his opportunity. By the help of a forged authority and through the negligence of the Paris bank's clerks—perhaps there was bribery as well—Hayes succeeded in getting hold of the American bearer bonds in which Mr. Oulton had invested the whole of his wife's fortune. The idea was to dodge paying income-tax. There are plenty of business men who consider themselves perfectly honourable but are perfectly willing to swindle the income-tax if they can manage it by any legal dodge—and plenty of clever lawyers to think up one-man companies, sham repayments of loans, bond washing, and so on, to help them. Anyhow, Hayes got hold of the bonds. Mrs. Oulton had no way of identifying them—she didn't even know what concerns had issued them—and Hayes, always in character, forgot to inform Bennett of his success. He vanished instead into the country, meaning to live there in peaceful retirement, with coupon clipping as his recreation.

" Young Oulton—Thoms—wasn't sitting down to it

though. He traced the Mr. Moffatt mentioned in the letters to Sevens, and at first suspected him of having the bonds. His half-sister, Miss Henrietta, wanted to start a poultry farm, as something had to be done to earn a living for herself and her mother and sister, and Thoms, while making inquiries about Mr. Moffatt, came across the farm she has now and suggested she should take it. It was quite suitable, and it would give him a good opportunity for watching Mr. Moffatt and waiting a chance if possible to recover the bonds. But then it began to dawn on him that he was on the wrong track, and that Mr. Moffatt knew nothing about what had been happening.

" But the same discoveries that convinced Thoms—young Oulton, that is—that Mr. Moffatt had had nothing to do with it put him on the track of Mr. Hayes. He managed to get employment with Hayes as chauffeur with the idea of watching him. Then, visiting his mother and sisters, he heard of the Way Side property, and mentioned it to his employer, who was, he knew, looking out for a secluded country residence. Hayes liked the place, and settled down with the idea of spending the rest of his life in peaceful seclusion, with nothing to do but clip coupons off bearer bonds. He never attempted to sell them, for fear of being asked questions, and the income was quite comfortable.

" Two things went wrong with his idea. The country bored him. Mrs. O'Brien, his housekeeper—really Mrs. Bennett—wanted him to marry her. Finally he began to get suspicious of Thoms. Thoms had been displaying a certain curiosity, wandering about upstairs and so on.

" All this time Larson was pursuing his schemes, with Mr. Moffatt's big holding in consols as his objective. The first step was to win Mr. Moffatt's confidence. On one of the Atlantic voyages Larson, who had been watching Moffatt carefully and knew a good deal about him—not difficult; Mr. Moffatt talked a good deal; it was something Mr. Moffatt said in a liner's smoking-room that first put Larson on the trail of his consols holding—found that Moffatt had been losing fairly heavily at poker. To Larson, losing money at poker had only one meaning—that the game was crooked and that Mr. Moffatt had fallen in with card-sharpers. That seemed to Larson a heaven-sent opportunity to win Moffatt's confidence by rescuing him—besides further establishing himself with the steamship companies by exposing the supposed card-sharpers. As a matter of fact, Mr. Moffatt had been playing with two extremely important and wealthy financiers, both of them really influential and well-known men, but travelling under assumed names to attend some conference in New York the papers were not wanted to know about—something about meat supplies. Larson had no idea of that. He told Moffatt he was being swindled, joined in the game one night, and soon saw the game was perfectly straight. A bit awkward; so, to prove his case and keep his influence with Moffatt, he proceeded to make it crooked by stacking the cards, but in Moffatt's favour, not in his own. Moffatt won quite a bit that night—all he had lost before and some more as well. Larson told him what he had done, explained that he had hoisted the card-sharpers with their own petard, and suggested telling the captain all about it. But, as Larson knew would be the case, Moffatt had got his money back, didn't want his family to know of these visits to America, and didn't like the idea of any publicity. So Larson said all right, it would be enough to drop a hint to the purser, and put him on his guard against the supposed card-sharpers—really these two financial magnates of the City of London.

"The financial magnates had their wits about them, though—financial magnates would have, naturally—and had seen that the play was crooked. Only they suspected Moffatt, the winner, not Larson, who had been a loser, like themselves. Larson, finding suspicions roused, took alarm, and, with his usual impudence, laid a complaint against Moffatt himself—by that time he knew the identity of the City magnates and daren't accuse them—and, for proof, produced cards that had been used and that he had marked himself. The guilt was saddled on the unconscious Moffatt, but the two City magnates insisted that nothing must be said. They said it would ruin the important conference they were attending if anything got out about their presence, and most likely as well they weren't anxious for it to be known they played poker with strangers on Atlantic liners. The two magnates were too important for their wishes to be disregarded. So all that happened was that their incognito was respected, Larson was thanked, and Mr. Moffatt blacklisted without his knowing anything about it.

"Larson passed out of Moffatt's life for a time. When he thought things were ripe, he appeared again. By now Pegley had also got in touch with Moffatt. The usual plan was contemplated. Pegley was to advise reinvestment. Larson was to give a warning. Moffatt was to be so grateful therefor he would be ready to take Larson's advice—saved from Pegley, he was to be caught on the rebound by Larson. It's an old game, of course, but it works.

"Not this time, though. Mr. Moffatt had first brought

himself to Larson's notice as a possible victim worth trouble by talking of his holding in consols—£100,000. Worth trying for; worth any confidence man's attention. Unfortunately, Mr. Moffatt never explained that it was a trust fund he had no power to touch, and Larson never thought of that possibility.

"His plans were coming to a head and he still had no idea of the trust fund snag when Bennett turned up again. Bennett was hard up now. Oddly enough, it was through Molly Oulton that he had heard of his old associates. He recognised his wife's signature on the back of some of Miss Oulton's sketches. He began to make inquiries. He found out Thoms was Hayes's chauffeur and tried to pump him. Having no idea that there was any connection between Thoms and Miss Molly, and, as he had heard vague, ill-natured gossip about her, he said something to Thoms about Miss Molly for which Thoms tried to knock his head off. I fancy they had both been drinking. Bennett was a bit tough himself; he fought back, and only the interference of the Cut and Come Again staff prevented serious damage to one or other. It was because of this—because Thoms heard in this way there was gossip about Miss Molly—that he tried to warn off young Noll Moffatt—with the pretty little scrimmage between them as a result that I had to stop.

"By that time, however, Bennett knew enough of what was going on to think the time had come for him to muscle in, as they call it. He knew enough to feel Larson could not afford to defy him. He added hints that if necessary he could produce proof that Larson had murdered Mr. Oulton. That probably decided Larson. He felt Bennett was better out of the way, and when he found out that Bennett had an appointment to see Mrs.

O'Brien he saw his opportunity. He calculated that anything that was discovered would lead to Hayes or Mrs. O'Brien, and that his connection with Bennett would remain unknown and unsuspected.

" On his way to meet Mrs. O'Brien, from whom he hoped to get some more information, Bennett stopped to have a look at the Sevens party through his field-glasses, so as to have an idea of what Mr. Moffatt was like.

" Not only Larson, but Hayes also, knew of the meeting arranged with Mrs. O'Brien. Hayes had been doing some watching on his own account. Bennett himself had asked Larson to meet him at the same place and almost the same time. Hayes was there with his camera, took his snap, and slipped away, with the evidence he required to give him an excuse for getting rid of Mrs. O'Brien. Larson was there, too, with Mr. Moffatt's automatic. He waited till Mrs. O'Brien had gone, and then dealt with Bennett in the approved gangster way for dealing with other gangsters who try to ' muscle in ' on a good thing and are rash enough to use threats of raking up old stories. He pushed the car and the dead man over the edge of the chalk-pit and had the bad luck as he was leaving to notice a labourer working in a field near by in full sight.

" That was a bit of a shock, but he had the dead man's hat and the labourer wasn't very near. He held the hat before him to hide his face, dodged away, found the bicycle he had hidden in readiness, and got away on it by sheltered paths through the woods."

Bobby ceased, his long story concluded.

Colonel Warden was consulting a map and his notes. He said:

" Would Larson have had time to get to the spot where

his gold cigarette-case was found, then to the spot where Miss Moffatt and Mrs. Markham saw him, and then back to Sevens for tea ? Defending counsel will put that. Also he claims to have witnessed the accident that afternoon at Winders Green and to be able to give details."

"There is no proof the cigarette-case was left at the time he claims," Bobby answered. "I suggest he went back that night to put it where it was found. He could climb out of his bedroom window, cover the distance, put the cigarette-case in position, and get back to his room unseen. He had to risk it being found by a dishonest person and kept without anything being said. Or he may have thought, if that happened, it would strengthen his alibi finally if it became a police case—as he would have taken care it should. And I think there is good proof that his story of the Winders Green accident is merely a repetition of a story told by a man named Hooper, and told freely by him in the local pub. I think that's proved by the fact that Larson repeats Hooper's story exactly, though in fact Hooper is either lying or mistaken. Larson would have to explain why he made exactly the same mistake and why he, too, thought a dog was a cat."

"That means," commented Colonel Warden, "that his alibi is broken, a motive established, a photo shows him on the spot with in his hand the weapon actually used. Seems watertight, with identity of time and place established. What made you suspect him first ? It was long enough before I began to think him a bit fishy."

"Well, sir," said Bobby slowly, "Miss Moffatt said when he passed her and Mrs. Markham he raised his hat. That was how—it was growing dark then—she realised it wasn't one of the farm labourers going home. But apparently he never wore a hat. If that was so, how did he happen to have one when he bowed to Miss Moffatt? It was that first made me think of him. But for that I don't think I should have suspected him. He seemed so confident; his presence seemed so well accounted for; there seemed no connection. Probably he raised his hat on purpose to attract Miss Moffatt's attention and help to establish his alibi."

"Well," the chief constable observed, "this is the first time I've ever heard of taking off his hat to a lady proving a man guilty of murder."

"It was a long time before I saw what it meant," Bobby admitted. "I left it out of the statement I drew up of the for and against the different suspects, and yet that was when I first thought of it seriously. I was going to mention it later on, too, only then Mrs. O'Brien turned up with her accusation of Hayes and rather pushed the hat incident into the background."

"I suppose Larson was hard pressed for money, and all that talk about his City interests mere bluff," the colonel went on. "He always made one think he was a rich man—part of his technique, I suppose."

"Yes, sir," agreed Bobby. "I think the failure of his Moffatt plans brought him down pretty nearly to his last penny. That was another pointer. At first he used a Rolls-Royce. Then once, when I met him, I gathered from what he said he had come down here travelling third on the railway. That time, too, I noticed he was wearing no hat, though it was raining, and he told me he never wore a hat in the country. So I started wondering still more why he had had one that day to take off when he met Miss Moffatt and Mrs. Markham. I expect, too, when he was looking so murderous in the way Miss Moffatt told us about, it was because he had just found out about the trust fund that put the lid on all his elaborate schemes. Probably he was feeling like murder that day. Bit of a knock-out, probably, to find he had been scheming and planning all those years and all for nothing, since the trust fund was well secured."

"The case seems complete," the colonel agreed. "I don't think even Treasury counsel will be able to talk about weak points. I see from your report the Moffatt butler, Reeves, was at Way Side, too?"

"Yes, sir. He admits he went there to help Thoms. Incidentally, he got his job at Sevens through Thoms. It was Thoms who supplied him with the references he showed. The Oultons knew him when he was butler to a friend of theirs. When he left there he went to the place where the trouble happened about the lost ring. When he was accused of the theft, he appealed to them to say his character had always been good. Didn't help him much, but he was grateful. They believed in his innocence all the time, and of course still more so when the ring was found afterwards. After his last release from gaol he made up his mind to run straight, and tried to find the Oultons again to see if they would help. But they had lost all their money and young Ted Oulton—Thoms—who was planning to get the bonds back, by force or fraud if he had to, asked his help instead. Reeves had done time for burglary, and Thoms was contemplating burglary. He knew Mr. Moffatt was looking for a manservant, and he helped Reeves to get the job in the hope that Reeves would be able to help him presently."

"Larson was after the bonds, too, I suppose?"

"Oh, yes, he knew from Mrs. O'Brien, who was wanting to get her revenge on Hayes, that Hayes had them. She told him, too, about the photograph Hayes had taken of her and Bennett, though, as she had only had a glimpse of it, she had no idea Larson appeared on it, too. She wanted to implicate Hayes, if possible. She may have had some idea of offering later on to prove his innocence on condition of his marrying her, now she was actually free with Bennett's death. Larson was quite willing to pack us off on any convenient wild-goose chase, but his real interest was the bonds. He had to get money somehow. He paid a visit to Hayes to have a look round, sold him the ring—that gave him an excuse to come again to redeem it—and no doubt took the opportunity to plant the automatic stolen from Mr. Moffatt where I found it. Hayes was getting more and more nervous though, and it was his determination to clear out of the country that brought things to a general climax. Larson and Pegley came along to get the bonds. They calculated that if they could once lay hold of them—and they knew from Mrs. O'Brien where they were kept—Hayes wouldn't dare to take any action to recover them.

"Ted Oulton—Thoms—knew, too, that Hayes was going. Hayes told him so himself when he sacked him. So Thoms knew it was a case of now or never if he was to recover his mother's property. He had arranged to meet Reeves at Way Side for a talk that night, so he came back from the poultry farm where he had gone and was seen by Noll Moffatt, who was prowling round, and by Hayes himself, who was very much on the look-out. It was the Larson-Pegley outfit who got rid of the cook by a faked wire, but I'm not sure who cut the phone wire or who it was kept the Mrs. White woman away by sending a message she wasn't wanted. Thoms and Reeves were at a disadvantage compared with Larson because they didn't know where the bonds were kept. They got into the house unseen—while he was there as chauffeur, Thoms had fixed the drawing-room windows so that they could be opened from outside—and Reeves, who was in a bad state of nerves and saw another long-term sentence ahead, gave their presence away, and Hayes a bad scare, by drinking the contents of a glass of whisky Hayes had just before poured out for himself. I was there, thanks to Hayes having applied for police protection, and I searched the house, but they had slipped out again. Then Noll Moffatt turned up. Miss Henrietta had never approved of her half-brother's plans, and she asked Noll Moffatt to try to find him and get him to give it up and come back to the farm.

"Thoms and Reeves returned to the house to have another look for the bonds. They went upstairs, and while they were there Larson and Pegley turned up, found the drawing-room window open, went in, and went straight to the study I had just left by the window after Noll Moffatt. Hayes, as soon as he saw them, bolted after me through the window—I heard him running for dear life, though I didn't know who it was—and the amiable Larson saw a chance to collar the bonds for himself, knocked Pegley out, and ran into Thoms and Reeves in the hall. That was not till Reeves had spotted me in the study and locked the door on me. Larson got away through the front door he shut after him and wedged somehow to prevent pursuit. Thoms made a bolt through the study to cut him off. Reeves got the front door open again and the general mix-up continued outside, Hayes, who was still in the garden, getting knocked out in the course of it. Larson wasted his cartridges trying to scare Thoms off. Thoms didn't scare, and managed to catch up with Larson just as Larson got to his car. In the rough and tumble that followed, Thoms managed to get hold of the bonds and vanished with them. Hayes turned up, shouting he had been robbed. Larson accused him of murder and produced the photo he had found in the house—again on Mrs. O'Brien's information—and I thought it good enough for an arrest."

"Larson will hang," Colonel Warden repeated. "What about Pegley?"

"I don't see there is any charge we can bring against him," Bobby observed. "Found on enclosed premises for unlawful purposes perhaps. He would deny knowing anything. He will be no good as a witness; he'll just deny everything."

"We can do without him," said the colonel. "What about Hayes? Is there anything we can charge him with?"

"I don't think so, sir," Bobby answered. "He stole Mrs. Oulton's bonds, undoubtedly, but it would be awkward to prove, and, anyhow, he has lost them now. He is threatening legal action against the Oultons, but of course he won't dare. He can't prove lawful possession, and they can prove the bonds are those they lost—Mr. Oulton's signature is on some, with a note of when bought and where. I suppose Thoms could be prosecuted for unlawful entry or something, but it wouldn't help Hayes any. He'll lie low all right."

"He'll have no alternative; nothing he can do," decided the colonel. "What was Miss Molly Oulton doing, though? Your report mentions her."

"Yes, sir," Bobby answered. "I think she came up after Noll Moffatt as soon as she knew her sister had sent him to Way Side. She wanted to make sure nothing happened to him. It was Miss Molly he was with on the afternoon of the murder, when he didn't take any of the photos he went out for—except one that turned out to give him a good alibi."

"Oh, well," said the colonel, "ends in wedding bells. Odd case all through, and odd for a murder case to end in a wedding."

THE END

Made in the USA
Middletown, DE
11 August 2017